PASSION FLOWERS

He was going to have to draw on all his strength. "I don't think we should be discussing this in your state. Go to bed."

"Don't order me around." She leaned toward him, her warm breath feathering his face.

"If you don't go down that hall right now, I'm going to kiss you. At the very least."

"Kiss me?" She giggled. "First it's arrows and bullets. Now kisses."

He was only human, damn it. He drew her to him and covered her mouth with his. She pressed herself against him, wrapping her arms about his neck. He kissed her deeply, appreciating the sweet softness of her lips, the intoxicating taste of her.

But this wouldn't do. He walked her backward across the hallway, took a deep breath and broke away. Then he even pushed her gently toward her bedroom.

"Go to bed. Lock your door."

By Roslynn Griffith

Pretty Birds of Passage
The Wind Casts No Shadow
Heart of the Jaguar
Shadows in the Mirror

Published by HarperPaperbacks

Harper
Monogram

Shadows in the Mirror

⊰ ROSLYNN GRIFFITH ⊱

HarperPaperbacks
A Division of HarperCollinsPublishers

HarperPaperbacks   *A Division of* HarperCollins*Publishers*
10 East 53rd Street, New York, N.Y. 10022

Cover illustration by John Ennis

First printing: October 1995

Printed in the United States of America

HarperPaperbacks, HarperMonogram, and colophon are trademarks of HarperCollins*Publishers*

❖ 10 9 8 7 6 5 4 3 2 1

Thanks to Edward Majeski for his research.

Prologue

Points to Ponder Along the Way

Prologue

West Texas, 1887

The darkness trembled.

Frightened, Xosi Baca awoke to find herself thrown against hard, unyielding walls.

Walls? The space was narrow enough to be a coffin. She felt cold enough to be in a grave. Was she dead? Xosi wondered, scrabbling at the surrounding barriers with desperate nails. Her actions were futile. The dark walls were impenetrable.

Then her enclosure shook again, harder, as if it were being moved by a terrible unseen force.

Memories stirred, slowly surfacing . . . even as Xosi scraped and scratched. She remembered her raw fear as a snarling, horrible face loomed over her.

Fear that turned to terror.

That face had belonged to a man with a knife . . . a primitive blade polished to killing sharpness. The knife had ached for Xosi like a lover.

She flinched and screamed, "Ai-ee-ee!," reliving the moment the knife had descended, sheathing itself in her breast.

She was dead. Her beautiful body had been mutilated, her vibrant life stolen from her! And where was she now?

In hell?

Wailing, screeching, she flung herself from side to side. "El Diablo!" She challenged the devil himself. "Come for me! I will scratch your eyes out!"

She would not burn willingly!

But, though her space heated, the king of the demons did not appear. Instead, one side of her enclosure began to glow. Xosi stared as the barrier shone with light, shifted . . . became translucent. She could see shadows looming outside.

"Ai-ee-ee!" she howled, hurling herself against it with all the force she could muster.

"Yow!" came an answering yell from outside.

Then Xosi was falling, tumbling over and over and over . . . finally coming to a jarring, crashing halt . . .

"Damn it all anyway!" he said through his teeth, shaking the fingers that still burned.

Spooked, he stared down at the little silver mirror. First the thing had turned icy cold, then fiery hot. A shaft of moonlight shining through the nearby open window made it glow like a little face in the dark.

He wanted no more of the cursed thing, sent it skittering beneath a chair with a booted toe.

He'd only picked up the bauble—some piece of Mexican work, a pendant in the shape of a hand mirror on a silver chain—because he'd found nothing else of value in Monte Ryerson's old roll-top desk.

When a floorboard in the hallway behind him squeaked, he tensed and glanced over his shoulder. Had he awakened one of the sleepers in the ranch house?

Such as Monte Ryerson himself? He wanted no showdown with the owner of the spread, at least not now.

Stealthily, he headed for the window and heaved himself up and over its deep sill.

He might not have accomplished what he'd come for this time.

But he'd be back . . . with a vengeance.

1

Upstate New York

Iphigenia Wentworth reached for the hand mirror beside her bed and moaned at what she saw. Her skin was dead white, her eyes sunken with fatigue, her masses of golden blonde hair as tangled as if a hurricane had roared through her Aunt Gertrude's twenty-room summer cottage in the Adirondacks.

With a shaky hand, Iphigenia placed the mirror back on the cherrywood nightstand and gazed about the guest bedroom, her prison the past four months. A breeze wafted through one tall shuttered window, fluttering lace curtains.

Light also crept into the room, though Iphigenia had no idea whether it was morning or afternoon. With all the pain she'd suffered, she only remembered that night had been descending about the time the doctor arrived the day before.

She'd thought she was going to die. In agony, she'd begged the man to shoot her.

Obviously, he hadn't.

Gingerly, she stretched a little, to see if her body remained intact. Her limbs seemed to have survived, though she felt sore and weak. She couldn't be certain of other parts of her anatomy.

Giving birth had been the worst experience in all her twenty-seven years.

She hardened her jaw. Damn Lamar Blake! Damn the day she'd been stupid enough to think having relations with a man would be enjoyable. What little pleasure she'd derived with the good-looking scoundrel had been canceled by nine months of increasing discomfort, followed by fifteen—twenty?—hours of sheer, unadulterated hell.

When the door creaked open, Iphigenia started, "Aunt Gertrude?"

"It's me, Miss Wentworth." Mary Flannery, Gertrude's plump, good-natured Irish maid, stepped inside, carrying a bundle swathed in a blanket. Smiling, she headed for the bed. "I am thinking you might like to see your new baby girl."

"Baby girl?" Iphigenia wasn't ready to confront the small burden Mary placed in her arms.

But she looked anyway.

Huddled inside the blanket lay an infant with a wrinkly pink face and a few wisps of fine, pale hair lying across her bald pate. A tiny hand clutched at the edge of the blanket, four perfect miniature fingers and a thumb.

"Ah, and isn't she beautiful now?" cooed Mary.

To her surprise, Iphigenia answered, "Yes . . . she is."

Furthermore, the weight of the baby in her arms felt . . . natural somehow. Staring down at the tiny nose and soft cheeks in fascination, she forgot about the pain she'd gone through for the moment. Her feelings turned to awe as she realized this miraculous little creature had actually come from her own body.

She swallowed, running her fingers lightly over the baby's head. "What a wonder you are."

"Isn't she, Miss?" Then Mary sobered, clearing her throat. "Or beggin' your pardon, would you rather I called you Ma'am?"

The maid probably was concerned because Aunt Gertrude was such a stickler for social niceties, especially when they served to cover unpleasantness. Perhaps she thought Iphigenia was planning to pretend she'd been mysteriously married and widowed.

"Address me as *Miss*, please. I am not one to tiptoe around the truth," Iphigenia stated.

Lamar Blake was long gone, had returned to Georgia or Alabama, wherever the charming rogue had originally come from. He had disappeared from the New York society scene as soon as Iphigenia had told him she was pregnant.

Mary leaned closer. "Babies are always lovely. They are God's blessing and people's hope for the future."

The maid's tone and expression seemed so nostalgic, Iphigenia wondered if Mary had experienced motherhood herself. The maid claimed to be single, though that didn't mean anything.

Mary straightened, obviously aware she was being scrutinized. "I should be drawing the curtains back." She moved away. "'Tis a fine, bright day outside."

Mary needn't have worried. Iphigenia hadn't planned to ask any prying questions. She remained fascinated by the child she held, and was content to let the world beyond them fade away.

"My hope for the future, hmm?" she said softly, examining each hand, each tiny finger.

Then she reached beneath the blanket to find matching toes. The baby stirred, making a soft noise. A smile trembled about Iphigenia's lips. She was a mother, though that had never been her ambition.

Her desire since she'd reached adulthood had been to live an independent life. When her attempts had been met with resistance from her difficult father, she'd become a rebel who drank and gambled more than a lady should. She smoked as well, and said and did things that embarrassed the family.

Would she have felt differently if her own mother were still alive? Would she have considered an alternate course?

Her memories of Dahlia Wentworth were few: a soothing voice, a loving touch, the comforting voluminous skirts that Iphigenia had clung to as a toddler. But all that clinging hadn't stopped death from tearing her mother away. At five, Iphigenia had wept over her mother's grave. An only child, she'd grown up in a cold, darkly furnished house in New York City where servants and nannies had been her companions.

"At least you have *me*," Iphigenia told the baby, filled with unusual warm, expansive feelings. Now she was glad she hadn't died during labor. She was also alight with new determination. God willing, this child would always have her. Gingerly, she inhaled the baby's sweet scent. "I shall call you Hope." She told Mary, "Thanks to the sentiment you expressed."

The maid beamed.

"I shall have to decide where we will live, of course," Iphigenia mused. "I do not think New York would be the right place." Where she'd existed in mild disgrace long before the final, humiliating incident with Lamar Blake. "The Continent will be better." She had learned from traveling that Europeans were more open minded as long as one had money. "Perhaps Paris or a villa in Florence."

Surely her father would turn over her trust fund now. Surely he realized she would never marry.

Iphigenia glanced up when the bedroom door suddenly opened again, admitting Gertrude Wentworth Cummings. Her silver hair crimped back from her austere face like wings, her patrician nose raised in the air, her spine straight inside her tightly laced corset, the older woman looked every inch the confident society hostess she was.

Iphigenia had never liked her paternal aunt very much, though the woman had been fairly civil during her months of confinement.

Aunt Gertrude spied the baby and raised elegant brows over steely eyes. "What do you think you are doing?"

"Mary brought me my daughter Hope to see—"

"You have named the thing?"

Iphigenia bristled. "How dare you call my child a thing."

But the older woman paid no attention, had switched her attention to the maid. "I should dismiss you. Get out of this room immediately."

Looking frightened, Mary obeyed.

Iphigenia remained angry. "That was cruel. I will employ Mary myself if you don't want her."

"You are not employing anyone. Your father controls your money."

"I believe he will be quite happy to turn over my trust fund if it means getting me and my disgrace out of his hair. I plan to go to Europe—"

"Europe?" her aunt cut her off. "You have no right to make plans, especially pleasant scenarios wherein you enjoy yourself. You need to be punished." Then she approached the bed and reached for Hope.

Appalled, Iphigenia turned on her side, clutching the baby. "Leave her alone! You have no right to touch her."

"You are the one with no rights." Aunt Gertrude sniffed. "A soiled woman. You have disgraced us enough and will be lucky to find some toothless, dim-witted widower who can be tricked into marrying you. And that will only come about because of your father's influence."

Before Iphigenia could react, Aunt Gertrude lunged for the baby, easily pulling her from Iphigenia's weak arms.

"No!" Iphigenia tried to rise.

But her aunt was already hastening away, long black skirts rustling.

"Where are you going?" Iphigenia cried, still struggling to get out of bed. A sharp pain shot across her abdomen. "I want my baby!"

Hand on the doorknob, her aunt turned. "It is not your baby. It is a bastard with no parents at all. Too bad you had to see it before—"

"Before what?"

Gertrude Wentworth Cummings didn't answer. Exiting quickly, she slammed the door behind her. The baby started to wail.

The sound cut through Iphigenia like a knife.

Moaning anew, she got to her feet, imagining all sorts of desperate scenarios, such as drowning her little girl in a well. Surely her aunt could never do such a thing. That would be murder.

Panicked, cursing at her unaccustomed feebleness, she dragged herself toward the door, clutching at the carved wooden bedposts, then an upholstered chair.

"Hope isn't an *it*! She's my daughter!"

But there was no one to hear. And as Iphigenia

finally grasped the doorknob, she glanced down to see fresh blood staining her nightgown. Then she collapsed, sliding down to the floor.

Perhaps she would die after all.

West Texas

Death haunted him.

Monte Ryerson tossed and turned in his brass bed. Though a chill gust blew through the ranch house, he was sweating. And along with the wind's rush came the soft sound of throaty female laughter.

Familiar laughter . . . as was the presence that rippled along with the breeze.

Xosi Baca.

Monte shuddered, once more reliving Xosi's death. His standing there watching, rifle in hand, unable to lift a finger to stop her mad killer. He watched the knife rise, quiver, descend in a lethal arc . . .

He groaned. Xosi hadn't deserved to die, especially not in the full bloom of life.

Monte . . .

He started, thinking the voice actually sounded real.

Monte . . .

And seemed to be coming closer.

Monte, my beautiful man.

Although hollow, the voice seemed to be near.

He opened his eyes to a shimmering vision, hardly able to believe that Xosi Baca stood before him. He heard her throaty laugh again as she slipped her *camisa* over her head. Then she let her skirt drop to the floor before sitting down beside him. Voluptuous, she had full breasts, a small waist and lush hips and thighs. Her long mahogany hair coiled about her back and shoulders.

A dream? A frightening vision? For he was frightened.

Monte, she whispered again, amber eyes glowing with warmth. She reached over to caress his chest. He had to be dreaming, so why did her cold touch feel so real?

"W-what do you want?" he managed to choke out.

You, querido. She slid farther into the bed and draped herself over him. *You know I have always wanted you.*

"But you're dead!" The accusation came out a strangled whisper.

He lay there stunned as she rubbed against him like a cat, her flesh cold as ice. Then she angled her mouth over his, kissing him with frozen lips as she reached beneath the sheet for his manhood.

"No-o!" He winced, trying to draw away.

Yes-s-s! she hissed, attempting to anchor him. *You are mine!*

"No!" he yelled again, horrified that he was being aroused by a nightmare. With every ounce of strength, he pushed her away.

Once again, she stood beside the bed, this time glaring with anger, disappointment . . . and more.

Do not send me away, querido, she said softly, yet with underlying threat. *You will be sorry.*

Still he dared, drawing the sheet about him. "Go!"

She seemed ready to fight with him, but her anger faded even as her image did. He lay back against the mattress, eyes squinched tight, breath labored, heart pounding, waiting to hear her voice calling his name.

The moment never came.

Opening his eyes, Monte stared into the darkness of his empty bedroom, then swore he heard light footsteps pad down the corridor outside. He rose and went to the door, his worries over what he might see battling with his concern that some noise had awakened his kids. But no one traversed the long hallway that connected the haphazardly adjoining rooms of the sprawling adobe ranchhouse. Though Monte swore that the scent of a woman lingered in the air. The hair on the back of his neck rose to attention. His flesh crawled.

A ghost rather than a dream?

His Comanche heritage allowed him to believe in such beings.

Though how Xosi Baca could have followed him to his abode he didn't know. Backing into his room, he lit the kerosene lantern beside the bed and checked the shadows as he pulled on a pair of denim pants.

Then he went through the house, peering at shadows, staring into corners. Everything seemed quiet. A dim moon and a skyful of stars shone outside. An open window let in a gust of cool spring wind.

Cool, but not cold. Not freezing.

Thinking of Xosi's chilly lips, Monte shivered.

Had he actually seen a ghost?

Or was the guilt that already haunted him taking a new form?

He'd prefer thinking it was guilt, he decided, heading back to bed. Though the black moods that had possessed him the past winter were almost as bad as ghosts. He had to do something about the situation. Guilt was rotting his insides and, worse, pushing away his children.

He didn't want to destroy their lives, too.

"Pa is lonely, that's what's wrong with him," thirteen-year-old Cassie Ryerson told her brother Stephen as they rode toward Pine Bluff to pick up supplies and the mail.

"It's more than that," said Stephen, reining in his sorrel to keep pace with her smaller paint. The horses clopped through the brown dust side by side. "He's got a lot on his mind. For one, he's worried about making a living." He assumed his wiser, older brother expression, though there were only three years between him and his twin sisters. "There's too many ranchers now—cattle prices have been forced down. Pa's probably afraid we might go broke."

"We aren't going to go broke," Cassie said, trying to be positive. "And Pa wouldn't think so either if he had someone really nice to talk to." Remembering something she'd read in one of the many newspapers her father subscribed to, she quoted, "He needs 'a soft hand to soothe his fevered brow, a sweet bosom on which to rest his head.'"

Stephen made a face, narrowing his eyes. "What in tarnation are you talking about? A woman?"

"Of course, she'd be a woman. A *lady*." That was especially important. "Pa needs a new wife." And she herself a new mother, Cassie had decided, though she thought it best not to admit so to either her brother or her twin, Ginnie, who'd stayed home today.

"Ma's only been dead for three years."

Three long years that had felt like a lifetime to Cassie. "I think Pa's mourned enough."

"And *I* think it's up to Pa to decide how long he should mourn. You should mind your own business."

Cassie only grinned and kicked the paint's side, sending her mare trotting ahead. The rough road they followed rose steadily as they climbed the spare, rocky foothills toward the tiny town of Pine Bluff. The basin in which the best part of the Ryerson spread lay—a grassy expanse created by a spring-fed creek that wove through many of the acres—was giving way to desert with its gray-green creosote bushes, cactus and mesquite.

Stephen also picked up the pace as they spotted the town ahead. Actually, town was too big a word for the small cluster of weatherbeaten, adobe buildings that made up Pine Bluff—a general store, a blacksmith shop and a cantina. Larger when it had been a stagecoach stop, the place had shrunk considerably as soon as two railroads—the Southern Pacific, then the Texas and Pacific—cut iron swathes across the state. The stagecoach line no longer existed but the needs of the surrounding ranches kept the remaining establishments in business. Each week, a rider made the one-hundred-and-forty-mile round trip to El Paso to deliver and return mail.

Cassie could hardly wait to see if there were any special letters addressed to her father. She hoped the storekeep hadn't gossiped about the one she'd sent to an Eastern newspaper a couple of months ago. As she and Stephen dismounted and tied their horses in front of the general store, she tried to hide her excitement but made sure she beat her brother through the door.

He didn't seem to notice. He stopped to examine a silver-trimmed Mexican saddle on display near the dry-goods shelves.

"Mail for Ryerson?" Cassie approached the counter to ask the storekeeper.

Her heart beat faster when he returned with a fairly large bundle, most of it sure to be the usual newspapers.

"Thanks," she said.

"You're welcome."

Quickly she undid the twine that bound the bundle and sorted through it. Two letters and a flat packet caught her eye. Glancing behind her to make sure Stephen remained busy, she headed off for a corner to rip open her prizes.

When she returned to the counter, Stephen was checking off a list of supplies. "Molasses, flour." He glanced at Cassie. "And didn't Carmen say she could use a new butcher knife?"

"Uh-huh."

For some reason, various utensils had been disappearing. The superstitious housekeeper claimed evil spirits were taking them, but Cassie paid her no mind. Excited, she could hardly wait while Stephen counted out some coins and told the storekeep to put the rest of the supplies on the Ryerson tab.

"Wait a minute, I forgot something," Stephen told the man, then looked at his sister. "How about a peppermint? Would you like a treat?"

"Uh, sure."

"You don't sound very enthusiastic. If you don't care, we should save the money."

Cassie sighed. "I'll take a peppermint. Please?" Though she wished her brother would hurry up so they could talk in private.

Glancing at her curiously, Stephen laid another coin down for the candy. He stuck a striped red and white stick in his mouth and handed the other to Cassie. Then he carried the supplies outside.

He was loading their saddlebags when she told him, "I found a wife for Pa."

"Uh-huh."

"I'm serious, Stephen. I put an advertisement in a New York newspaper. She held up the letters. "And I got some answers."

Surprised, Stephen stopped what he was doing. "Advertisements? Are you loco?"

Cassie frowned. "I'm not crazy and I'm not stupid. I know there's such a thing as mail-order brides. Mr. Rolfson sent for one and she came all the way from Sweden."

"That was different. That was someone his family knew."

"But other men have sent away for wives," Cassie insisted. "Just listen to me, Stephen." She waved the envelopes again. "These women are willing to come to Texas and marry Pa and take care of us."

"I'm near full grown."

"But I'm not." She lifted her chin. "And I'd like a real lady for a mother. Someone who can teach me the right things to say and do."

Someone who could help her be more feminine. She was sick of drudging about in dusty boots and tying her hair back in a braid. She didn't want to end up wearing trousers all the time and riding with the men like her twin sister Ginnie.

"Look at this." Cassie pulled the biggest prize of all from the mail bundle—the fancy daguerreotype that had been in the flat packet. She could tell her brother was impressed when his eyes widened. "Isn't she beautiful? And I bet she's smart and sweet, too."

"Not to mention rich." Frowning, Stephen fingered the daguerreotype. "Who else could afford to send something like this?"

Now they'd gotten to the hard part. "I don't know how she got her portrait taken or how she managed to send it, but this lady must not be rich." Or else she was taking the advertisement at its word. Cassie paused. "What happened to the money you saved up from those horses you broke last fall?"

"Why?"

"We need to send her money for the train."

Stephen's frown turned to a scowl. "No."

"Stephen!" To get this close and be unable to carry out her plan would break her heart. Though she hadn't known what she'd do when the time came, she'd been depending on her brother's help.

"This is crazy. You're crazy," he fumed. "That woman's probably crazy, too."

"She's not!" Cassie didn't want her to be. "Please,

Stephen!" To her embarrassment, she felt her eyes fill. "It will change things, you'll see. She'll change Pa. He won't be so sad . . . and faraway." At times her father withdrew so much, Cassie couldn't reach him at all. She simply knew it was more than worries about the ranch. "I can't help missing the way he used to be."

Stephen's expression became more sympathetic. He knew what she was talking about. "Don't cry."

Cassie sniffed and swiped at her cheeks. "I'm not crying." Again she held up the woman's image, pressing her case for all she was worth. "Pa won't be able to ignore a lady like this. She's as beautiful as an angel."

"Well—"

"Please!" She could tell her brother was weakening. "Please, please, Stephen. I'll pay you back, I promise."

"It's so crazy," he muttered. "And we'd have to ride all the way to El Paso to buy the ticket."

We. Now she knew she had hooked him.

"That town is dangerous," he went on. "It's full of gamblers and gunmen and shysters these days."

"But no one will bother us, Stephen. You're sixteen, a man," she said, flattering him. "You'll see that we're safe."

And Cassie would see to changing the direction their lives had taken the past year or so. She'd been wishing for change, praying for it, working toward it with all her might.

2

TEXAS RANCHER SEEKS A WIFE AND A MOTHER FOR
HIS THREE CHILDREN. WILL PAY TRAVEL EXPENSES
TO EL PASO. THIS WOMAN SHOULD BE PRETTY AND
NICE, AGE 25 TO 35, AND BE A REAL LADY.

Once again Iphigenia read the rather child-
ishly worded advertisement she'd cut from *The New
York Crier*, then placed it back in her reticule. She
hoped she hadn't made a terrible mistake. Ever since
the Southern Pacific train had left central Texas, the
land outside had grown wilder and rougher and more
foreboding. Dry and dusty, often mountainous, nearly
barren except for twisted trees and harsh-looking plants
that pushed their way between outcroppings of raw
rock, the place seemed unfit for human habitation.

Where had she gotten herself?

As close to her child as she could manage, came the
swift answer in her mind.

As soon as she'd discovered that her aunt had sent

Hope to live with poor relations out west, Iphigenia had left no stone unturned finding out exactly where the Fricketts lived. Fort Davis seemed to be some distance from El Paso on the map, but Iphigenia was certain she would find a way to get there. Just as she'd happened on a way to get to Texas from New York.

The newspaper advertisement had been a miracle. The proffered railway ticket a godsend.

Especially considering Horace Wentworth had been measuring out the most meager of allowances, no doubt expecting his daughter to bolt. But Iphigenia had been careful to hide her feelings concerning her baby. She was certain that her aunt and father would have headed for the wharves, thinking she had found some means to book passage to Europe, when her empty suite in the New York mansion was discovered.

They would never believe the cold, sharp-tongued Miss Iphigenia Wentworth was on her way to retrieve her illegitimate baby. They would never think she'd go so far as to marry some uncivilized Texas rancher to get her daughter back—possibly the only unselfish act she'd ever done in her life.

She could hardly believe the latter herself. Perhaps if she'd never seen her daughter . . . but she had. Those few moments when Hope had rested in her arms were the most precious in her memory. She'd felt a love she hadn't known she was capable of. Taking a deep breath, she pulled another piece of paper out of her reticule, the letter that had come with her ticket. The enthusiastic scrawl was also childish and the wording similar to that of the advertisement, but at least this Monte Ryerson had enough education to write at all, which was undoubtedly unusual in the wilderness.

Iphigenia put the letter away, then attempted to dust some of the dirt and train soot off her fawn-colored

Redfern traveling costume. The white lace at her throat had already turned nearly the same color as the jacket and skirt. She was exhausted after endless days of travel and looking forward to who knew what when she arrived in El Paso in less than an hour.

She assumed she'd meet with Ryerson's approval. She'd actually try her best to get along with him until she had her child in her arms again. And she was prepared to do whatever else she must to achieve the reunion with Hope. She had no illusions left about romance. She need not fear another pregnancy—the doctor had told her that the difficult birth had ended her chances of ever becoming a mother again.

Which made Hope's being taken away from her even more traumatic.

Her baby was the only person who would ever truly belong to her. Picturing Hope's innocent little face, the precious little fingers that had clutched the blanket, brought tears to her eyes.

Then, lowering her veil, she glanced about to make sure that none of the other passengers had noticed. She was a proud woman who rarely wept. But her traveling companions, a quiet young couple holding hands and a white-whiskered old man snoring against his seat, paid no attention.

The conductor entered the car. "El Paso," he announced, looking at his pocket watch. "We arrive in ten minutes."

Ten minutes. Iphigenia clutched her reticule tightly. She tried to be optimistic, assuring herself that whatever predicament she faced would only be temporary. Eventually, a legal marriage would release her trust fund, and she could offer financial compensation to Monte Ryerson before she left him. If he objected anyway, she would show him what her father called the true, acidic side of her personality. Then he'd probably be willing to pay to get rid of her.

A flicker of doubt crossed her mind when she went over her plan again. What if this Monte Ryerson got attached to her in truth? She would have to steel herself to any soft emotions toward the man. She would approach this as a business deal, just as Horace Wentworth would.

Not wanting to be reminded of her father, certainly not wanting to think she was in the least like the cold man who'd been her only parent, she looked for a distraction and was relieved when the conductor strolled down the aisle.

"I have two trunks in the baggage car," she told him. "Make sure you unload them both."

"Yes ma'am."

She'd packed at least half her wardrobe, not knowing what kinds of situations or weather to expect. She'd brought all her jewelry, sewn into her petticoat, having read that West Texas was a next-to-lawless land. And for protection, she carried one of her great-uncle's ivory-handled dueling pistols in her carpetbag. Reputedly, he'd died in a scandalous shooting incident before he was thirty, but at least he'd had courage.

Courage Iphigenia hoped she'd inherited, she thought, upon alighting in El Paso a few minutes later. The conductor offered her a hand stepping down from the passenger car. The depot—if one could call it that—was nothing more than a mud-brick shed. Or adobe, she had heard it called. Larger adobe buildings rose some distance away. A gaggle of Spanish-speaking people embraced the young couple who'd ridden in her car. Nearby, an ugly, filthy, greasy-haired man spat a stream of tobacco onto the ground and stared at her with bloodshot eyes.

Monte Ryerson? *Please God, no.*

Frozen with trepidation, Iphigenia hardly noticed the two youngsters approaching.

"Miss Iphigenia Wentworth?"

She raised her veil and stared at the girl who addressed her, a pretty one of twelve or thirteen with soft brown eyes and wavy brown hair tied back with a pink ribbon that matched her simple dress. The girl's companion was older, a tall youth with wide shoulders, long limbs and an air of awkwardness.

"I am Miss Wentworth, yes," said Iphigenia.

"Oh!" The girl's eyes widened and lit up, while her lips curved into a tremulous smile that couldn't help but touch Iphigenia. "You're even more beautiful than your picture."

The youth tipped his hat. "Pleased to meet you, Miss Wentworth."

Gazing into the boy's blue eyes, Iphigenia was confused. "You're, uh . . . Monte Ryerson?"

"Me?" He blushed beet red, looking terribly embarrassed. "Of course not. I'm Stephen, his son."

The girl stepped forward to offer her hand. "My brother and I are here to take you back to the ranch. I'm Cassie. I'm thirteen. My twin sister Ginnie stayed at home. We brought a buckboard to take you and your luggage to the ranch—"

The poor girl was babbling. "What about your father?" Iphigenia cut in.

"Well . . . Pa was busy." Cassie sobered and glanced at her brother. "He was sorting cows, wasn't he, Stephen?"

The boy merely grunted.

Though they were friendly, Iphigenia thought the two were acting a little odd, in an anxious sort of way. Ryerson actually preferred sorting cattle to meeting his future bride? But she had little chance to ask questions as she followed the youngsters to the team and wagon they had left near the depot.

No buggy? Perhaps people didn't use them in West Texas, or Monte Ryerson simply didn't have the money to buy one. He would be pleased then if she came up with a cash settlement later on.

"El Paso isn't very pretty," Cassie told her as Stephen took care of having the trunks loaded. "And it can be dangerous, especially at night—gamblers and drunks and even outlaws walk the streets."

Iphigenia raised her brows and thought of the filthy man who'd spat the tobacco.

"But don't worry," Cassie went on. "Stephen brought a rifle. He'll take care of us." Then she stared as Iphigenia opened her parasol against the bright sun, her expression obviously awed. "Do ladies use those sort of things?"

The girl was so innocent and seemed to be looking for guidance. "Most ladies have parasols," Iphigenia told her, "to protect the skin from the sun. It is fashionable to remain on the pale side, rather than to turn brown or freckled."

Cassie's smile wavered. "Really? I guess I'm not very fashionable then."

"You're also in West Texas," grumbled Stephen, who'd come around to help them up onto the wagon's seat. "Out here, things with pale hides usually make their homes under rocks."

Always ready to trade barbs, whether good natured or not, Iphigenia wondered if he were indirectly needling her. "Are you comparing me to toads and snakes?" she asked.

"No, Ma'am." The boy flushed as he climbed the wagon himself and took up the reins. "I was only teasing Cassie. I didn't mean to insult you."

He was so serious, so easily discomfited, Iphigenia felt sorry she'd said anything. She also found herself wanting to reassure Cassie, as unusual as that seemed. She guessed it was the girl's innocence and honesty. She'd never dwelled on class differences the way Aunt Gertrude did anyway. She mistrusted all people equally.

She smiled at the girl. "Fashions vary in different parts of the country. I'm sure you are quite the mode for West Texas." That brought a grin to Cassie's face. Soon, she was maintaining a stream of conversation as the buckboard rumbled along. They passed small houses with chickens scratching within adobe-walled yards. A man wearing a huge hat and leading a burro loaded with baskets got out of the narrow road when the buckboard approached him.

"He's wearing a sombrero." Cassie pointed at the man. "A Mexican hat."

"There seem to be many Mexicans here," remarked Iphigenia. "But then I suppose that is natural, considering the Spanish settled this part of the country in the beginning." She'd read her history.

"Mexico itself, the town of Paseo del Norte, is on the other side of the Rio Grande," said Stephen, who seemed content to remain silent most of the time. "The river is right over there," he added with a gesture.

The buckboard was heading the opposite direction and soon left El Paso behind. Cassie continued to chatter, asking questions about New York, as well as pointing out local landmarks, and naming flora and fauna. Iphigenia tried to converse politely, though the buckboard's lack of springs made her teeth rattle. Besides, one stark mountain range or painted mesa pretty much looked like another and she wasn't very interested in creosote bushes or prairie dogs.

Cassie regained her full attention when she said,

"Our Ma died three years ago. She was killed in an accident." She sighed. "We've really missed her."

A pang engulfed Iphigenia for a second. "I expect so. I lost my mother myself when I was a small child."

"It's important for a girl to have a female influence in her life, don't you think?" Cassie asked, sounding hopeful.

"Well, yes, I suppose so." Though the inference that Cassie might need her made Iphigenia distinctly uncomfortable. She hadn't considered the repercussions her presence might have on Ryerson's children. "Other female relatives can also be helpful for a girl. I have cousins and an aunt." She didn't add that her cousins were stuffy prigs or that Aunt Gertrude was a cold, cruel lady.

"We don't have any other relatives, at least not in this part of the country," Cassie said. "My Pa has a half sister named Louisa up in New Mexico Territory, but we've never gotten around to visiting her."

"That's too bad. I'm sure you will meet her one of these days." But her assurances didn't seem to impress the girl, who continued to observe her eagerly, like a half-grown pup waiting for a pat on the head. When the buckboard hit a big bump, Iphigenia bounced on the seat and hastened to change the subject, "How long will it take us to get to the ranch?"

"It's quite a piece," said Cassie. "We're hoping to get home before dark."

It was mid-morning now. Iphigenia's heart sank. "How far is quite a piece?"

"Seventy miles," Stephen replied.

Iphigenia's mouth nearly dropped. "Good God!" Then she remembered she should watch her language. "Er, good heavens."

"We'll stop and rest, have a meal at noon," Cassie told her. "We brought tortillas and some chili."

"Chili? Tortillas?"

"Chili is a spicy stew," Cassie explained. "This one has more beans then beef. Carmen, our housekeeper, also made the tortillas."

Stephen put in, "Tortillas are a type of flat bread."

Iphigenia was more interested in the mention of a housekeeper. "So your father has someone to cook and clean and do the laundry?"

"Of course. You won't have to do any of that." Cassie's tone was full of pride. "Our Pa owns one of the biggest ranches in this area of the country—three thousand acres. Our house has glass windows and real wooden floors. It's very nice. That's why Pa wants to marry a real lady."

Glass windows and wooden floors? That made Ryerson well-to-do for this part of the country? Iphigenia told herself to be thankful for small favors. She was already appalled at her surroundings, a seemingly endless wilderness where nothing existed for seventy miles beyond El Paso, a horrid place in and of itself. Gazing out on the road that wound around rocks and sometimes too near deep crevices, Iphigenia once again wondered about her decision to come here. At the very least, every bone in her body would be bruised by the time they reached the ranch.

Many hours later, Iphigenia was far too numb to feel any bruises. She hardly noticed that the land had changed subtly.

As the buckboard topped a gentle hill, Cassie announced, "This is my Pa's spread—the R&Y."

Iphigenia focused bleary eyes.

Before them stretched a surprisingly grassy vale crossed by a big creek, in places edged with tall broad-leafed trees. At the nearest end of the basin, inside a huge fenced enclosure, sat a sprawling house of timber and adobe. Several imposing trees shaded the back of the house, while some distance away from the residence, numerous barns or sheds stood, many connected to pens for animals. Horses grazed, as well as cattle. Within one of the pens, some mounted men were chasing cows, swinging ropes against their mounts and yelling.

Still sorting cows? Iphigenia wondered. She glanced up at the swinging sign over the gate as they rolled through—the name Ryerson had been carved into the wood.

She'd be meeting Monte Ryerson any minute. If she weren't so fatigued, she supposed she should try to brush off some of the new dust that had accumulated on her traveling costume over the filthy miles. Her hair probably looked like a bird's nest, but she'd grown tired of wearing her hat miles ago and had removed it, placing the fancy felt with feathers and veil in her carpet-bag along with her leather gloves. She'd also folded and laid aside her parasol when her arms grew too tired to keep holding it aloft. Doing so had exposed her to the sun, of course, and now the skin across her nose felt sore, probably sunburned.

Stephen slowed the team of horses as they neared the house, and turning to Cassie said, "You'd better tell her now."

The girl had been quiet for the last hour or so of their journey—Iphigenia assumed from weariness.

"Tell me what?" She frowned at both of them.

"Um." Cassie looked like she wanted to squirm. "Er, well, you're going to be a surprise."

"Some surprise," Stephen complained. "What is Pa going to say? I shouldnt've agreed to any part of this."

Cassie swallowed. "Pa didn't place that advertisement in the newspaper, Miss Wentworth. I did." Her voice was a little shaky. She added quickly, "Please don't be mad. He'll like you—you're so pretty—and he really does need a wife."

Iphigenia's mouth went dry. "I'm a surprise?" Suddenly her entire plan was cast in a new, more doubtful light. "Damnation!" Surely she couldn't have come all this way for nothing. She had to be reunited with her baby at all costs.

"There's Pa out on the porch," Stephen said.

Iphigenia looked dead ahead. A tall figure detached itself from the shadows of the house's front overhang and descended a short flight of steps to approach. The man's walk was all smooth muscle and, as he came closer, Iphigenia noted his bronzed skin, strong features, and shoulder-length black hair.

Good Lord, the man was a savage.

Monte Ryerson glared at all three people mounted on the buckboard, though his attention centered on Stephen. "Where the hell have you been all day? I thought you must have taken off with your little sister and sold her to some bandits."

"Sorry, Pa."

"Sorry isn't an explanation."

Stephen gave Cassie an angry look, prompting the girl to speak up. "We went to El Paso to fetch Miss Wentworth. She came all the way from New York on the train."

"Who the hell is Miss Wentworth?"

Ryerson's hostile gaze burned into Iphigenia. His eyes seemed as black as his hair. He was attractive in his own way, she admitted, but so wild and fierce looking, she could almost imagine him lifting her scalp. The only Indian she'd ever seen before had been in a Wild West show.

The man continued to stare, this time addressing her directly. "Who are you?"

For the first time in her life, she was nearly speechless. "Well—"

Cassie intervened. "Miss Wentworth came here to marry you, Pa. She's looking for a husband and you need a wife."

Surprise suffused Ryerson's features, followed by an expression that seemed far from pleased. Again, he spoke directly to Iphigenia. "What kind of trick are you trying to play here? I oughta run you off my property."

Run her off the property? After days of uncomfortable train travel, then hours of a bone-crushing ride on a buckboard?

Leery of the man's latent ferocity, Iphigenia nevertheless managed to find her tongue . . . along with a righteous flare of anger. "I am not running anywhere, Mr. Ryerson. I am exhausted and frustrated, as much a victim of your daughter's ruse as you yourself." She reached for her carpetbag and threw it to the ground. "I am getting off this chariot from hell and walking into your primitive excuse for a house. If you don't like it, then you must do what you will—drag me behind your horse or shoot me full of arrows."

Now it was her would-be husband's turn to be speechless. As Iphigenia dismounted from the buckboard, she saw the light that flared in the depths of his dark eyes. Was it surprise, she wondered, or perhaps respect?

Monte stood stock still and watched the haughty blonde pick up her carpetbag and march toward the house. Despite the grime on her skin and her sunburn, Miss Iphigenia Wentworth was truly and elegantly beautiful. Her chiseled features revealed a bone structure as finely formed as any blooded horse's, and her masses of pale gold hair seemed to shine in the growing dusk. Most fascinating, she held herself with as much pride and fire as any warrior.

That thought reminded him of her reference to his Indian heritage. Before she'd gotten her back up, he'd caught a flash of fear in her expression. No doubt a mail-order bride from New York hadn't expected to be matched up with a half-breed.

That she was there at all, though, was the problem. Stephen, obviously feeling guilty, was blurting out all the details of the newspaper advertisement and the train ticket purchase. Monte returned his attention to his kids.

"Why would you do a stupid thing like that?" he asked his son angrily. "You're too old for such shenanigans." And he came around the buckboard to deal with Cassie, who was sliding to the ground. "Don't you think you're going anywhere, girl. You're in deep trouble. I oughta lock you up for a year."

She gazed up at her father, mouth trembling. "I thought you would like her!"

Cassie had always been more dreamy than practical, but Monte had never thought she'd do something crazy. "You can't match people up like a cow and a bull. And where did you get the money for the ticket anyhow? Did you dig around the bureau in my room? Search my pockets?"

A tear seeped out of Cassie's eye and slid down her cheek. "I wouldn't steal! I borrowed the money from Stephen." Then she broke into sobs and took off at a dead run, holding her pink skirts up out of her way.

"Come back here!" Monte roared, striding in pursuit.

But the girl only ran faster. Behind Monte, Stephen called, "She *did* borrow the money from me, Pa, honest."

Monte stalked on, until he heard a new, icy voice. "Enough! Stop right there!"

He whipped around.

The blonde woman had dropped her carpetbag to run after him. "Leave the poor child alone! Perhaps she has made a mistake but she doesn't deserve to be beaten."

"I'm not going to beat her," Monte growled, upset that anyone would think so. Did his anger seem that ferocious? "I never beat a young one in my life." He only intended to catch up with Cassie and give her more of a talking to. "Go back to the house and mind your own business."

"This *is* my business." Iphigenia Wentworth retreated a couple of steps, but no fear glinted in her eyes. She stuck out her chin and placed her hands on her hips. "I answered an advertisement in good faith, whether it was placed in a newspaper by you or your child. The damage has been done. I am here. It would seem more sensible to work out this matter between the two of us, not rant and rave at her."

"I won't have my daughter thinking she can do whatever she gets into her head."

"Then talk to her when you have calmed down. *If* you are ever calm. With a father who shouts and makes accusations and wishes to think the worst, it is no wonder she longed to obtain a parent who was softer and more liberal."

The woman's speech sounded impassioned, as if she had some personal experience with the subject.

But Monte wasn't about to be told what to do, and by a stranger. "Who says she wanted another parent?"

"She did. She wanted a wife for you and a mother for her. That is how the advertisement was worded."

At this new bit of information, Monte scowled, though his anger was slowly fading.

"You do not have to worry about the imposition of my presence here anyway," Iphigenia went on. "I had a good reason for traveling to Texas. As soon as I have taken care of it, I shall be most happy to return to New York."

That didn't sit well with Monte. "You're not taking off until I say so. Besides, you just stood there and admitted that my daughter wants a mother."

"But you don't want a wife."

He couldn't tell if that was a relief to her or not. If she *was* relieved, he couldn't help feeling annoyed. "Don't plan on going anywhere yet. I don't know what I'm going to do."

Her eyes widened. "You don't mean to say that you would consider marrying me?"

"You came here under that assumption. And my daughter paid for your train ticket. She must be expecting something from you. You're gonna have to stick around, at least for a while, until things get sorted out."

"But . . ."

Good. That shut her up. "Go back to the house. I thought you said you were tired. Sit down and wait until I come back." He still wanted to talk to Cassie, if not give her the tongue-lashing he'd originally intended.

"Sit?" She took a big breath. "I am no dog to be ordered about."

"Look, lady, I don't know how you want me to talk to you. Go sit, lie down, prance up and down, dance on the roof. I don't care."

He turned his back and walked away, surprised to hear low cursing behind him, a string of words that would make a churchman blush.

Miss Iphigenia Wentworth might be a lady—she certainly looked like one and spoke with education—but she could use language that would do justice to an old cowpoke with the seat of his longjohns caught in barbed wire.

*   *   *

Ginnie Ryerson said nothing as the blonde woman clashed past her on the porch. What a stupid thing for Cassie to do—send away for some mail-order bride through a newspaper. She couldn't understand what her sister was about. But then, they'd been growing apart the last year or so.

Ginnie herself wasn't very interested in the whole show. She'd only watched because everybody was making so much noise.

Who cared about the ordinary world, when a person had a secret that went far beyond it?

Filled with anticipation, she slid into the house and sneaked down the long corridor that connected most of the rooms. Her own territory beckoned, the small space she'd carved out for herself in the attic under the eaves. She ran up the narrow stairs that led to her makeshift lair, flopping down on the narrow bunk she'd moved out of the room she used to share with Cassie. Her bed was right under the window where she had a view of grazing land and mountains looming in the distance.

But the landscape she was most interested in could lie in the palm of her hand.

Reaching beneath the mattress, she pulled out the little mirror necklace she'd found beneath a chair downstairs. She polished it with a sleeve and stared into the mirror's silvery face.

"Are you there?" she said softly, searching for the spirit who inhabited the thing. Then she reworded the question in Spanish.

There was no answer in either language.

But maybe that was only because it wasn't dark enough.

Xosi Baca would eventually appear, Ginnie could

count on that. And once again, she would tell Ginnie not to worry, that Ginnie was very smart and important, that Xosi would help her get whatever she wanted.

Of course, Ginnie had asked what Xosi wanted in return. The answer was: freedom.

Xosi had already had a taste of that last night with Ginnie. But Ginnie suspected that Xosi had also managed to free herself from the mirror at other times to wander through the house in the dark.

Unless the footsteps and the laughter had only been a dream. Ginnie wasn't sure exactly who or what Xosi was, but she was fascinated by the mirror and its inhabitant, respectful of Xosi's power. Fed up with her own boring existence, disheartened by the gap that had grown between her and the rest of her family, Ginnie would give just about anything to possess some power herself.

She felt certain the little mirror and its magic could give that to her.

3

"Señorita Wentworth?"

"Hmm? What?" Dozing, Iphigenia started, wondering where she was.

A dark-haired, middle-aged woman peeked shyly through the doorway. She spoke with a soft accent. "I have made a late supper. You may join us at the table if you are hungry."

Hungry? Iphigenia's stomach growled. "I shall be there. Thank you."

Rising to her elbows, she gazed about the bedroom that Carmen, Ryerson's housekeeper, had made up for her. Exhausted and thankful she hadn't been trundled into the master's quarters—although that would have been unlikely since he hadn't known of her existence before today—she'd barely washed up, removed her outer clothing, and shimmied out of her corset, before she'd fallen on the bed to drift into deep sleep. She had no idea how long ago that had been.

But she wasn't about to pass up food. The chili stew and insubstantial tortillas felt like distant memories. She groaned at the feel of her stiff back and sore muscles, as she threw aside her covering and sat up to put her feet on the floor. Then she turned up the wick of the kerosene lamp that glowed beside the bed. Her trunks lay in the middle of the room, having been carried there by some surly looking, mustached men.

She'd been so comfortable sleeping in her petticoat and camisole, she hated to get dressed. But supper beckoned. She stood, stretched her sore body, and hobbled for the washstand to scrub her face and arms again. Then she rummaged in the carpetbag for keys, opened a trunk, and pulled out the first garment she found, her brown riding habit.

That seemed appropriate for a ranch, where, she was certain, people didn't dress formally for dinner. She was also fairly sure that no one around here wore corsets. She thought she could squeeze into the riding habit's skirts if she left the top buttons open and wore the shirt outside.

She was equally casual with her thick waist-length hair, brushing it back quickly and tying it with a ribbon before leaving the room.

Delicious aromas wafted through the corridor. She would have been able to find the kitchen and the dining table by the smells alone, even if she hadn't seen those areas of the house when she first entered. Carmen had stared at her curiously but had been helpful, providing her with a pitcher of washing water as well as a place to rest.

The woman still wore a questioning look when Iphigenia entered the dining room. Monte Ryerson stared openly, his black gaze disconcerting. His three offspring were already seated, Cassie's face swollen from weeping. Still, the girl managed a shaky smile.

Iphigenia couldn't help feeling sympathetic toward the girl. She had found her emotions surprisingly stirred when Monte had carried on, yelling at his daughter when they'd arrived.

She took the chair next to Cassie's. "Good evening."

"Good evening."

No one else said a word. Stephen merely nodded, Monte maintained his silent stare, and Cassie's twin sister, Ginnie, didn't even raise her glance to the visitor. Iphigenia had caught sight of the slimmer, darker girl upon entering the ranch house. Acting as furtive as a wild animal, Ginnie had then quickly disappeared.

Well, Iphigenia shouldn't care if her presence was or was not appreciated at the moment. Her goal was sustenance.

"Please help yourself." Cassie passed a heaping platter of roast beef that made Iphigenia's mouth water.

There were also beans, rice, some sort of sausages, and corn bread. Iphigenia dug in with enthusiasm.

While she ate, she covertly observed her intended "husband." He was definitely handsome, if wild looking, with his long raven-dark hair and exotic rugged features. He had wide shoulders and strong arms. For some reason, Iphigenia found herself imagining what those arms would feel like wrapped around her body. What in Hades was the matter with her? she thought, face growing warm.

Monte was also watching her. Finally, he asked, "Have a nice nap? Now that you're rested, I figured we could get down to the dragging behind horses and arrow-shooting."

He spoke so bluntly, she couldn't tell if he was being sarcastic. "I assume you mean to be humorous."

"What if I don't?"

"Then I suppose I shall have to fetch my pistols and defend myself."

"You have pistols?"

"And I know how to shoot."

"Oughta fit right in out here in the Wild West then."

He chuckled, though no one else laughed. And Iphigenia felt no real fear. Ryerson simply had to be needling her.

The man then directed his attention to his son, asking the boy about some ranching duties. Stephen answered soberly, obviously continuing to feel ill at ease because of his part in Iphigenia's arrival. He didn't look much like his father, except for his height and large-boned build. He had blue eyes, rather than brown like the girls', and Iphigenia guessed that their mother must have been white.

She wondered if Monte Ryerson would make good on his threat about marrying her. Although she needed her trust fund to support her and Hope, she found the idea of wedding a stranger disconcerting now that she faced the reality of such a situation. And Monte Ryerson scared her . . . for reasons other than his mock threat about exchanging arrows and bullets. The man's Indian heritage might have something to do with it. He certainly was wild and in a true sense wilder than the reckless man who'd fathered her baby.

Moreover, Ryerson exuded a fierce power Iphigenia found frightening, if fascinating. She wasn't certain whether that came from the attraction she felt for him—against her will—or whether there was something deep and dark within him, secrets that called out to a woman who had never particularly been happy, who had lived through some deep, dark moments herself.

But Iphigenia wanted to set aside her worries. She needed to maintain calm. Making Cassie feel more at ease might help. Not that she approved of the girl placing the advertisement. But she could identify with someone who got into trouble with her father, not to mention a child who had wanted a mother so badly she was willing to go to so much effort in the first place. She realized that that was what had caused her intense reaction to Monte's yelling earlier.

Helping herself to more beans, she asked the girl, "Is this dish another sort of chili?"

Cassie shook her head. "Just black beans and pintos with some bacon and seasoning."

"Spicy seasoning," said Iphigenia. She thought the taste rather interesting, but she got a surprise when she took her next bite of corn bread. "Oh!" Eyes watering, she stared at the bread, noting a bit of green in the middle. "What in Hades . . . er, what on earth is in here?"

"Jalapeño peppers," said the young girl. "Do you like them?"

Actually, she didn't, but Iphigenia struggled to be complimentary. "They certainly make the bread interesting." She nibbled at it more gingerly, avoiding the jalapeño.

"Mexican cooking uses a lot of chilies," Cassie went on. "That's what they're called—where the name for chili stew came from. There's all kinds of chilies, green and red. Jalapenos aren't so bad but watch out for the little, bitty green ones. They'll set your mouth on fire."

"Thank you for the warning," said Iphigenia, feeling as if steam would start to come out of her ears any second. The jalapeños had already burned her mouth. But she acted like she was having a good time and smiled, pleased when she got a return grin from Cassie.

"I guess they don't have peppers in New York," Ginnie remarked from across the table.

Iphigenia turned her attention to the other twin. At last the girl had said something. "We use sweet peppers, rather than hot."

"What would the usual meal be like in New York?" asked Cassie.

Iphigenia thought of the formal way her father and aunt always dined, even when the number of guests at the table was limited. "We would probably start with a soup course. And we would frequently have a seafood dish, stuffed fowl, and perhaps lamb or beef."

"And a fancy dessert, I suppose?" inquired Cassie. "We're having plain old apple pie tonight."

"Apple pie sounds wonderful," said Iphigenia, though she was already nearly full.

Ginnie stabbed at the food on her plate for a moment, then made a rude noise. "You don't really like our food," she told Iphigenia. "You hated the jalapeños and I bet you think apples are boring. I bet you'd love to go back to New York. Why did you really come out to Texas anyway? You don't belong here."

Cassie looked stricken. "Ginnie! That isn't nice— insulting a guest."

"She's *your* guest, not mine," Ginnie returned. "And I can say whatever I want."

Though Iphigenia had had plenty of experience with speaking her mind when she shouldn't, she felt moved to put Ginnie in her place. "You can indeed say anything you want but you would do well to think about the repercussions of being unpleasant. The more civilized and clever way to insult someone is by being indirect. Your victim will receive the message, yet often be caught too much off-guard to respond in kind."

Ginnie was not deterred. "You use big words, but that doesn't make them important."

"Ginnie." Now Monte Ryerson stepped in. "I don't like arguments at the table. And I also don't like children mouthing off to their elders. If you can't behave yourself, you can take a walk."

"All right." Throwing her fork down as Carmen was clearing the dishes and starting to serve pie, Ginnie gave Iphigenia a look of pure hatred and strode out of the room.

That's when Iphigenia noticed the girl wore trousers. Was the style normal for girls and women in this wild country?

"Insults are mean, whether they're indirect or not," Monte went on, looking directly at Iphigenia. "Everybody gets along in this family or they have to deal with me."

Iphigenia wasn't about to be told what to do and she wasn't a member of Ryerson's family. "I believe we already have an assignation for the exchange of arrows and bullets. Do you want to step outside immediately?"

"Those words don't sound too indirect."

Iphigenia shrugged. "Sometimes I fail to follow my own advice."

Monte scowled, looking like he wanted to say something else, but was holding himself back. Finally, moving his dark, penetrating gaze to the pie, he dug in. He'd only gotten a few bites, however, when one of the ranch workers, a short, bow-legged man, appeared in the kitchen doorway.

"Mr. Ryerson? Found out what happened to those hosses in the north pasture last night. You might wanta come take a look at what's left of 'em."

Monte seemed startled and pushed aside his plate. "Okay, Shorty. I'll be right out." When Stephen started to rise, he said, "No, you finish your food. I'll take care of things."

Thus ended the first real meal Iphigenia had eaten in West Texas, as well as her second conversation with Monte Ryerson. Exhaustion seeping slowly back into her limbs, she decided she'd finish the pie and make a run for her bedroom so there wouldn't be another go-round tonight.

*   *   *

Monte frowned at the lathered animals his wranglers had herded into a corral. Nearly saddle-broke, the small herd had been grazing some distance from the buildings before being run off in the wee hours the night before.

"Whoever them hombres was, they didn't really wanta steal these cayuses," said Norbert Tyler, one of the cowboys who'd returned the horses. "Or they would've headed 'em for Mexico. They jest wanted to spook 'em."

Monte had already figured that out, having tracked the smears the invaders' horses had made until they split off from the herd. The thieves had covered their mounts' hooves with cloth Indian-style, so their prints couldn't be identified. The only problem left to deal with had been to round up the horses, which is why he'd sent some of his men and hadn't gone along himself.

"Them sum-bitches did a damned good job of spookin'," said Shorty, the leader of the round-up crew. "We couldn't catch three or four hosses. High-tailed it like the devil hisself was after 'em. And found a mare layin' on a mesa, dead. Plain run herself to death."

"Run to death?" Monte was surprised. And angry. The fact that Iphigenia's arrival had gotten him all riled up earlier didn't help any. "Who would want to run a horse to death when they were valued everywhere out west? And how could they run the mare to death anyway? They didn't follow the herd that far."

"Don't think it was jest the thieves," said Norbert. "Somethin' else scared the hell out of them animals in the first place."

"A cougar? Wolves?" Though Monte hadn't seen any signs of either predator around the ranch in a long time.

Shorty shook his grizzled head. "Bill says there was some kinda spook light out there last night."

"Spook light?" Monte felt a chill.

"Pablo here seen it, too," Norbert said, nodding toward another wrangler. "We was up late, takin' a smoke outside when we saw some kinda greenish light flutterin' around way up on the hill. I think it made them hosses take off and the thieves jest followed 'em."

More men had gathered from the bunkhouse, including Monte's foreman, Jake O'Brian.

"Guess ghosts and evil spirits and such sure can scare an animal," muttered Jake, stroking his bushy mustache. He pointed at a sweating bay. "Look at that horse's eyes. They're still rollin'."

Monte couldn't give in to superstition, at least not in front of his men. He didn't believe Jake or Shorty would have either, if the three of them hadn't made that fateful trip deep into Mexico the previous fall.

Though he wasn't certain about the situation himself, he insisted, "I don't know what you saw, Norbert. Or you either, Pablo. But there weren't any spooks."

"Then how do you explain what happened?" Jake asked, giving him a slant-eyed look. "And why did that waterhole over east go bad all of a sudden? And why are we findin' cows laying dead for no reason? Things aren't doing so well around here."

"Don't know that I have an explanation but I don't believe we're talking about anything unnatural." Monte hoped not anyway. "Waterholes go bad every once in a while in desert country. You know that. And cattle die."

Not to mention that he had some enemies, the worst of which was Jonah Barkley, his estranged stepfather. Monte's grandfather Ryerson had paid Barkley to marry Monte's mother and take her away from the Comanche warrior she fancied.

Growing even angrier at the thought of Barkley, he ordered, "Let's get these horses cooled down, see that they don't make themselves sick by drinking too much water."

Some of the men started to go about the task, but several of them muttered among themselves.

"Sure that one of your enemies didn't put a spell on you, Mr. Ryerson?" Norbert asked. "Luis Padilla ain't too happy that his brother got kilt in Mexico."

"None too happy about it myself," said Monte, having felt low as a snake when he'd had to talk to the family. "Roberto was a good man."

"And it ain't Mr. Ryerson's fault what happened," added Shorty.

Monte was glad to hear that vote of confidence but noticed Jake had nothing to say. His foreman had been acting odd the past months, maybe a bit spooked himself. Possibly because the man had seen things that didn't agree with his view of what was real and what was not.

"Nobody likes losing someone they love," said Monte. "Tobias Perez was shot out of his saddle by the bandits we chased into Mexico, the ones who began all the trouble. His family buried Tobias and mourned him, but they don't blame anybody for his death."

Though he sometimes couldn't help blaming himself. Still, he had to keep his men in check. Because cattle prices had been low, he'd been working with a skeleton crew whose hours were long and wages were late every month. They were already edgy. Figuring those who'd been grousing would calm down if he helped with the work tonight, he went into the corral and got busy.

"Say, who was that pretty lady I saw ridin' in with your kids on the buckboard?" one of the men asked.

"A visitor," was all Monte would say. About the lady part, he wasn't certain.

"How long she stayin'?" asked Shorty.

"Don't know for sure. Probably no more than a week or so."

He hoped to talk Cassie into that, as long he could avoid giving in to the temptation to keep the tart-tongued but beautiful blonde around so he simply could look at her.

He had enough problems already.

Iphigenia undressed and returned to bed but she couldn't sleep. Though she remained exhausted, she felt all wound up, worrying about her baby, thinking about Monte Ryerson and his children, considering all the complications that had cropped up. Tossing and turning, she wished she'd packed a flask of smooth bourbon in one of the trunks. Actually, even a glass of wine would do.

Wondering if Monte Ryerson kept spirits somewhere in his house, she rose and peeked out into the corridor. Finding it empty, she threw a wrapper over her night-gown and went out to explore. The place seemed completely deserted, the children having gone to bed and Carmen having returned to her own abode after cleaning up. Cassie said that the housekeeper and her husband occupied a small house on the grounds.

Kerosene lamps burned in the kitchen and in the parlor area that opened off the dining room. Orange-gold light flooded the whitewashed adobe walls.

Iphigenia searched every cupboard and cabinet, all to no avail. Wandering through the parlor, she ran her fingers along the edge of one of the blanket-covered sofas. The throws were colorful, obviously of Mexican or Indian make, as were the rugs covering the wooden floors.

Beside a well-worn chair stood a stack of newspapers and other publications. Iphigenia spotted an issue of *The New York Crier*. Monte Ryerson might be a savage, and he hadn't written either the advertisement or the letter enclosing the train ticket, but Iphigenia assumed he was literate. He spoke intelligently enough, if not intellectually.

Sighing with frustration at the way her well thought-out plan had taken an abrupt turn for the worse, Iphigenia entered the corridor again and approached a half-open door not far from her own. Even in the dim light, she could tell it wasn't a bedroom. She brought the lamp from her own quarters to see a roll-top desk standing against one wall and a tall cabinet occupying the farthest corner.

She approached the latter, smiling when she spotted a bottle of yellowish liquid that had to be liquor. It was labeled in Spanish but she didn't care what the contents were, as long as they were alcoholic. Conveniently enough, there were also several squat glasses in the cabinet.

Pouring herself a generous serving, Iphigenia took a big swallow, closing her watering eyes as the liquor burned a path to her stomach. The liquor had an odd salty flavor, but did its job. Warmth seeped through her limbs. Soothed already, she finished the glass and poured herself another before sliding down into the chair before the roll-top desk.

"You drink, too?"

The question suddenly coming from the shadows of the corridor would have made Iphigenia jump if she weren't so relaxed. She wasn't too relaxed, however, not to feel slightly nervous at the sound of Ryerson's voice.

"Surely you don't object to a guest having a glass of spirits. After all, no wine was served with dinner."

"Guess West Texas doesn't live up to New York standards. Didn't have all those courses, either," he said, stepping into the room, his face dark and enigmatic.

The way he loomed over her made Iphigenia think his height topped six feet. On the tall and willowy side herself, she'd already noticed he bested her by several inches. With broad shoulders and long muscular legs, he was a fine figure of a man. She watched him as he went to the cabinet and picked up the bottle.

"Mexican tequila. Ever had this stuff before? Kinda strong for most ladies."

"Society women in New York have been known to drink spirits when they so desired, at least in the privacy of their own quarters or at gambling parties."

"Society?" Monte poured himself half a glass and turned to gaze down at her. "Are you saying you're from upper-class type of people?"

Iphigenia took a big sip herself, smiling as another wave of warmth stole over her. She felt proud that she could hold her liquor and remain in control. "My blood runs true blue."

"Hmm, never knew that blue-blooded ladies cursed like sailors."

Was he actually doubting her? Iphigenia gave him a haughty look, realizing at the same time that he was running his eyes over her. And she wore only the thin silk wrapper and nightgown. "I am not the usual lady," she said sternly, sitting up straighter, pulling her wrapper tighter. "But I *am* a lady. My father is Horace Wentworth of Park Avenue. He is the owner and president of New York Central Maritime Bank."

"Never heard of the man."

"You will find his name in some of those papers you have stacked in the parlor."

"Yeah? And that's where you could have read about him, too."

Now Iphigenia was beginning to feel angry. "Are you questioning my veracity? You, who are nothing more than—"

"A savage?" He pulled another chair out from where it sat against the opposite wall and sat down. "Get your names right, *lady*. I'm a half-breed, not a full-blood. Half Penateka Comanche and half Ryerson. Will, that was my white grandfather, was one of the founding pioneers around here."

She nodded, pretending she wasn't that interested in the information. "What is a Penateka Comanche?"

"The Penatekas were a tribe that used to live in Southern Texas. They owned thousands of horses. Introduced them to the Plains Indians up north."

"A service for which they should be commended by the U.S. Army, I'm sure," she said, sarcastic.

"The Comanche already paid plenty to the U.S. Army—lost their land, their people, a lot of them their very lives."

He didn't sound bitter, though.

"Are you still on the warpath about that?" she asked, using a term she'd read about.

"I'm half white, too. I'd have to be at war against myself." Then he turned the conversation back to her. "Lady or not, I'd appreciate your watching your mouth around my kids."

She could hardly believe he dared chastise her. "I said no more than you. I know you spoke two 'hells' to one of my 'damnations'."

"You said a lot more than that when we were arguing out there. And you never know who's around to hear. I'd also appreciate your trying to hold back the insults, especially about Indians. At least in front of my kids. They've got Comanche blood, too. Have it out with me, if you want, but don't be mean to them."

Her eyes were green, but he'd already realized that at dinner. Green and shimmery as emeralds. Now, in the lamplight, they sparkled with anger. Iphigenia Wentworth definitely had a temper.

"I have no intention of being cruel to your children," she said tightly. "I would never yell at them, unlike you."

Now she was hurt, he realized. "I'm only asking for *decent* where behavior is concerned."

"Are you insinuating I am indecent?" She really had her back up. "In my vocabulary, indecent means lewd. What do you think I am? A harlot?"

No, he thought. Not unless she was a high-priced one.

But he didn't get a chance to say anything before she went on. "I *am* the daughter of Horace T. Wentworth. My Aunt Gertrude Wentworth Cummings is a hostess in the finest Knickerbocker tradition."

He recognized the term from having come across it in the New York newspapers.

Iphigenia's hand shook, sloshing the tequila around as she became even more upset. "I have given you absolutely no reason to think I am a lightskirt. I have not so much as flirted with you."

No, though he couldn't say as that would be unpleasant. "Don't get your tail in a spin—"

"My tail?" Now she leaned forward, as if she were going to strike him or throw the liquor in his face. "How dare you!"

He took hold of her hand, appreciating its softness. "Calm down. I'm talking like a Texan. Tail is only a word, not lingo for your behind." Pretty as it surely must be, he added to himself. "You musta known that somebody would have some questions about what a woman like you is doing out here. Never seen an outfit like the one you were wearing when you arrived tonight, not even in Kansas City." That was the biggest city he'd been to, and just once, when he'd driven cattle there.

When he reluctantly let go of her, Iphigenia seemed to settle down. She took a long swig of tequila, draining her glass. "I had a disagreement with my father. We aren't close."

"Enough of a disagreement to take off for Texas to be a mail-order bride? I'd never let one of my daughters do a thing like that." Even if she was older—Iphigenia was at least twenty-five.

She lowered her gaze. "My father doesn't know that I am here."

"So you ran away?" That explained why she'd needed a train ticket. She had two trunks of clothes or belongings but obviously no cash.

He waited for an answer to his question but she placed the glass down on the desk and gazed off into the shadows. Probably not wanting to admit anything. He gulped down some liquor himself.

Then he probed, "You said you had a good reason to be in Texas, something you had to take care of."

"A business matter."

"What type of business matter?"

"I do not have to explain."

"To an intended husband? I think you do."

She looked at him, eyes widening, once again impressing him with her fine-boned, fiery beauty. Her golden hair shone about her face like a halo, though he suspected she was no angel.

"Are you truly going to insist that I marry you?" she asked.

"What did you expect? Did you think you could take a train ticket from somebody, come clear out here and renege on your promise?" Not that he actually *did* intend to marry her, but he'd needle her plenty. "You can't waltz onto my place and take advantage of my hospitality, without giving anything back."

"What do you want?"

He could tell exactly what was going through her mind, but he hedged. "I'm not sure what I want. I told you I'll have to think about it."

Especially where Cassie was concerned. He'd seen how upset his daughter was when they'd had a talk earlier.

"I suppose I could stay on as a sort of governess, to teach your children some of the finer social graces. If you don't think that would be insulting them, that is."

She stood up, swaying a little. But who wouldn't, unless they were used to strong tequila? From his count, she'd had two hefty glasses.

She looked at him, her mouth pouty. "And I'll have you know that teaching social graces is all I will do. I don't want to be your wife, but I am certainly not going to share your bed unless we are married."

He felt a spark of desire. "I didn't ask you to." Much as he'd enjoy getting his hands on her.

"You may say what you will. But from my experience with men, I know that it is not beneath any one of them to ask for a woman's . . . body, in trade. I am certain that was the reason you inferred I might be a harlot in the first place."

"I didn't call you any names. You took things the wrong way. I only asked a few questions. I have the right."

"No, you do not have the right. Insulting a woman's reputation is something that is not done, at least it is not spoken of openly."

He stood, too, liking the fact that she was so tall. She only had to raise her face a little bit to look him in the eye. "Maybe they don't talk about such in New York, not in Knickerbocker society. But if that's the case, I get the feeling you don't always follow the rules. You seem to speak pretty straight about anything you want to."

She sighed. "I suppose I do have a sharp tongue at times."

This was the first admission of any fault or weakness he had heard from her. Actually, he liked her spicy personality. It gave her an extra dimension, like spirit in a good horse.

"Well, you don't need to be dancing around bushes out here. We usually talk straight, speak our minds."

"As long as I do not swear or insult your heritage."

"Use common sense. We wouldn't have had this whole conversation in front of the kids."

She started to leave but wobbled and caught the edge of the roll-top desk.

He reached out to take hold of her arm. "You've had too much tequila."

"I can hold my liquor," she insisted. "I have always been able to do so." But her voice was slurred.

"Still, you'd better be careful with this. It's a might stronger than you're probably used to. And you've had an exhausting day."

He took hold of her shoulders and pointed her toward the door. A strand of her golden hair lay against his hand. He touched the curl lightly, appreciating its softness.

"Um-m." She turned toward him, her perfectly shaped lips half parted.

He felt a hot wave of desire but fought it, and pointing said, "Your room is in that direction."

Still, she stared at him. "You are handsome in your own way, I'll admit that."

He wondered if she was picking up the sensations that sizzled through his veins, but he refused to take advantage of a drunken woman. "I should be flattered, I guess," he said tightly.

"You like my looks, too."

He was going to have to draw on all his strength. "I don't think we should be discussing this in your state. Go to bed."

"Don't order me around." She leaned toward him, her warm breath feathering his face.

"If you don't go down that hall right now, I'm going to kiss you." At the very least, he added to himself.

"Kiss me?" She giggled. "First it's arrows and bullets. Now kisses."

He was only human, damn it. Reaching for her, he drew her to him, covering her mouth with his. She pressed herself against him, winding her arms about his neck. He kissed her deeply, reveling in the sweet softness of her lips, the intoxicating taste of her. The curves of her body pressed against the thin material of her gown. He became instantly aroused.

But this wouldn't do. He broke off the kiss and walked her across the hallway. He even pushed her gently toward her bedroom.

"Go to bed. Lock your door."

She mumbled something unintelligible but went inside the room, thank God. Monte glanced over his shoulder, taking a deep breath. He still wasn't certain Iphigenia Wentworth was a lady, but he knew he was more of a gentleman then she would ever appreciate.

In the dead of night, Iphigenia awakened to the sound of soft footsteps in the corridor. Monte? But the soft throaty laugh she then heard seemed to be female. Strange . . .

She jumped when something suddenly thudded against her door. It was locked, thank heavens. Her mind was muzzy, but she remembered following Monte's orders.

Click. Click.

The doorknob was turning, rattling.

"What? Who's there?" Iphigenia raised her head.

Only to hear the same female voice mutter something in Spanish.

"Carmen?"

But there was no answer and Iphigenia was suddenly too tired and dizzy to care. Even in the darkness, the room spun. For the first time in a very long while, she'd managed to get drunk.

"I am having hallucinations," she decided, letting her head flop back down. She shouted at the door, "Go away!"

Then she squeezed her eyes shut and pulled the pillow over her head, hoping she wouldn't feel too badly in the morning.

4

"*Great-gramma Ryerson* had silver plate and pretty china," Cassie told Iphigenia. "Ma showed me some pieces once, said she was scared to lose or break them. I don't know where everything is stored, maybe in the attic."

"Then we'll take a look there." Seated at the dining room table, Iphigenia sipped another strong cup of tea, attempting to clear her head.

She'd risen that morning with jumbled, embarrassing memories of the night before. Monte questioning her identity, challenging her claim to social position, chiding her for use of strong language . . .

Then soundly kissing her goodnight.

Iphigenia only wished she could recall the details of that kiss and exactly how it had come about. Surely it had been his idea, though the man hadn't taken further advantage of her. Mortifyingly enough, she realized she might have let him.

"So we're going to have a *real* dinner," Cassie said excitedly.

"This very evening, if I can make the proper arrangements." And even if it killed her, she would show Monte Ryerson a thing or two about society and manners. "We will have several courses and they will be served correctly."

But first, Iphigenia felt the need to wash the dust out of her pores. The kitchen had a pantry with a door that could be closed for privacy. Rushing to her bidding, Carmen heated water, spread an oilcloth on the pantry's floor, and carried in a round metal tub. It wasn't big enough to sit in but Iphigenia took a bath as best she could, using some scented soap she'd brought from New York.

Cassie bathed next and, as their hair dried, the two of them went over the types of foodstuffs available on the ranch. Iphigenia made up a list, which she gave to the housekeeper.

"This will be our menu for tonight."

The Mexican woman seemed perplexed, a little flustered. "Pardon, Señorita, but I do not read English so well."

"Yes, of course." Iphigenia felt badly that she hadn't realized this. "Start with soup—you said you have some squash that would do. Mix in cream and season it with salt and pepper." At least she thought that was what Cook did in her father's Manhattan kitchen. "Then we shall have an egg dish."

"Eggs? For supper?"

"Dinner," corrected Iphigenia. "Seafood is better but God only knows what sort of fish they have around here." *Oops.* She'd forgotten her language again—though obviously the same rules didn't apply to men as to women, considering how Monte often spoke. "Just boil the eggs and slice them. Serve them with a sauce."

"Salsa?"

"Um-hmm." She assumed that was the right Spanish word. "Hollandaise would be good. After the eggs will come sliced beef and stuffed quail. You said your husband shot some birds?"

"*Si*, Señorita."

"I suppose we shall have to have rice and beans again as side dishes. But you said there are greens that can be used for a salad. That's the traditional fourth course of a five course meal."

"I know where we can gather the greens," Cassie offered.

The girl had been following Iphigenia about, her constant shadow.

"Good. I think we should have fresh bread made with flour, not cornmeal," Iphigenia continued. "And what was the pudding you suggested for dessert, Carmen? Flan?"

"*Si*, Señorita." Though agreeable, the woman continued to look flustered.

But Iphigenia was certain everything would come together beautifully. Since Carmen was considered a good cook, how difficult could it be?

"I shall come back to the kitchen to help you a bit later," she promised. And to instruct the housekeeper on the proper way to serve. She patted Carmen's arm. "I know this is all new for you. We really should have a maid, as well as a cook and housekeeper."

Carmen merely nodded.

Iphigenia tied her hair back and headed for the dining room with Cassie trailing her and asking, "You really had a maid in New York?"

"Several of them, including a girl who saw to my wardrobe and my hair."

"A maid just for your clothes and hair." Cassie sighed. "My, aren't you going to miss all that in Texas?"

Iphigenia hoped not to stay so long that she would miss it, but she wasn't going to say so to Cassie. "Life is simpler here. I'll adjust."

Meanwhile, she and the thirteen year old climbed the narrow stairs to the attic, where they found a surly Ginnie stretched out on a small cot beneath the sole window.

"What are you doing here?" Ginnie asked, tone sour.

"We have to get into the storage area." Cassie gestured to the low door set in the inner wall. "We're going to bring out Great-gramma Ryerson's china and silver for a real fancy dinner."

"I don't want a fancy dinner."

"Then I guess you shouldn't eat," said Cassie.

Iphigenia felt the same way but she tried to handle things in a more polite, adult manner. Not that Monte's complaints about cruelty to his children had anything to do with it. She was simply in a better mood today.

"I am sure you will like the food, Ginnie, as well as the new experience."

Ginnie muttered ominously as Cassie stepped over the clothing scattered across the narrow floor and opened the big latch of the storage door. Iphigenia followed. Inside, Cassie lit a candle to illuminate the darkness. There was a large trunk and stacks of numerous crates, musty and covered with cobwebs.

Cassie handed Iphigenia the candle and opened the trunk. A cloud of dust rose, making both of them sneeze. After a few minutes of sorting through layers of fabric and paper, Cassie came up with a silverware case and located her grandmother's china plates.

It was an old design but authentic, Iphigenia noted, holding a plate up to the light to see the mark.

They found the rest of the china set packed in a crate, as well as lace-trimmed damask tablecloths with matching napkins. The fabric goods were wrinkled and yellowed with age. They wouldn't have time to try to wash them, but Iphigenia suggested they be shaken out and smoothed with a hot iron from the fire. Another task for Carmen.

The last treasures they located were some stemmed glasses and silver candleholders. Cassie held up a glass. "Isn't it lovely?"

"Very." Monte's grandmother clearly had had decent taste. But now there was the problem of bringing everything downstairs. "We'll have to make more than one trip . . . unless Ginnie can help us. Ginnie?" Iphigenia called, raising her voice.

In answer, she heard retreating footsteps.

"Isn't she disgusting?" Cassie whispered. "She didn't used to be like this. We used to have a good time together."

"Girls go through spells." Iphigenia could recall the times that excuse had been applied to her. "When did Ginnie change, anyway?"

"I'm not sure. She was always a tomboy who liked being outdoors. Sometimes she even rode with the cowboys. I can't remember when Ginnie started keeping to herself and acting so nasty." She sounded thoughtful. "I guess a couple of months ago."

But they had better things to do than worry about Ginnie. On their last trip to the attic, though, Iphigenia tripped over a shirt lying on the floor of Ginnie's room, sending something skittering across the floor.

Cassie picked up the object. It was a butcher knife. "What's this doing here? Carmen thought she lost it."

Iphigenia frowned. What purpose would Ginnie have with a knife?

Then again, on a Texas ranch where weapons were kept in the open, perhaps a girl having a knife wasn't anything to remark upon. She certainly hoped that was the case.

As she and Cassie walked down the long corridor downstairs, they passed Monte's bedroom. The door was open, and a gunbelt and revolver hung on the brass bedpost—no doubt a Colt .45. Having learned to shoot on country outings, Iphigenia knew something about guns. She could even identify the Springfield rifles on the rack on Monte's wall.

Ginnie was now lurking in the dining room. She gave Cassie and Iphigenia a scowl before starting to walk away.

"You could help us fill out menu cards, Ginnie," Iphigenia said, yet again trying to include the girl. "They will list the courses and we will need one for each person."

"I don't want menu cards."

"Then you could help fold napkins." And before Ginnie could come up with another excuse, Iphigenia informed her, "You will have to dress for dinner, you know. I assume you have a skirt or a frock of some sort."

Ginnie stopped and whirled around. "I'm not wearing any stupid dress!"

Iphigenia became more stern. "Then you will have to eat in the kitchen."

"Pa won't make me eat in the kitchen."

"I think he will," Iphigenia bluffed, wondering if he would think banishing Ginnie there too cruel. "I must be strict. He specifically asked me to share my knowledge of social graces with you children."

"I'm not a child!" Ginnie shouted, rushing toward one of the doors that opened to the outside. The wooden panel slammed behind her.

Cassie raised her brows, but Iphigenia said nothing. She'd wait until the evening to see how things went. She had a feeling that Ginnie wouldn't be the only disgruntled person, but she didn't care.

The morning and early afternoon passed quickly. Since Stephen and Monte had chosen to take "grub" with the men in the bunkhouse, Cassie and Iphigenia shared a light lunch of cheese and tortillas and got to know one another better. After eating, they rinsed the china and silverware, dealt with the tablecloth and napkins, set the table, made out menus, gathered greens, and helped Carmen cook.

Later in the afternoon, Iphigenia found time to unpack a few of her things. Cassie insisted on helping. The young girl oohed and awed over the beautiful clothing.

"I wish I had something like this." Cassie held up a silk tea-gown.

"Are there dressmakers in Texas? Perhaps we can have something made up for you."

"Do you think so?" The girl looked thrilled.

Again, Iphigenia felt touched. Cassie seemed so sweet and open. It seemed that the smallest nicety pleased her. "Maybe someone could even cut down one of my gowns," Iphigenia offered. She was rewarded by the girl's dazzling smile.

"Would you really let me have one of your dresses? Oh, that's too much. They're so beautiful!"

"But I have many. One less wouldn't hurt." And would obviously give the girl a great deal of pleasure.

Iphigenia wasn't certain how much a dress would ease the pain once Cassie's new "mother" was gone, however.

After spending two days together, she was getting an inkling of how high the girl's expectations were, and she couldn't help feeling guilty that she didn't mean to stay. Perhaps she should keep more distance between them. For the moment, she decided to send Cassie away by asking her to find some pretty greenery or flowers for a centerpiece. The girl agreed happily, saying she'd look down by the creek.

On her own for the first time that day, Iphigenia searched a trunk for her little Swiss music box. When she found it, she held the wooden box for a few moments, running her fingers over the carved lid, then placed it on the bureau at the foot of her bed. The tune would no longer play but the item was dear, since it had belonged to her mother.

Motherhood.

Both the music box and Cassie's anticipations reminded Iphigenia of her baby. Determined to find Hope, she decided to look in Monte's office for the map of Texas she recalled seeing on the wall above the roll-top desk last night.

She crossed the corridor and opened the door to the office. There was a map indeed, a big one with the Ryerson spread outlined in red and towns clearly marked in black. Unfortunately, if it were true to scale, the map indicated some distance between the ranch and Fort Davis. More than seventy miles, since El Paso seemed closer.

And the country was probably rough.

Iphigenia sighed. She'd expected her new husband to gladly help her retrieve her child. But nothing was working out as planned. She had no idea what Monte had in mind for her—whether or not he expected to marry her, not to mention whether or not she was willing to marry him now that they'd met. After the unpleasant surprise of her arrival, he surely would not appreciate a second, more shocking one. Undoubtedly, he would refuse to take her to Fort Davis.

Well, she would just have to go it alone, then, and find Hope by herself. She would have to borrow a horse or trade a piece of jewelry for one of the animals, as well as cart along her compass and aged muzzle-loading pistols. Still, the journey would be none too safe.

Nevertheless, to be reunited with her daughter, Iphigenia was prepared to do whatever she had to.

"I *must* wear a jacket to dinner?" growled Monte when Iphigenia informed him of the rules that evening. "The hell I will."

She gave him a withering look. "You are swearing."

"And I'm gonna swear more if you keep making me mad."

Miss Iphigenia Wentworth herself was all gussied up in a fancy, silky green dress that matched her eyes. And she was obviously up on her high horse, trying to prove something to him.

"Surely you'd like your children to know about the finer points of dining," she said. "Cassie and I have gone to a great deal of trouble setting the table and organizing everything."

Cassie? At least Iphigenia was helping one of his daughters enjoy herself. Monte tried to swallow his aggravation and glanced about, noting some weedy flowers that had been stuck in a vase and placed on the small table in the entryway. Iphigenia had tried to pretty the place up, probably meant well.

"Okay, I'll wear a jacket and tie," he finally said.

"Also be sure to wash up and slick back your hair."

He scowled. "I always wash, woman. Don't insult me."

"I am sorry. I forgot about the insults. Whether or not one washes has nothing to do with having Comanche blood, does it?"

He walked away, not even bothering to make a return comment.

When he came out of his bedroom a half hour later,

he was wearing the black broadcloth frock coat he'd
been married in, a white linen shirt that needed to be
starched, and a floppy silk tie that was probably out of
style. Monte read many newspapers but he had no use
for articles about fashion.

Stephen emerged from the opposite side of the corridor, wearing the only nice jacket he owned, a brown
wool. He'd grown like stinkweed the past year and the
jacket was at least two sizes too small. The boy looked
very uncomfortable, as well he might, considering the
seams of his coat could burst at any moment. Monte
forced himself to keep a straight face and accompanied
his son to the dining room.

What they found there was pretty impressive, Monte
had to admit. China that he hadn't seen in years had
been set out on his Grandmother Ryerson's old tablecloth. Cloth napkins had been folded at each plate, on
which also rested handwritten menus. In the center of
the table, candles burned in silver holders and a glass
vase held a pretty mixture of greenery and the same
weedy flowers Monte had seen in the entryway.

"At dinner, the host sits at the head of the table."
Iphigenia pointed out his place. "I shall sit to the host's
right and Cassie on other side. Stephen, you will sit at
the foot of the table."

Monte glanced about, looking for the other twin.
"What about Ginnie?"

"She has to eat in the kitchen, Pa," said Cassie. "She
yelled and said she wouldn't put on a skirt or dress."

Monte started to object, then figured getting banished to the kitchen wouldn't hurt Ginnie any. The girl
had been far too sulky lately, and he hadn't liked the
way she'd mouthed off at supper the night before.

Cassie herself wore a *camisa*—a Mexican blouse—a
full blue skirt and a great big smile. At least someone

was happy. Noting the way his daughter's wavy brown hair had been pulled up and pinned to the top of her head, he guessed Iphigenia had worked on it. Suddenly realizing that she reminded him of her mother, Monte felt his stomach knot.

When Stephen started to sit down, Iphigenia informed him, "A gentleman seats ladies first. Pull out a chair for your sister." Then she turned a challenging gaze on Monte. "And you may pull out a chair for me."

Oh, he may, may he?

Monte went along agreeably, enjoying a whiff of soap and light cologne as he helped Iphigenia into her chair. He liked the way her upswept hair curled about her pretty neck.

He finally sat down himself and noticed the amount of silverware. "What are we gonna do with three spoons, two knives, and two forks?"

"If you'll read your menu, you'll see we are having soup and salad, as well as pudding," Iphigenia explained. "Simply use the utensil that fits the course and work your way in from the outside." She added, "Of course, one of the knives is for bread and butter, the other is for meat."

Of course.

Iphigenia ended up guiding them through the whole meal. Monte just about wanted to yell bloody murder before they even got to dessert, what with all the orders, such as "spoon the soup away from you," "break your bread before you butter it," and "do not pick up your quail—fowl is not eaten with the fingers."

He gave Carmen a sympathetic look as the woman attempted to "serve from the left and remove from the right" and was questioned about the red salsa she served with the sliced eggs. Monte thought the dish tasted odd but ate it anyway.

Iphigenia ran the housekeeper silly by demanding that

an empty plate sit before each guest at all times, while platters and serving dishes remained on the sideboard. By the end of the meal, strands of the Mexican woman's gray-streaked hair had escaped its tight bun and she seemed about ready to cry as she poured coffee and tea.

"You did a real good job," Monte told her. "I'm gonna give you an extra day off for all of this."

Carmen's lips quivered but she held herself proudly. "You cannot give me another day off, Señor Ryerson. The children can eat bunkhouse food for one day, but they should have more than beans and bacon for two days in a row. Their father is a *rico*."

A rich man. That term might soon refer to past glories, Monte thought. Texas had been flooded with new ranchers and herds of cattle over the past ten years. The prices on beef might never go up again.

Monte made another suggestion. "Miss Iphigenia here can cook for us. That way, you oughta be able to get some rest."

Iphigenia looked startled. "I do not cook."

"Learn," said Monte, a satisfied grin splitting his face at her chagrined expression.

"I'll help," Cassie hastened to say, acting as sweet and helpful as usual.

Monte hadn't wanted to ruin Cassie's expectations, but now he started worrying that the girl would get too attached to Iphigenia, a woman he didn't know enough about to trust even halfway. And that temper of hers—the blonde seemed to be doing a slow burn.

Stephen leaned forward and reached for the sugar bowl sitting in the middle of the table.

"You should ask to have items passed to you, Stephen, not prostrate yourself across the tablecloth," Iphigenia said sharply.

Stephen turned red and lost hold of the delicate china

bowl. "Darn!" Trying to catch it before it hit the floor, the boy made the thing flip up into the air, then nearly fell out of his chair as it crashed anyway, spewing sugar and bits of china everywhere. His color deepening, Stephen bent over, ripping the entire shoulder out of his jacket. "Damn!"

"Don't go on about swearing," Monte warned Iphigenia before she could open her mouth. "The poor kid could say a lot worse in this miserable situation."

"Miserable? That's what you call having a proper dinner?"

She was itching to fight, he could tell. But Monte didn't want to have another set-to in front of the kids.

"Let's step into my office and talk about this." He got up, throwing his napkin down on the remains of his flan, whether or not he was supposed to. "We need some privacy."

She made no objection and rose to flounce off ahead of him. Cassie and Stephen merely watched.

Iphigenia strode into the office with her head high. Monte followed and slammed the door behind them. When she turned to face him, her expression resembled that of a cornered cat. Did she think he meant to harm her?

"You don't have to be afraid." He'd seen fear flicker in her eyes before. "Half Comanche or not, I don't beat kids and I don't hit women."

"I'm not afraid. I am furious that you have no care for all the time and trouble I have taken today."

"Proving you know all the social rules? You might have demonstrated something, I guess, but you did it at the expense of everyone else's comfort. Carmen was about ready to cry and you made Stephen feel about two inches tall."

"Aren't you going to add that I forced your other daughter to eat in the kitchen?"

"That's different. She sassed you. The rest of us made an effort—we don't deserve the sharp side of your tongue."

"Sharp tongue? Hah! You sat there and *ordered* me to learn how to cook—"

Which was what had got her going in the first place, he suddenly realized. He supposed he could have been nicer and asked but he didn't feel like apologizing now.

"You showed no concern for Carmen. She's a hard-working woman."

"I have concern for Carmen—I helped her all day long. And I would be most willing to help her again. I also care about Stephen, who is a nice young man. You are the person who does not care about other people's feelings." Iphigenia tossed her head. "You have been rude and offensive toward me from the very beginning. Your first words were to accuse me of playing a trick on you. Then you threatened to run me off your property." Her voice rose nearly an octave. "And, *then*, you insinuated I wasn't even a decently bred lady!"

"Which was the reason for this damned dinner."

"Yes, this damnable, miserable dinner."

Her eyes glistened—with tears? he wondered.

But still she wasn't done. "I am so sorry that I cannot seem to please you!"

She started to leave but he caught her arm, trying his best to be gentle. "Hold on." Now he was beginning to feel sympathetic, though he didn't really believe pleasing him was so important to her. Impressing him seemed more accurate. "Settle down. We could clear everything up here with some honesty."

She shook off his hand but didn't try to flee. "I told you the truth about who I am, about who my father is."

"Uh-huh, but you didn't say what the disagreement was all about between the two of you. Did it have anything to do with that business matter you won't explain?"

"I told you I will not speak of that."

"Then we're in trouble, because until you do, I don't see as I can trust you. No matter what you say, I've got no idea what a woman like you would be doing in West Texas. I can't believe a New York lady would become a mail-order bride, not unless she was in a predicament of some kind."

She blushed. "I am not in a predicament . . . if you are implying that I am expecting a child."

He hadn't meant that at all but found it interesting that she seized on the subject. "That would be a pretty good reason for coming here all right."

"I am not pregnant."

Though from the look on her face, he would bet she wasn't in the least innocent about the act that made babies.

She glanced away, touching the edge of the desk with a finger. "I do not know everything about you. Why should you know every single detail about me?"

"I've been straightforward enough about the basic things."

"Blunt would be a better word for it."

"I don't know how to talk pretty, like they probably do in New York," he admitted. "But people usually know where they stand with me." Then he took a different tack. "I expect everyone has secrets real deep in their hearts." Including a few he prayed he could forget someday. "That's not what I'm asking you to tell me. I just want to hear a good, simple explanation for why you came out here."

"All right." She paused, apparently thinking. "Would you accept that I believed marrying would be the solution for me?"

"Solution to what?"

"*Not* being married."

"Uh-uh. That doesn't sound simple. Not unless you and your father got into a big squabble over your being a spinster. What are you, twenty-five?"

"Twenty-seven."

His guess had been close. She was about ten years younger than him, but no spring calf. "Besides, if your old man's as important as you say, he could surely hustle up a husband for you."

"And what if I wouldn't marry the man he had in mind?"

Monte considered that for a moment. Though he wasn't that educated—he had learned to read from just a few lessons, and then lots of practice on his own—he was smart. He was also fairly shrewd when it came to figuring people's motives.

"Nope. Don't think you'd leave New York because of that. Don't even think your pa would try to pull a forced marriage on a feisty woman like you." His eyes raked over her fancy dress. The skin above the lacy, modestly cut bodice was smooth as ivory, and had never been cooked by the sun. "You're obviously used to a fine way of living. Texas wouldn't be your first choice of a destination."

Her expression hardened. "Since I cannot seem to come up with an explanation that pleases you, perhaps you should decide on one yourself."

"I'll settle for the truth," he insisted once more. "If you keep refusing to give it to me, I won't be able to stop myself from thinking the worst."

"Such as my being a woman of ill repute?"

"Given up on that. Now I'm wondering if you committed a crime of some sort."

"You think me a criminal?" Her voice shook.

"You're something all right."

"Enough! No more interrogation." Again, her eyes glistened and her lips trembled. "Furthermore, you need fear no more miserable dinners. That was the last I shall ever foist on you!"

She whirled around and swept out. She left the office door open but she slammed the one to her own room across the hall.

Shaking his head, Monte headed back for the dining room. Miss Iphigenia Wentworth was impossible and possibly desperate, but he didn't really think she was a criminal. The only danger she posed was her ability to upset his kids.

Not having been the best parent himself since coming home from the disaster in Mexico, he figured he owed it to them to go back and finish dessert in peace, at least get them settled down for this evening.

He'd heard spook lights glowed in the windows of the Ryerson ranch house at night.

When he asked a cowboy about it, the man had said, "Yup, witch lights. I saw 'em. There must be some kinda evil stalking the ranch. Some say there's a curse on Monte Ryerson hisself."

Spooks. Witchcraft. Eerie balls of fire.

He thought of the little mirror he had found a few months back, the way it had become cold and then hot. He wasn't sure he believed in anything devilish or supernatural, but the rumors gave him an idea.

"Real interesting." The situation could fit in perfectly with his plans. "Spread those rumors of evil around and I'll see that it's worth your while."

The cowboy grinned. "I'll have 'em shakin' in their boots."

Good. Monte Ryerson definitely deserved to be cursed.

5

Iphigenia lay in the semi-darkness of her room and smothered her sobs with a pillow. She cursed Monte Ryerson, the most infernally difficult, cruelly blunt man she had ever met.

She simply couldn't bring herself to explain the existence of Hope to him, nor the events leading up to the decision to come to Texas. Monte had said she need not bare her heart, but that's exactly what she would have to do if she told the truth.

She had never bared her heart to anyone.

In fact, Iphigenia thought sadly, no one had ever wanted her to do so before. Since she had suffered her father's shouts and accusations as a child, her aunt's coldness, the servants' indifference and society's general artifice, she had learned to keep her own counsel. She would have to become another person entirely if she were to actually share her hopes and fears.

Not to mention that she felt certain Monte Ryerson would not approve of a woman who'd set out to marry a man she didn't love and then trick him, regardless of the desperate nature of her motive or her intention to offer that husband financial reward.

The entire scenario would be humiliating.

Iphigenia hated humiliation. That's why she'd developed her protective skills—a cool demeanor, the ability to sting with words, the show of reckless courage that dared anyone to challenge her.

None of which Monte Ryerson paid much attention to.

Iphigenia would have to leave him and his horrid ranch as soon as possible.

That very night.

Still thinking about that, much calmer after an hour or so, she heard the footsteps of the young Ryersons as they headed for bed, then the heavier tread of Monte himself.

She waited a while longer before she rose to find the compass, the dueling pistols, and the petticoat that contained her jewelry. She stuffed all these into a cloth bag. After changing her clothing to the brown riding habit and boots, she sneaked down the corridor, took a candle and matches from the kitchen, then let herself out.

A full moon glowed high in the sky. Thankful for that, she went directly to a pen where she'd seen cowboys put their horses. She would have to borrow a mount if she were to reach Fort Davis. Once there, she'd fetch little Hope and trade a string of pearls or another piece of jewelry for a train ticket to New York. To prove she was not in the least a criminal, she'd also send Monte Ryerson enough money to replace the horse and its equipment two times over.

A horse. Choosing one was going to be difficult, Iphigenia thought, peering into the fenced pen. She was a good rider, and able to keep her balance on a spirited mount tacked up with a sidesaddle. But she'd prefer taking more time to look over an animal that was to carry her more than a hundred miles. In the darkness, she'd have to settle for whatever she could get hold of.

She lit the candle and went inside the barn that stood next to the horse pen. There, she picked out a bridle and a length of rope. The only saddles were heavy, with high pommels and cantles, and would have to be straddled. She'd hike up her skirts.

Letting herself into the horse pen, she chose the first steed that allowed her to approach. She petted his nose before slipping a looped piece of rope over his neck, then calmed him before sliding the bit between his teeth. After saddling him quickly, she took one of her pistols from the cloth bag and stuck it in her waistband. Hanging the bag from the saddlehorn, she led the horse out of the pen to mount.

The animal snorted but trotted off when Iphigenia nudged her heels into his sides. After she'd ridden through the entrance gate and gotten a couple of furlongs down the road, she started to breath easier. She could almost imagine she was inhaling freedom. The great bowl of stars sparkling overheard stood for adventure. She could envision the explorers who had come to this country in the first place.

She could almost identify with them, except what she sought was far dearer to her heart than new lands could ever be—possession of her child and freedom for them both.

The moon kept slipping in and out behind clouds, but Iphigenia could tell the land became more rugged as she left the Ryerson ranch behind. The road narrowed and climbed. Hoping the horse would know his way, Iphigenia loosened the reins, tensing only when he stumbled.

When a lonely howl suddenly pierced the night, she nearly jumped out of the saddle entirely. Hand on the pistol at her waist, she peered into the surrounding darkness, hoping the wolf or whatever it was would leave her alone. Intent on that threat, she didn't see the riders approaching until they were nearly upon her.

She reined in and gave a little cry as two hulking figures took shape in the darkness.

"Well, well, what do we have here?" asked one man in a raspy voice.

Thinking it best not to answer, Iphigenia kicked her horse to go ahead, only to rein in again when the other man moved directly into her path.

"Seemsta be a female," the second man said. "Who are you, Missy?"

Iphigenia thought fast. "A traveler," she answered, keeping her voice firm and cool. "I would appreciate your moving out of my way."

The man blocking her path laughed roughly. "A traveler? Now ain't that strange? Nobody rides at night unless they're running away or have something downright unlawful on their minds."

Certain that these men themselves had unlawful thoughts, Iphigenia carefully removed her great-uncle's dueling pistol from her waistband. A long-barreled, old-fashioned muzzle-loader that required powder and handmade bullets, it sometimes misfired and was far more awkward than a revolver like a Colt .45. But Iphigenia couldn't worry about such problems as she cocked the weapon's hammer.

The action made an audible click.

"What the hell is that?" the first man asked just as the moon came out from under a cloud. The light showed him to be lean and bearded. "The woman's armed. Take her out of the saddle and teach her a lesson, Newton."

Iphigenia aimed the pistol at Newton's chest as the man came at her. But as the weapon fired with a great cracking noise, her arm jerked and the horse shied. The animal's movement combined with the pistol's recoil nearly knocked her to the ground. Eyes smarting from the gunpowder, she grasped the weapon and hung onto the saddlehorn for all she was worth.

"Damned bitch tried to kill me!" shouted Newton.

"Get her!" ordered the man with the beard.

Thinking she was about to be ravished or die, most probably both, Iphigenia reined her horse in a circle, desperately trying to cock the pistol's hammer again.

That's when yet another rider approached, the hooves of his mount pounding over the ground in nearly the same thumping rhythm as her heart. Even by moonlight, Iphigenia recognized the proud, powerful carriage of Monte Ryerson.

The other two men cursed and reined in, backing away as Monte came to a sudden halt.

"What the hell's going on here?" Monte leaned forward in the saddle, a rifle in his hand. He pointed it at the bearded man. "What do you think you're doing, Barkley?"

Barkley snorted. "I'm not the one who's up to no good. Ask this witch here—she pulled a gun on my foreman and tried to shoot him."

"Iphigenia?"

"Effy what?" muttered Barkley.

"Iphigenia Wentworth—my fiancée," said Monte. "Try anything with her and you'll answer to me."

Iphigenia felt a mixture of relief and gratitude toward the man overflowing in her heart. "They threatened to attack me. Otherwise, I wouldn't have used the pistol."

"Attack you?" said Barkley. Then his aggressive tone became all smooth and civilized, "Why, you must have misunderstood, Ma'am. My foreman and I merely questioned your identity." He told Monte, "You don't usually find women riding around in the dark."

"You don't usually find most people out at this time of night," Monte retorted. "Where are you going?"

"That's my own business." Barkley's voice tightened a bit. "The roads belong to everyone. But enough of this nonsense. Let's get going, Newton."

The other man grunted and the two riders headed off, going back in the direction from which they'd come.

"Let's sit here for awhile," Monte told Iphigenia in a low voice. "And keep watching until you think they're out of sight."

"Are they outlaws?" Iphigenia whispered.

"Only a little better. Jonah Barkley owns a ranch in this county but he's not known for his friendly ways." Finally, he motioned. "Come on. They went over the rise. Let's ride for home."

He turned his horse, not even bothering to ask if returning was what Iphigenia wanted to do. Not that she intended to travel a road on which Jonah Barkley and his man Newton were lurking. Subdued, she kept her mouth shut and slipped the awkward dueling pistol back into her waistband.

As they trotted on, the moon slid under a cloud again but Monte seemed to have no trouble seeing. He also had no trouble speaking his mind.

"So what cockeyed idea made you think you could steal a horse and take off in the middle of the night?"

Iphigenia swallowed, knowing there was no way she could admit the truth. "I—I wasn't stealing the horse." Particularly after she'd vehemently denied being a criminal. She steadied her voice. "I was angry. I merely wanted to take a ride and let off some steam."

"In New York, do ladies usually go for rides by themselves at night?"

"Sometimes. At least on country estates." They

didn't, actually, but Iphigenia decided Monte wouldn't know the difference.

"Well, this isn't a country estate. This is West Texas. You never know who you're going to meet up with or what he'll want from you."

"I realize that now."

"The land itself is dangerous, full of crevices and drops. Sometimes you can't see the road, even when the sun's out. You could've easily gotten lost. I bet you're not even carrying a canteen."

"A canteen?"

"A container for water," he snapped, sounding amazed that she didn't know what one was. "Wells and waterholes are few and far between. And there aren't any creeks, either. My spread is blessed with the only one for a hundred miles on either side."

How stupid she had been. Iphigenia supposed she should thank Monte for coming to her rescue. She opened her mouth to do so, but she couldn't bring herself to grovel.

Instead, she asked, "How did you know I had left the ranch?"

"I heard noises, got up and noticed the door of your room standing open. When I realized it was empty, I went outside and saw you heading down the road."

"You must have keen senses." She'd been as quiet as she knew how to be.

Monte made no response as they rode on, the horses' hooves kicking up dust. The moon slid toward the west. Soon the dark outlines of the Ryerson buildings were visible. Feeling a combination of relief at being alive and sadness at failing in her mission, Iphigenia wished she could hurry into the house, go to bed, and forget about her ineptitude.

But Monte seemed to want her company. "Let's take

the horses over to the main corral," he said, moving his mount closer so she had to veer in that direction. "I'll unsaddle them. Where did you get the gear? From the barn next to the corral?"

She murmured her agreement. When they dismounted, her legs felt shaky and her hands numb. Seeming to know she was weak, Monte placed his hands at her waist. She imagined she could feel the hard, warm imprint of his fingers and chills crept up her spine.

"Thank you," she said. But she still couldn't bring herself to thank him for saving her life.

She tried to remove the cloth bag she'd hung from the saddlehorn. Monte had to help with that, too, their fingers brushing as he untied the knot she'd made. The man definitely attracted her. After what she'd been through, she decided she must be insane to feel anything other than fatigue and relief.

He hefted the bag and handed it over. "Sure you weren't taking off? This feels like serious business."

"My other pistol is inside."

"What kind of guns do you have? Muzzle-loaders?"

"How did you know?"

"From the sound your shot made. We used to carry old-fashioned pistols in the army." Before she asked, he admitted, "I served the Confederacy. So we were on opposite sides."

Did he think she cared? "I was only a child during the war—I never thought much about sides." Nor had her Yankee upbringing stopped her from getting involved with Lamar, a descendent of planters from the deep south.

"Guess I should have known you weren't real patriotic or you wouldn't have come to Texas." He paused as he took off her horse's saddle and laid it on the ground.

She supposed she could leave now but wasn't certain that he was finished talking. She could at least listen, be respectful, since she couldn't thank him.

"I can buy you a train ticket back to New York, if you want."

Her mouth dropped open. First he'd saved her life. Now he was trying to be decent.

Too decent.

Thinking of her mission, seeing Hope in her mind's eye, Iphigenia knew she simply couldn't do as he asked, even though getting out of his life and the lives of his children would be the best thing.

"I do not wish to return to New York . . . at least not yet."

"Then what are you gonna do?"

Meaning he had no thoughts of marrying her at all? She couldn't help feeling disturbed if he'd so swiftly come to a negative decision. At the same time, she would be upset if he told her he *did* wish to wed her. It was a ridiculous and illogical conflict.

"I don't know what to do," she said finally, honestly. "Must a decision be made this very moment?"

"I don't want Cassie's heart broken."

"Neither do I." And she meant that sincerely.

"I thought she'd be happy if you stayed for a few days, but now I'm afraid she's becoming too dependent on you."

"I know." She'd felt guilty all the while she'd been saddling up the horse and riding off.

Monte faced her in the dimming moonlight. All she could see were the stark, strong planes of his face.

"Let's make a deal then. Since you're not leaving right away, but there's a big question as to our getting hitched, you're gonna have to try to wean Cassie away. Being nice about it, of course."

"Of course." Iphigenia would be happy to agree to that. "A girl her age should be establishing a little independence anyway. I think I can help her."

"Try to explain that two people don't get along just because she wants them to. I've already told her that but she doesn't believe me."

And Iphigenia knew why. "She misses her mother terribly."

"Missing somebody don't bring them back."

And in the pregnant silence that hung between the two of them, she instinctively felt that Monte had suffered as much as his daughter. Possibly more. His remark held a dark undertone, as if he were feeling guilty himself . . . or angry. He wasn't a hearty, smiling type of man. Had he ever been? Cassie claimed that her father used to enjoy much better humors, and had taken the time to have fun with his children.

"You could pay more attention to your family," Iphigenia suggested, hoping he wouldn't be offended. "That would help Cassie feel less dependent on me."

"Probably. With the ranch work, though, I have to spend a lot of time away from the house."

"But you could try to be in a better mood when you're there."

She realized he wasn't going to make any promises. He turned away to unsaddle his own horse. Stifling a yawn of exhaustion, Iphigenia decided to make a break for it. "Good night."

He mumbled some words in return, his back turned toward her.

Something was bothering him.

But then, Iphigenia had the feeling that something had been bothering Monte Ryerson before they'd ever met. She wasn't being completely honest with him, but she now felt certain he wasn't being honest with her, either.

*   *   *

With a great sigh of relief, Xosi Baca escaped from the mirror and gazed about the small room that belonged to Ginnie Ryerson. Through the window Xosi saw the moon slipping toward the west, but the girl lay wide awake, waiting expectantly.

"You've got to get rid of her!" Ginnie cried.

Xosi knew who the girl was talking about, the blonde gringa who had moved into the ranch house. "What has this woman been doing?"

"She's hateful! She made Carmen prepare a horrible dinner and she made me eat in the kitchen!"

Xosi tried to be soothing toward the child. So far, able to escape her confinement only when spurred on by strong emotion, she was dependent on Ginnie. Though the girl need not be awake.

"Do not worry, chica. If you wish, I will scare her until her gold hairs fall out."

Ginnie smiled. "Good. Then she won't be so pretty. Pa likes her."

Xosi felt a blaze of jealousy. "Monte . . . your father likes this woman?"

"She's a mail-order bride. Cassie sent away for her."

Monte, Xosi's beautiful man, was planning to marry another woman? Xosi's heart—or what should have been her heart—turned over in her cold breast. If she were ever to find some sort of existence, to live again, she believed her former lover's desire to be necessary.

So she spat, "This cannot be!"

"I despise her!" Ginnie said. "Make her go away. I don't care what you do to her!"

Strong words. Did the girl speak of murder? When she had been alive, Xosi had killed to defend herself. But she hesitated now, not needing more blood on her *soul. Still, was not the present situation as desperate as life and death?*

Though she questioned how much harm she could do.

Xosi could not always appear when she wanted, no matter how badly she wished to do so. She might make threats but she could not be certain about scaring anything but animals, who seemed to sense her presence. Perhaps it would have been better if she had studied brujeriá *when she had been flesh and blood.*

"You can do something really bad to her, can't you?"

Xosi didn't want to cast any doubt, so she remained vague. "Keep my mirror near your heart at all times, chica." *The girl must feed her with living emotion. "Meanwhile—"*

"Meanwhile, what?" Ginnie asked anxiously.

"Perhaps we should try some spells," said Xosi, wondering if the simple ones she knew of would actually work. Magic had to exist in some fashion or she wouldn't be confined to the mirror in the first place. "Go into this woman's room and collect some personal things from her."

"Like what? Hair? Pieces of fingernails?"

"That would be good. Anything that has been close to her or that she loves."

"I'll do it right away. Tomorrow."

"Good." Xosi assumed her most motherly tone, knowing that was what this girl wanted. She hovered over Ginnie, stretched out a ghostly finger to stroke her face. "Sweet little chica. *Now go to sleep and do not worry anymore."*

For once released, Xosi liked to wander on her own for as long as she could. She had no control over the length of time she could flit about the outside world, though she was confined to the darker hours.

Thank Dios *Ginnie saw fit to sink down to her pillow with a satisfied sigh. The girl was breathing heavily even as Xosi floated down the narrow attic staircase.*

The corridor lay before her, deep with night and shadow. Yet she knew exactly where the invader's room lay. She flew toward it, wishing she could scream in the blonde woman's ears and keep her awake all night.

6

Iphigenia slept restlessly, tossing and turning her way through strange dreams. As a result she rose later than usual the next morning.

Not that she should be in a hurry. After last night's ride, she realized she needed to prepare and get her bearings before attempting a journey to Fort Davis again. It would take days to study the map, prepare a simpler version for herself, and collect supplies. Not to mention that she would have to make arrangements for the return of a horse and anything else she borrowed from Monte.

The man had finally acted decently toward her. She would be decent in return.

Further, she intended to keep her promise regarding Cassie. But her heart sank when she went into the kitchen and found the girl waiting for her. The eager expression on Cassie's face touched her more deeply than she wished.

She cleared her throat and reached for the tea kettle sitting on the back of the stove. "Do you have tasks to do about the ranch?" she asked diplomatically, pouring herself a cup of hot water, then steeping some tea. "I hope my arrival has not interrupted your schedule."

"Tasks? You mean chores? Sure, I collect eggs from the hens for Carmen. And I help her with the cooking whenever she asks. Sometimes I even help Stephen or Pa outside. Now I can help you, too. Are we going to have another fancy dinner tonight?"

"I don't think the rest of your family enjoyed the last one very much."

Cassie shrugged. "Pa has to get used to new things, you know."

"And sometimes people can't or won't get used to the new. Your father prefers more informal dining."

"Well, I thought the meal was beautiful."

"Thank you." The girl was so sweet. And so unaware of Iphigenia's other motives. She suggested compromise. "Maybe your father will agree to having a fancy dinner from time to time, such as on holidays. That would be a nice way for you to celebrate."

Cassie nodded, not noticing that Iphigenia had used the word *you*, rather than *us*. "That might be possible."

But the conversation came to a halt when the back door sprang open, admitting a wide-eyed, pale-faced Carmen.

Iphigenia couldn't help feeling alarmed. "What's the matter?"

Carmen twisted her hands. "Two men have quit. Señor Ryerson rode after them but I do not think he will change their minds. They believe someone has put a curse on this ranch, a spell to raise the dead."

"Why on earth would ranch workers come up with a story like that?" Iphigenia asked.

"A terrible thing happened. A herd of cattle on one of the high ranges stampeded off a cliff last night," Carmen said, her voice shaky. "Cattle do not do such things—they must have been very frightened. The men were miles away but they saw fiery lights and heard loud sounds."

"Explosions? Those are man-made and have nothing to do with curses."

"There were no marks on the ground, the men said. It was not explosions." Carmen paused, lips trembling. "And there have been other things."

"Like those horses?" Cassie turned to Iphigenia. "A bunch of them spooked and ran off the night before you came. But Pa says there has to be an explanation."

Carmen crossed herself. "I do not think anyone can explain. Horses know when spirits walk. All animals know and some of them die of fear. I myself found two chickens lying dead in their coop."

"Perhaps they had a disease," Iphigenia suggested.

Carmen shook her head. "Their necks were broken. Blood ran from their beaks and some of it had been used to paint strange signs on the building."

"Then someone killed them." Someone horrible or sick, Iphigenia thought.

Cassie looked troubled. "When did the chickens die? I've never seen any blood."

Carmen sighed. "It was yesterday. My husband washed the signs away as best he could."

The housekeeper looked like she wanted to collapse. Iphigenia pulled out a chair for her. "Why don't you sit and rest?"

The woman sank down gratefully, but wasn't finished with her tales. "I do not know whether these bad things were done by the living or the dead. At night, many people have seen lights flitting from window to window in this house. Even I have seen such, and heard noises when I did not leave before dark."

Iphigenia felt a little thrill. "Noises?"

"It's Ginnie sneaking around," asserted Cassie. "She's been acting strange for months."

Ginnie? It was possible. Then again, maybe not.

Iphigenia realized that the restlessness she'd suffered the night before had been due partially to an annoying, rattling doorknob, and what seemed to be laughter and footsteps in the corridor. Recalling that she heard the same sounds the night she was drunk on tequila, she'd gotten out of bed and opened the door, only to see no one.

Carmen obviously noticed her brooding expression. "Have you seen lights, Señorita Wentworth? Or heard noises?"

Iphigenia wasn't about to admit to such irrational fears, especially if cowboys were quitting because of them. "I do not know what spooks horses or stampedes cattle but I do know that houses make unusual sounds as they settle." As for the lights, she also remembered waking and seeing something greenish-white flash in her bureau's mirror. She'd been chilled to the bone and had pulled the bed's extra blanket over herself. Yet she insisted, "There are always logical reasons for unusual occurrences."

"Perhaps they do not believe in ghosts and curses in New York," said Carmen.

"Curses I can't speak for. But there are houses that are reputedly haunted in New York, just as anywhere else. Including one that belongs to a second cousin of mine. I stayed there several times and all the doors on the second floor refused to stay closed some nights. There were also unusual noises."

Cassie listened attentively. "And you weren't afraid?"

"Ghosts can't hurt you. They can only scare you. That is, if you let them. That was my cousin's opinion, and it made sense to me." Though she'd never had to think much about it since that time. "Did someone die on these premises? The ghost in my cousin's home was supposed to have been a servant who committed suicide."

Carmen shivered.

But Cassie said, "Great-gramma Ryerson died in this house, then Great-grandpa, but it was years and years ago."

"And why should they haunt us now?" asked Carmen.

"Who knows?" Needing to warm herself from the inside, Iphigenia sipped at her cup of tea. "We should pay no attention to restless souls. If you ignore them, they will go away." At least, that was the case according to her cousin. And the noises in the New York house had ceased once Iphigenia had adopted that attitude. "We have enough problems with living people and the situations they create."

She thought of the threatening men she'd met the night before. Who knew how many lawless individuals populated West Texas?

Iphigenia realized she would need a better weapon than a dueling pistol when she set out to find her baby again. She would also do well to learn any skills that seemed useful for this wild country.

This curse rumor had to stop.

Angry because he hadn't been able to persuade his two wranglers into staying on with him, Monte rode several miles to Luis Padilla's small ranch. Little faces peering out of the windows watched him tie his horse to the fence in front. Luis Padilla's children were watching . . . and, possibly, the late Roberto Padilla's kids, as well.

Taking a deep breath, he walked up to the door, noting some equipment lying to one side on the floor of the adobe house's covered *portal*. A bullwhip coiled among several lengths of rope like a snake.

The response to his knock was a shout, "Go away!" No doubt Luis himself.

"I want to talk. I'm not leaving until you come out here."

Dark muttering rose from inside the house but footsteps clumped to the door. The wooden panel opened, revealing Luis's angry face. "You are not welcome in my home, Señor Ryerson. No one invited you—"

"I'm not asking for hospitality. I told you I want to talk."

"There's nothing to talk about. My brother is dead."

"Which you seem to think is my fault. Roberto was my friend as well as one of my best ranch hands. When he was kidnapped by those bandits, I went down into Mexico to get him back."

"But you failed, didn't you, Señor Ryerson?" Luis said bitterly. His large dark eyes were accusing. "And my brother died a horrible, bloody death. He left a wife and two children—"

"I gave them compensation." A year's wages, in fact. Roberto's widow must still have some of the money, since she'd moved in with her husband's brother and his wife.

"No one can bring Roberto back," Luis said. "He was a good man." He added, "Let his death be on your head."

"Are you saying you're cursing me?" Monte tried to keep his anger in check. "Have you told others that you wish me ill?" *And might Luis have even helped the bad luck along a bit?* he wondered silently.

The man crossed himself. "I do not make curses. I am a good Catholic. God will take care of those who are evil."

Monte figured the man was referring to him. When Luis had first heard about Roberto last fall, the Mexican had made remarks about Monte's "savage" upbringing.

And Luis obviously believed Monte had some connection with Roberto's ritualistic death. Monte had turned to Shorty and his foreman Jake O'Brian for backup, only to have Jake refuse to talk while Shorty got the same reaction from Luis as Monte himself.

"Do you believe the spirits of the dead are haunting you?" Luis asked, sounding hopeful.

Monte himself had once glimpsed the spooky kind of light the men often spoke of, but he said, "More likely somebody alive is persecuting me."

Luis didn't bat an eye. "Perhaps you should pray for help with your problems, Señor. Perhaps God can help you."

The man's tone indicated he'd far rather see the devil on Monte's trail. Eyes burning, Luis Padilla slammed the door in his face.

Monte mounted his horse, feeling no better than when he arrived. Luis had always been the more hotheaded of the two Padilla brothers, but he was also religious and conservative. Monte hated to think the man would try to harm him in any way.

Still, peculiar things continued to happen on his spread. Eerie lights. Spooked horses and cattle. Either someone clever was pulling these stunts and making them look strange. Or else someone or something was haunting the R&Y . . . possibly even spurred on by an evil witch who'd been hired to put a spell on Monte.

Having been raised to believe in Comanche magic and spirits, he couldn't quite dismiss the possibility. He'd heard the ghostly laughter and footsteps in his corridor at night. He'd dreamed of Xosi Baca, or else had actually seen her.

Xosi. Gooseflesh rose on his arms. He'd assumed guilt had brought her forth at the time, but now he wondered.

Not that he intended to admit any such uneasiness to his men. Many of his cowboys were more than uneasy, they were just plain superstitious or even out-and-out fearful. If enough wranglers quit on him, he'd go out of business for sure.

"Whirl the lariat over your head, then toss it over the calf's neck," Stephen told Iphigenia.

Trying to concentrate, she focused on the scampering brown animal the boy drove toward her from the other end of the corral. She whipped the loop around and let it fly. The rope hit the calf, but merely grazed his side, sending him bucking back in the other direction.

"Good try," Stephen grinned.

Iphigenia laughed. "You're trying to flatter me." She wasn't certain that roping was a useful skill but she was having fun anyway.

She'd been on a walk after trying to calm Carmen and leaving Cassie to do some chores, when she'd spotted Stephen practicing looping a rope around a fence post. He'd been most happy to explain his technique. Between that discussion and Iphigenia's apology for making him uncomfortable the night before, he'd suggested that he show her how to make slip knots.

From there, they'd gone on to full lariat lessons. Iphigenia had done surprisingly well on the fence post, but was disconcerted when they moved into a corral to face a living, moving target. She'd tried and failed half a dozen times, earning Stephen's amused chortles. She hadn't cared that he was laughing at her. She appreciated this more relaxed, humorous side to him. After what she'd been through lately, she enjoyed humor of any kind.

"Try it one more time." Stephen yelled and waved his arms at the calf.

Iphigenia gathered her rope again, aiming it at the calf's head. When the rope whirled through the air and actually circled the animal's neck, she cried out with surprise and pleasure.

Then the calf took off and jerked her off her feet. She hit the ground with a thump and an "Um-mp!"

"Let go of the rope!" shouted Stephen.

"I will not!" said Iphigenia, laughing, gripping the rope even as the calf bleated and circled, dragging her several feet. He was much stronger than he looked. "I have worked too hard!"

"You are one stubborn woman."

Even in her predicament, Iphigenia recognized Monte's voice. She stared up as he loomed over her, his expression dark and enigmatic. She couldn't seem to find words, then caught her breath as the calf jerked her a little further.

"Guess we'll have to tie this critter down," Monte drawled, grabbing hold of the rope. Then he used one smooth motion to pull the calf toward him, flip it over and tie its legs with a loose loop.

It bleated piteously.

Iphigenia struggled to her feet, unable to keep from reacting to the noise, "Let it go. That's cruel."

"He's not hurting. He's scared and mad. But he'll have to get used to being roped and tied, since he'll need to be branded some day."

"More cruelty."

"Would you rather he was rustled off, maybe eaten before his prime?"

"Ugh, must you mention the poor animal's final purpose?" She glanced at the calf's silly face. "I don't think I could eat roast beef if I had to stare my dinner in the eye first."

Monte chuckled, his sober expression softening.

"Actually, this guy looks pretty healthy and well made. Instead of turning him into a steer, I just might let him grow up into a nice bull. A lover rather than a dinner. Does that make you feel better?" His tone was light, bantering.

Did he mean to toy with her? "Any circumstance which extends the animal's life is certainly a more positive prospect for him."

Monte untied the calf and let it buck away. "So you've got a soft heart beating beneath that frostbitten skin of yours."

Iphigenia knew she should probably disagree, should probably say that her heart was as cool as her demeanor. That was the flippant sort of answer she had given men in the past. But she and Monte weren't trading barbs in an elegant New York parlor. As new as their relationship was, the man had touched an elemental part of her.

Not wanting to show her mixed emotions, however, she stared down at the skirt of her brown riding habit and dusted it ferociously.

"Haven't you got anything else to wear besides that thing and the fancy green dinner dress?"

"Of course." She kept dusting. "I have many ensembles. I packed at least two more riding habits if I remember correctly." Though both were fancier and considerably tighter at the waist. Having gotten used to going corsetless, Iphigenia hated to think of returning to stays and laces. "I did not realize you expected me to dress fashionably."

"Don't give a hoot about fashion. Only thought you might want to loosen up and get more comfortable, especially if you're spending time outside."

"She could wear a split skirt," called Stephen, who had busied himself at the other end of corral, as if to give them privacy.

"Where would I get something like that?" Iphigenia had noticed the garment Cassie wore today—a trouser-like affair with flaring legs that ended some inches above the ankles and showed the wearer's boots.

"Have to have one made," said Monte. "And that would take a while." He eyed Stephen. "My son's probably got an old pair of pants and a shirt that would fit you."

"I can wear trousers?"

"It's a free country."

"For men." Not that she intended to lecture him on women's suffrage. She wasn't the sort to become involved in political affairs. "I have to admit I find the idea of trousers appealing. I once wore a man's suit to a country party. Except for the starched collar, I found it amazingly comfortable."

"A man's suit?" Monte knit his brows.

"I was trying to prove an annoyance to several people."

"I bet you succeeded."

"Indeed. I was amused."

He gave her a disbelieving look. "Amused because you annoyed people? Was that how you had fun in New York?"

She stiffened. "I participated in other activities, such as going to the theater and the opera. Though the crowds could be a bore." She added, "And I rode whenever I could, either in the country or through Central Park."

"Sidesaddle," he said, a statement, not a question.

"It taught me a great deal about balance."

"You ride real well," he admitted. "Did you go hunting in the country, too?"

"I didn't care for that." Maybe she *did* have a soft heart. "I learned to shoot by aiming at stationary targets or at skeet."

"Clay pigeons thrown up in the air?" Monte kept his gaze on her, which was disconcerting. "And did you do all this riding and shooting with other people or by yourself?"

What was he getting at? "I pursued such pastimes alone or with a few companions." Mainly men she flirted with or relatives she was getting along with at the moment.

"Hmm . . . so you don't like crowds. Enjoy shocking people at parties. Sounds like you were some sorta rebel."

Iphigenia murmured, "Perhaps."

"The West is full of rebels. It's a free kind of life, as long as you can pay the price." He obviously noticed her questioning look. "Everything in life costs something. You don't get anything for free."

As if she didn't already know that, as if she hadn't already paid more than she had ever expected. "What is the price of rebellion?"

"Loneliness, if you're too mulish and cantankerous."

Did he think her cantankerous? Lonely? Not wanting to ask, she bent over to pick up the rope. Stephen remained standing at the other end of corral.

"How about one more pass at the calf?" she called.

"I think we've had enough games here," Monte said. "The boy has work to do."

"Aw, Pa, let her try one more time."

Monte glanced from his son to Iphigenia, then relented. "Okay, once more."

The boy shouted and ran at the animal, sending it scampering. Aware that Monte was watching her, Iphigenia suddenly wanted to show off, to prove that she was capable of accomplishing something she set out to do. She whirled the loop around her head and let it fly. When the lariat again settled about the animal's neck, she yelped with glee and dug in her heels. But instead of running away from her like it had last time, the calf came straight on and passed her by.

Startled, Iphigenia backed up and stumbled as the tightening rope threw her hard into Monte. Caught off-guard himself, he grabbed her but couldn't keep from falling. In a tangle of arms and legs, they hit the ground with a great thud.

The breath knocked out of her, the rope torn from her hands, Iphigenia somehow found herself lying beneath the man and staring directly into his eyes. Up close, she noticed those eyes were actually dark brown, not black, though the difference between the irises and pupils was a matter of subtle shading.

His gaze was mesmerizing. Time stopped. His breath feathered her face. His lips poised over hers. Warmth spiraling from her middle, she couldn't stop herself from letting her own eyes drift closed.

She expected a kiss.

Which never came.

"You oughta add a hat to your wardrobe, along with a shirt and pants, city lady." Monte's voice rudely brought her back to reality. "Or your ivory complexion is soon gonna be pink."

He rose to his feet, then offered a helping hand. She ignored his gesture and rolled to the side to scramble upright, her face hot with embarrassment rather than sun.

A kiss? With Stephen looking on? What in Hades was wrong with her?

Worrying her even more was what she might have expected if the boy hadn't been around at all.

7

Iphigenia made sure she started wearing one of her straw hats whenever she went outside. She supposed the Texas sun, being farther south, glowed warmer and closer than the one in New York. A parasol would also make sense but would look silly in this rough country.

She was thinking about that the next day, as she enjoyed a picnic lunch with Stephen and Cassie under a large cottonwood tree behind the house. Comfortable in the old wooden rocking chair Stephen had brought out for her, she glanced up at the bright gold and blue sky. The boy and Cassie sat on some rocks piled about the base of the cottonwood. Ginnie lounged on the ground a few yards away, close enough to eavesdrop, though seemingly uninterested in their conversation. Cassie's twin had very dark hair, olive skin, and a strong-bridged, slightly hooked nose that resembled her father's.

Reminded of Monte, Iphigenia thought about the embarrassing titillation she'd felt when she'd assumed he was going to kiss her in the corral. "Where is your father today?" she asked Stephen.

"Out with some of the men cleaning up the mess after those cattle got rimrocked. I think they got help going over that cliff," Stephen said. "Pa does, too. Anyway, some of the meat might be salvageable. I guess I should be helping. I kinda sneaked away when they set off early this morning. I'll catch it when Pa comes back."

"You've been working around the buildings."

"Yeah, but I should have rode with Pa. He decides what's most important and he's shorthanded." Stephen took a bite of a tortilla filled with meat and mild chilies. "Don't know what got into me. I don't usually slough off my duties."

The boy was as serious as he was nice. Iphigenia wanted to cheer him up, bring back the grin he'd had on his face when they'd roped the calf.

"It's spring. Who wouldn't want to enjoy oneself on a beautiful sunny day." And she felt flattered that Stephen seemed happy to spend some of his time with her. Her gaze wandered. "Why aren't there any flowers planted near the house? They would be blooming now."

"I bet you're used to roses," said Cassie.

"Later in the spring. Now there would be tulips and lilacs and irises."

"There's flowers down by the creek," said Stephen. "I think I saw bluebonnets."

"Can such flowers be set into beds near the house?" Not that Iphigenia was any gardener. She'd only stood around and watched the professionals who took care of the Wentworth townhouse and the country estate.

"I guess flowers can grow here," said Stephen. "You'd have to carry water to them, though."

Cassie smiled. "I bet they'd be pretty."

Iphigenia scrutinized the rocks at the foot of the tree. They bordered a ring of deep sandy soil which was damp from a rain shower they'd had the night before.

"This would be perfect for a flower bed. I can imagine blooms growing right here."

Then she realized she was making plans when she wasn't going to be staying on. And she truly felt regret.

Who wouldn't, with such company? Cassie and Stephen were such unaffected, cheerful young people. They were far kinder and more personable than any of Iphigenia's cousins had ever been. She might have been a different sort of person if she'd had Cassie and Stephen as relatives. She could even imagine having them as her own . . .

Children?

Amazed, Iphigenia realized she actually felt motherly, though she was too young to be either youngster's parent. Perhaps her baby had awakened such deep emotions.

At that thought she sobered, and once again worried about Hope and the people she'd been given to. Iphigenia knew they'd been paid for their trouble, but she hoped they were taking good care of her child. She'd kept count of every day and hour since the baby had been torn away from her.

Cassie patted her hand. "You look sad."

Remembering going into Monte's office that morning to draw a simplified version of his map, Iphigenia forced herself to smile. "I'm fine. I am only thinking of my former home."

"I guess a person would get homesick traveling so far," said Cassie. "Maybe we should do something to cheer you up this afternoon."

"You two could go flower-picking by the creek," Stephen suggested. Then he paused, narrowing his eyes. "Say, what's *he* doing here?"

Iphigenia glanced up, noting the three strangers riding through the front gate.

"Jonah Barkley." Stephen rose to his feet.

"Barkley?"

Iphigenia remembered the name well, and that Monte had said the man was as bad as an outlaw. If so, a sixteen year old shouldn't be facing him and his cronies alone. She sprang out of the rocking chair, gesturing for Cassie to stay put as she hastened after Stephen. She caught up with him before he reached Barkley. By daylight, she saw that the man was sixtyish and that his beard was as gray as his hair. He wore a revolver holstered at his hip and had a bullwhip coiled around his saddlehorn.

"You'd better go into the house, Miss Wentworth," Stephen said tightly.

"And you'd better go and fetch reinforcements. There are three men. You're not even armed."

Barkley seemed to be riding for the bunkhouse, but he reined in his horse when he spotted Stephen and Iphigenia. Tipping his hat, he dismounted directly in front of her while his two cohorts halted to watch.

"Miss Wentworth, isn't it?" he said, ignoring Stephen. "Mr. Ryerson's fiancée?" His impudent gaze slid over her body. She wore a white batiste afternoon frock with ribbon trim, another dress that was too fancy for a Texas ranch. "How lovely you look. How nice to see you."

Iphigenia would recognize that raspy, edgy voice anywhere. "Unfortunately, I cannot say it is nice to see you."

Barkley's smile didn't reach his eyes. "Now surely you aren't going to hold our misunderstanding against me. Men can't help being suspicious when they're faced with strangers who fire on them."

"You shot at him?" Stephen gazed at Iphigenia with surprise, his tone tinged with admiration, then turned to Barkley. "You'd better leave. Pa says you're not welcome here."

"My, my," said Barkley. "The young pup is barking like a full-grown dog."

Iphigenia felt a chill, fearing this man would have no qualms about harming a sixteen year old. She bluffed. "Monte will be returning any minute."

"I don't think so." Barkley lightly fingered his holster. "I saw him riding out to the range this morning." He gave Iphigenia another thin-lipped smile. "I mean no harm. I'm merely making a little social call."

"Nobody invited you." Stephen's tone was threatening. Which made Barkley raise his brows and Iphigenia grow concerned.

She took Stephen's arm in a firm hold. "Go to the bunkhouse and get the men." There were a few around. Iphigenia had spotted Monte's foreman Jake O'Brian this morning.

Stephen seemed reluctant, so Iphigenia urged, "Please, Stephen," and breathed a sigh of relief when the young man finally walked off.

Barkley laughed. "How flattering. Does this mean you want to be alone with me?"

Iphigenia could think of several sharp responses but curbed her tongue. "Do I appear to want to be alone with you?"

Barkley's lips twitched. "No, my dear, you look frightened." He stepped nearer but she refused to move back. "Though it is your intended you should be concerned about, not me. Ryerson killed his first wife."

Eyes widening in surprise, she stood there in shocked silence.

"I don't know where you came from," Barkley said, "or how you and Mr. Ryerson met. But he has a terrible temper. Probably comes from being half savage. He and his wife fought like cats and dogs. Rumor has it her ghost still haunts the house."

Gooseflesh rose on Iphigenia's arms. "A ghost?" She told herself she would do well to remember she had a living menace to deal with right now.

Barkley smirked. "I don't believe for a moment that you were going for any pleasure ride the other night, armed as you were with a pistol. Did you and Ryerson have a fight already? Did he threaten you?"

Iphigenia had indeed argued with Monte, but he'd never tried to harm her. It was Barkley who had, by ordering his cohort to take her out of her saddle and teach her a lesson. She became angry again simply thinking about it.

"You and your man are the ones who threatened me. That's why I pulled out my pistol and took a shot."

"You should be more careful. Your aim isn't very good."

"Not with a muzzle-loader." She lifted her chin and stared him in the eye, tired of watching what she said. "You ought to see what I can do with a revolver by daylight. I'd blow a hole right through you."

"My, my, you are a . . . spirited female, aren't you?"

Barkley was the first to break off their mutual glare, as one of his men spoke up. "Here they come."

Barkley stared toward Stephen, as Jake O'Brian and Norbert Tyler approached. All carried rifles. One of his own men drew his revolver.

Barkley scowled. "What the hell?" He made a motion. "Put the gun away. It's not worth it today." He smiled down at Iphigenia as he gathered the reins and remounted. Leaning over, he lowered his voice conspiratorially. "You should think about what I told you. Your future husband is a killer."

"From you, that opinion doesn't hold for much."

At least she hoped and prayed so.

*　　　*　　　*

Though she wasn't involved with Monte Ryerson, and certainly wasn't going to marry the man, Iphigenia hated to think that he could have murdered his children's mother.

Still, she brooded about the possibility as she sat at the table watching Monte wolf down his supper. When he'd arrived that evening, he'd berated Stephen for staying behind, as the boy expected. Then the man had withdrawn into himself, merely grunting a noncommittal response to Cassie's remark about planting flowers and growling when he heard about Barkley's visit.

Iphigenia glanced at Ginnie across the table. The girl was sullen as usual. Perhaps father and daughter were alike in dark temperament.

She was tempted to remind Monte that his son had been ready to risk his life to protect the ranch, then thought better of it. Stephen would probably be embarrassed if she defended him.

But when the meal was over and Monte went out onto the porch to catch a breath of fresh air, she followed. Leaning his large frame against a rough wooden column, he didn't even turn to look at her, but merely gazed out into the night. He seemed remote, unapproachable, a little frightening in his intensity.

Then, again, she'd already faced armed men that day. "You're certainly in a fine mood," she said to break the silence.

"Which means it's best to leave me alone."

"I can't stand by and see you treat your children with such coldness and lack of respect." It triggered something deep inside her. "Stephen was ready to face Jonah Barkley by himself."

"My son should have been out working with me today."

"Then there would have been no one to protect the

house. Barkley could have burned it down by the time the men came from the bunkhouse."

He snorted. "Yeah? You would have strangled him or shot him before he got that far."

She was surprised. "You were depending on me?"

"You were here. Heard you told Barkley off good, threatened to blow a hole through him."

She hadn't realized that anyone overheard. But she guessed she'd been speaking fairly loudly.

"I would never harm a human being, except to protect myself or someone I cared about." She paused, wondering about Barkley's claim. "Can you say the same for yourself?"

Now he turned toward her, though she couldn't make out his expression in the dark. "Back to accusing me of beating kids and hitting women?"

"What happened to your wife?"

Silence. Except for the wind soughing through the cottonwoods and the lowing of a cow in one of the corrals.

"Why are you asking about my wife?" he asked finally.

"Cassie said she died in an accident. In the house?"

"I don't owe you an explanation."

He certainly didn't. He hardly owed her honesty at all, considering she herself could not be open. But she persisted. "Jonah Barkley said you killed your wife. He said you have a terrible temper."

Monte made a derisive sound. "And you believed him?"

"He doesn't seem the sort who can be trusted, but—" She paused, uncertain of how to bring up a sticky topic.

"But what?"

"Barkley also claimed that your wife's ghost haunts this house." Again she paused, not knowing what his beliefs about spirits might be. "There *are* unusual events happening at night. I've lain awake and heard laughter and footsteps. Once I awoke to see an eerie light in my bureau's mirror."

"You, an educated city woman, believe in ghosts?"

"You don't?"

"I didn't say that. But I can tell you one thing, if there's a ghost in this house, she isn't my wife."

The wind rustled the cottonwoods' leaves. To the east, the line of mountain ranges started to glow as the moon rose. The night felt unsettled.

Monte felt strange and restless. Was Iphigenia startled? he wondered. Surprised that he admitted there might be a ghost? Amazed that he thought it was female, yet didn't think it was his wife?

Iphigenia had sure as hell shocked him by bringing up Amanda Ryerson in the first place. The pain of Amanda's death had become a distant throb, though Monte was still haunted by it.

Ghosts.

Standing there in the dusky dark, wearing a flowing white dress, Iphigenia resembled a wraith herself. But she wasn't cold or floating around on some other plane. She was here, fully flesh and blood. Monte could hear her breathing, could imagine he felt warmth flowing from her. And he was comforted, glad for her company, a living presence. To his surprise, he realized he actually longed to reveal some of his inner self.

"About my wife—she died three years ago in a buggy accident. It was winter and there'd been a rainstorm." The roads had been wet, slippery clay. "She was on her way to Pine Bluff, a little hole in the wall not far from here, and the buggy slid off into an arroyo. I was nowhere around."

He could add more but he wasn't ready. But he said this to allay Iphigenia's curiosity, in case she still wondered.

"I'm sorry," she murmured.

Sorry he'd lost his wife or sorry she'd made a false accusation? Monte didn't bother to ask. "Now, about this ghost business, over the past few months, I've heard laughter and footsteps, too. But I would know my wife's voice. I would sense her presence. It's not her."

He wasn't going to mention that the spook sounded and felt more like Xosi Baca. He wasn't going to bring up the dream he'd had about her. If it *had* been a dream. Xosi had seemed so real, if in a cold otherworldly way. Though he didn't see how she could be haunting him.

"So these incidents have been happening for only a few months," she mused. "There weren't always noises and lights in the night? I already gathered it's a fairly new occurrence from Carmen."

"Carmen?"

"Your housekeeper was upset about the cowboys who quit yesterday. She was talking about curses and raising the dead. She blamed the noises, as well as the horse and cattle stampedes, on a curse. She also mentioned some dead chickens."

"There's lots of superstition in this area of the country." Iphigenia moved to lean against the column opposite, her skirts making a soft, swishing sound. "Well, I can't speak for the beliefs in West Texas, but something sure doesn't make sense to me."

He frowned. "What do you mean?"

"I'm not an expert on spiritualism, but I've always understood that ghosts are unhappy spirits who haunt the places where they died," she explained. "No one passed away here except your grandparents. If your grandmother was going to wander the halls and flicker with light, she would have done so long before now."

Then she went on to explain her own experiences

with her cousin's house in New York. She seemed rational and accepting of the business. Monte was mildly surprised, since he usually found that most Anglos dismissed such things as spirits.

"It seems to me that the stampedes and other odd happenings about the ranch would be due to human mischief, not demons or ghosts."

"I agree."

"Did you find evidence of foul play where the cattle ran over that cliff? Carmen described explosions of some sort."

"The men who quit were camped out some miles away. They say they saw bright lights and heard loud cracking sounds. But when I rode out there today, I couldn't find anything." He tapped a finger on the wooden column. "But maybe that's because it rained last night and washed any tracks away."

That was one of the reasons he'd come home in a dark mood. He didn't want to complain about rain, living in an arid area as they did, but he wished nature could have waited until after he investigated.

"What about the horse stampede?"

"I know somebody intentionally spooked the animals. Couldn't tell who, though. They covered their own mounts' hooves with strips of blanket."

"Do you think it could have been Jonah Barkley?"

"Makes sense. You saw how he was out at night where and when he had no business being. He had no business coming by the ranch today. Never know what he's up to." From his conversation with the wranglers who'd quit, Monte had the idea that someone had tried to encourage them. "At the least, he's spreading bad rumors." Still, he had to admit, "Not that I don't have other enemies. Something happened last fall—a man got killed and his family is still blaming me for it."

As the moon rose, Iphigenia stood out pale in the cool, colorless light. "A man got killed?"

"It's a long story. I don't want to go into all the details." Though it felt good explaining something, letting go of a tiny part of the weight he'd been carrying. "I'll just say that in the beginning, some Mexican bandits took off with two of my men."

"Kidnapped them?"

"Something like that. Me and Jake O'Brian were set to go after the bandits, trail them into Mexico if we had to. I'm a good tracker. I learned that from my Comanche father." He paused. "Anyway, we were set to go when an army man showed up with a couple of fellows. They were also tracking the bandits. Said the pack were followers of a madman named Beaufort Montgomery who thought he was an Aztec god." Monte had known the man from years and years before, a former Confederate officer he'd served under. He'd already been notified that the man was on the loose. "Know who Quetzalcoatl is?"

"I have read about the Aztecs."

"Then you also know about the way they sacrificed people."

"By cutting out their hearts. Oh my God, that's what happened to your kidnapped men?"

"One of them." Which was terrible enough. And Xosi's sacrifice had been even worse. "Saw the whole thing myself and couldn't raise a hand to stop it." Not even when he'd held a rifle. "Roberto Padilla died a terrible death and his family is never gonna let me forget it."

"So you're saying Padilla's family might be trying to harm you?"

"Maybe." He added sincerely, "I hope not."

"Were you held captive by this madman yourself?" asked Iphigenia.

Shamefully enough. "He had a lot of followers. They got the drop on us."

"Then how could the Padillas hold you responsible?"

"They have to blame someone, I guess. Some people even think bad medicine—or curses, whatever you want to call it—followed me back to Texas."

"At least you escaped."

"By the skin of our teeth—me and Jake and Shorty, along with the army man and his woman."

Monte was referring to his own brother-in-law and half sister, but he didn't feel like explaining it all now. No more than he wanted to go into the details surrounding his long-time, sour relationship with Barkley.

Bad medicine.

"Sometimes I kinda half believe there's a curse on this ranch myself," he admitted. "My soul is Comanche, you know, probably more than white. Indians believe that power exists all through the universe and can be used for good or for evil, depending on the person who wields it."

"Power that is good or evil, hmm?" She leaned her head back against the column. "Well, then, if bad medicine exists, if you have actually attracted a dose, you must simply find out how to get rid of it."

"Sounds practical." If a bit too simple. But at least she hadn't dismissed the whole thing.

"One can say the same for ghosts. If they exist, there are ways to deal with them. For one, you must face their existence squarely and not let them frighten you. Spirits cannot truly harm you . . . they are not corporeal. They are lost souls who live a shadowy existence, as if they were mere reflections of real life—the other side of a mirror."

A mirror.

The word stuck with him even as he thought about objections to what she was saying. He couldn't believe that dealing with spirits and bad medicine was always so easy. He'd seen the new Aztec empire the madman had built and the miraculous growth of crops, supposedly nourished by drops of sacrificial blood. He'd swear that ancient death spirits had actually drawn breath through Beaufort Montgomery and the man's crazed followers. But then, even before Mexico, he'd known and experienced things that white men's civilization couldn't explain.

"I seem to have gained an inkling for the reasons you are moody," she was saying. "You have suffered many bad experiences in a short time."

She was making excuses for him?

His pride rebelled. "If you don't watch out, you're gonna become some kinda sweet, helpful woman instead of a rebel who wears men's suits and drinks and swears."

That shut her up.

He straightened and glanced at her dress. "Enough about spooks and such. Did Stephen give you those pants and that shirt yet?"

"Now you are complaining about my dress?"

"Not at all. It's beautiful."

Like her. He had the feeling Iphigenia possessed beauty inside as well, something he hadn't known when they'd first met. "I was asking, that's all. You might want to go riding."

Though he hoped she wouldn't run off. With surprise, he realized he had warm feelings for her and he knew one of the reasons why. "I appreciate you sticking by Stephen when Barkley rode in today. You probably saved the boy from getting beat up." Or worse. Monte would have died inside yet again if anything had happened to his son.

"Stephen deserves whatever support I can give him. He is a good-hearted young man." Then she gazed up at the sky and yawned. "It's getting late."

"Better turn in."

Which made him think about sliding into bed with her himself. What if she were actually his mail-order bride? He could imagine himself entangled with those smooth, ivory limbs. He'd love to run his hands through that mass of gold hair. He'd touch every inch of her soft, pampered flesh, join them in a union that would make them both tremble . . .

"Good night, Mr. Ryerson." She turned to go.

Her formality hit him like a pail of cold water. "Call me Monte. Surely we know each other well enough by now to go by first names." Especially with the way he was thinking of her. He shifted, uncomfortably aroused.

"All right. Good night, Monte."

"'Night, Iphigenia." He liked saying her name, as if the familiarity gave him some hold on her.

But it was a false familiarity. He watched hungrily as she glided off, just beyond his reach.

A mirror.

The word came to mind again when Monte went into the office to pour himself a short snort of tequila. He had to find some way to relax, to forget about the lovely woman sleeping across the corridor. He had to forget how long it had been since he'd been with a woman at all.

He hadn't had much luck with women the past few years. Amanda was dead. And so was Xosi Baca.

Not that he should really compare the two. He'd loved his wife and had merely slept with Xosi.

But he couldn't forget what had happened to Xosi the day after they'd made love. He could still see her climbing that bloody pyramid toward its altar.

A member of the band of Mexican bandits who had captured Monte and his men, Xosi had been a sensual woman, if a greedy and selfish one. She'd set her sights on Monte and writhed beneath his lovemaking, leaving long scratches on his back from her nails. Monte thought he must have touched her in other, less physical ways, as well, since he'd talked her into coming over to the prisoners' side and helping with an escape plan.

As a token of her affection, she'd given him the little silver mirror she wore on a chain. She warned him that the thing was magical, that you could sometimes see what people or spirits were doing in other places . . . possibly, other worlds.

The mirror.

Monte stared at the roll-top desk where he'd deposited Xosi's necklace when he'd returned to Texas. Opening the desk, he reached in and tugged at a small drawer. Empty. Thinking his memory must be playing tricks on him, he opened more drawers, frowning when the mirror appeared in none of them.

"Damn!" He placed the glass of tequila on top of the desk, scrabbled with papers. "Damn it all, anyway!"

He knew he hadn't taken the necklace out of the desk. He hadn't so much as wanted to touch or look at it again, since it stirred up bad memories.

The mirror simply had to be there. After turning up the wick of the room's kerosene lamp, he took hold of it and let the light flood the interior of the desk, using the other hand to scrabble some more. Finally, every single drawer and narrow shelf was empty, every paper tossed onto the floor.

The mirror necklace had disappeared.

And Monte was filled with foreboding. He'd never had a magical experience with the little mirror but he swore the object had once thrummed when he'd held it.

The glass of tequila sat untouched on the table as

Monte thought about the dream he'd had of Xosi, of the laughter and footsteps that shouldn't be floating around the house at night . . .

Moonlight flooded the deep-silled bedroom window when Iphigenia awoke. Had a noise startled her again? Ghostly footsteps?

She swore she'd been hearing them in her own room at times. Not to mention that she'd been finding some of her personal belongings out of place. But perhaps she'd simply been too fatigued to remember where she'd put things.

Then she heard a definite noise, a soft scuffing and sat straight up. If she followed her own advice, she should ignore such goings-on, but Monte's talk of curses and strange happenings in the past had only heightened her curiosity. She rose, cracked the door and glanced out into the corridor.

Her eyes widened when she glimpsed a slim figure sneaking in the direction of the dining room. It was Ginnie.

What was the girl doing up and about at this hour? Was she seriously troubled?

As Cassie had implied, the noises haunting the Ryerson house could very well be of living, breathing origin.

8

"*I can dig up some* bluebonnets and bring them to you later," Stephen told Iphigenia after breakfast the following morning.

"That would be nice." And it would give her something to do. Even Cassie and Ginnie had chores—Iphigenia was beginning to feel a bit uncomfortable lazing about while everyone else worked. "Can I plant them right away?"

"Sure. Dig some holes and put the flowers in, roots and all. Then keep them watered."

The boy had joined Iphigenia on the porch where she'd taken her cup of tea. A blaze of morning light purpled the distant mountains and inched across the subtle green and brown land.

Monte came outside. "Bringing a lady flowers, eh?"

Stephen colored, but smiled shyly at Iphigenia before darting down the porch steps. A host of cowboys had saddled up and were waiting some yards in front of the house. Stephen gave her a quick look before joining them. Monte and his son would be heading out to the range with the wranglers.

"You didn't have to embarrass the boy," Iphigenia said.

Monte chuckled. "Teasing is good for Stephen. He's old enough to go courting one of these days. He needs more confidence." Smiling at her with more than enough self-possession for both father and son, he stepped to the edge of the porch and shouted to the waiting men. "Ready, boys?"

Iphigenia had difficulty putting the courting comment to the back of her mind. Had Monte courted many women since his wife's death? she wondered. A woman would be hard-pressed to turn away his advances. Even she felt the power of his manliness, no matter how bitterly opposed they seemed at times.

"Hey, Ginnie!" one of the cowpokes shouted, making Iphigenia turn to see the girl standing off to one side behind her. "Wanna join us today?"

The girl shook her head. "I have important things to do here."

Important? Iphigenia had the feeling Ginnie was referring to activities other than chores. She stared at the girl, wondering if she'd had enough sleep after sneaking about the night before, perhaps creating mischief. Ginnie glared in return, then went back inside.

What cheek, Iphigenia thought. Yet she was reminded of herself at Ginnie's age. She'd hidden from her father and the servants, crawling out of her bedroom window onto the roof. She'd also "misplaced" some of Horace Wentworth's belongings and thrown away calling cards that visitors had left.

But then, she'd had an excuse, misbehaving because her father had been so uncaring. Horace Wentworth had never once said he loved her and he'd never seemed concerned for her well-being. He'd bristled and shouted as often as not whenever she approached him.

Monte Ryerson, on the other hand, was blunt and sometimes aloof, but Iphigenia firmly believed he loved his children. She was certain he would talk calmly, as well as listen, if they were patient and sought his counsel.

Ginnie should be happy she had a caring parent. In fact, Ginnie should be happy she had a parent at all. Iphigenia's own baby was essentially an orphan put out for adoption. She sighed, again praying the family who'd taken in her child was being kind to Hope.

Still, she was determined that it wouldn't be long now before they were reunited.

Monte glanced back at Iphigenia as he got ready to leave, noting her somber expression. He'd give a pretty penny to know what was going on with her.

"Where's Jake?" asked Shorty.

Monte had been about ready to mount up. "He's not here?" Now what was the matter? Yesterday, his foreman had claimed he'd felt "poorly" and stayed behind.

"Thar he be. He's a'comin'." Norbert Tyler jerked his chin in the direction of the bunkhouse. "But he shore looks as cross as a snappin' turtle."

In another bad humor? Monte tried to be open-minded, considering his own moodiness, but some of the men were beginning to complain about Jake's belligerent attitude. Mexico had changed the man. Monte didn't like the look of the big bullwhip Jake had wrapped around his arm. He saw no reason to be deliberately cruel to people or animals.

Jake stomped up, glaring at Shorty. "Where's my horse, you son of a bitch?"

The smaller cowpoke didn't take offense, probably

because he used to be Jake's good friend. He motioned. "Saddled 'im and tied 'im to that post over there."

Jake grumbled and headed in the direction of the roan that was his favorite.

At the same time, Cassie came running from the house. "Get extra bluebonnets this afternoon," she told Stephen. "So we can plant flowers under both cottonwoods."

Jake snorted. "Flowers? Nothing is gonna grow around here, girl, not with the curse that's on your pa."

Curse?

Startled, then furious for a moment, Monte had to fight his anger. He wasn't the sort of boss who yelled and pushed his men around. Voice taut, he ordered Stephen and the others to go on ahead. "Jake and me will catch up."

"Okay, Pa."

The men rode out, Norbert at the rear, looking over his shoulder as if he'd prefer staying for the coming show. Obviously sensing something was wrong, Cassie fled back to the house. From the porch, Monte heard Iphigenia jabbering, saying something about his daughter going inside because they were altering a dress for her.

He concentrated on Jake, stalking right over to him. "What the hell do you think you're doing, running off at the mouth about some damned curse?"

"I'm callin' it the way I see it."

"Well, I don't give a hot damn about the way you see it. You keep your trap shut around the other men. We've had two wranglers quit."

"And there may be more," said Jake ominously.

"What's the matter with you? If we don't have enough help, I'll have to sell off the cattle for whatever I can get and probably go broke." Jake had been with him for years or he wouldn't have been so forgiving the past months. "You'll lose your job. Is that what you want?"

Jake seemed to hesitate before saying, "Nope, can't say as it is."

And for a moment, the man seemed to soften, resembling the trustworthy, salt-of-the-earth ranch hand Monte had always known. He wondered if Jake had some intuitive feeling about what had been going on lately, some sensitivity that went beyond his own. He seemed to know something . . .

The foreman mounted, winding the bullwhip around his saddle's rigging, above his lariat. "I'll be going," he told Monte, not waiting to be dismissed. "And I'll shut up—not that it'll help you a whole damned bit." Then he kicked the roan and sent the horse galloping off.

Monte let out a long, disgusted breath, stepping toward his own horse, a big black. He stuck his foot in the stirrup, ready to spring into the saddle, when he decided it wouldn't be a bad idea to arm himself with more than the usual Springfield rifle in the saddle boot. He couldn't help feeling uneasy, never knowing what might go on anymore.

Striding back to the house to get his Colt and holster, he was waylaid by Iphigenia.

"Monte?"

He liked the sound of his name on her lips, but he wasn't in the mood to be held up. Still, he halted.

"Are you certain that Mr. O'Brian means well by you?" she asked. "Perhaps he is working against you, spreading rumors about the curse."

As if Monte wasn't already worried about that. But he told himself she was only trying to be helpful. "Jake hasn't been the same since we came back from Mexico. Don't know what happened to him. Maybe he lost a piece of his soul." If not the whole shebang, he added to himself. Before that doomed trip, the man had never been mean on purpose.

"Maybe you should fire him."

Monte held his temper. "Don't worry about what I should do. It's not exactly your business." He caught a glimpse of Cassie peeking out the window and lowered his voice. "You've got your own problems. Thought you were going to wean my girl away from your skirts. Spending the day sewing a dress for her isn't gonna do that."

Iphigenia raised her chin proudly, though her green eyes darkened. With hurt?

"I don't think a little kindness will harm Cassie," she said coolly. "I intend to talk to her, not push her aside ruthlessly."

"Just see that you keep to your agreement." He turned his back and stalked off.

As if things between her and his family, and between her and himself, hadn't already gone far beyond uncomplicated. She seemed too involved, sounded like she cared, as proven by her questions about Jake.

Shrewd as he was at understanding people's motives, Monte sure as hell couldn't figure out Miss Iphigenia Wentworth.

"It's so-o-o beautiful!" Cassie cried as Iphigenia and Carmen slipped a blue silk gown over her head. She wore only her simple muslin camisole and bloomers. "Only I don't have a nice petticoat to wear with it. Do you think anyone will notice?"

"I have an extra petticoat that I can give you, as well."

Cassie wanted to kiss Iphigenia on the cheek in thanks, but she felt too shy. Instead, she merely beamed at her as Carmen went about the fitting and pinning and cutting. Iphigenia had seemed a bit embarrassed when she'd said she wasn't good at sewing, but Cassie figured that was another skill a real lady didn't have to have.

"This will be *bonita*," Carmen said with delight. "My little Cassita will look so pretty. You watch out, the boys will be chasing you when they see you in this dress."

"Do you have some young men you favor?" Iphigenia asked.

She spoke so fancy. Cassie only wished she could learn to talk like that. "Young men? Oh, there might be a couple I wouldn't mind dancing with."

Iphigenia seemed interested. "There are dances you can attend?"

Carmen answered for Cassie. "There are always *fiestas*, parties. Señora Ryerson—Cassita's mother—liked parties. She gave them and went to other people's. If she traveled far, she took blankets so that her family could sleep at the home of the hostess."

"You knew Amanda Ryerson?" asked Iphigenia.

"*Si*. I have been with the family since before the twins were born." Carmen quickly pinned darts in the silk dress's bodice and took up the shoulders. "The girls were so sweet as babies. You should have seen them." She glanced up at Cassie. "This one is still sweet—"

Then she stopped, probably not wanting to say anything bad about Ginnie. Sometimes Cassie wondered if Ginnie had gone crazy. A while ago, as Iphigenia helped Carmen gather sewing tools, Cassie had glanced out a window to see Ginnie under the tall cottonwood. The girl had been carrying a burlap bag and digging in the rocks with a big stick. Cassie had no inkling as to why.

But she forgot about Ginnie as Carmen worked and visited with Iphigenia. The housekeeper answered questions about Cassie's mother, saying she'd met her husband when she'd come to Texas as a schoolteacher. Amanda

Ryerson had been good-natured and happy, the sort of woman who helped her husband be more social and who made him laugh. Iphigenia seemed awfully interested, but Cassie wished they'd talk about something else. Thinking about her mother always made her sad. She was about to open her mouth and change the subject herself when Iphigenia and Carmen got into discussing Pa's mother.

"She married a Comanche warrior? Isn't that unusual?" Iphigenia asked.

"*Si*. Though there are many kinds of people in Texas," said Carmen. "Mexicans, Anglos, and Indians before the army drove them out. Mestizos are people who are a mix of all three."

"But Monte, er, Mr. Ryerson isn't mestizo."

"He is a half-breed." Carmen added, "And he had a difficult time growing up, especially after his grandfather paid Señor Barkley to marry his mother."

"Barkley?" Iphigenia frowned. "Jonah Barkley?"

"*Si*. Old Señor Ryerson tore his daughter Señorita Sarah away from the Comanches, kidnapped her and—" Glancing at Cassie, Carmen hesitated.

Not that Cassie didn't already know that Barkley had been paid to marry her grandmother.

Carmen sighed. "It was a terrible mistake. Señor Barkley isn't a good man. Señorita Sarah was very unhappy and ran away. She died and no one even knows where she is buried."

"How horrible," said Iphigenia.

Cassie suddenly realized why Iphigenia was so intrigued by her family's history. As Pa's new wife, she probably wanted to know all about his background and how to make him happy. As her new mother, Iphigenia would probably be asking questions about her childhood when Cassie wasn't around. Despite the tragedy of the subjects being discussed, she smiled.

She only hoped Iphigenia didn't care about her family's Comanche blood. She wondered if the fact that her father looked more Indian than white bothered Iphigenia. "Do you think Pa is handsome?" she asked.

Iphigenia raised a brow. "He is attractive in his own way."

"And what about me?" Cassie asked bluntly. "Do you think my skin is too dark?"

"Of course not." Iphigenia frowned, as if she hadn't ever thought about it. "You are quite lovely, Cassie."

"There are good people of all kinds," added Carmen, obviously also concerned with Iphigenia's opinions.

"I know that." Then Iphigenia smiled at Cassie and fussed with the blue dress. "You will need a ribbon to match this gown, though fresh flowers are always appreciated at parties. You will certainly be a sight for young male eyes."

Carmen agreed, "Everyone will want to court you, Cassita."

"Good heavens, yes." Iphigenia nodded enthusiastically. "You're not that far from eighteen, the most eligible age for a young woman."

"Many women are married at eighteen," said Carmen.

Cassie wasn't certain she cared for the way the conversation was going. She liked the idea of male attention but she didn't want to think about marriage. She didn't want to grow up so fast. Especially not when she just got a new mother.

"I need to know a lot more than I do now if I'm going to be a real lady," Cassie said, noting how coarse her hands looked against the beautiful material of the dress. "It'll take more than five years."

"Not so long. Why, you've already learned a great deal," claimed Iphigenia. "And you have charm and a kind heart—that is what makes the greatest of ladies.

You're going to have many friends in the future. And, eventually, a man who is special to you."

Special? As in a future husband? Why all this talk about marriage? Cassie felt as if Iphigenia was trying to push her out of the house, when she'd just started making it a home.

"I'm not going to get married until I'm . . . how old are you?"

Carmen chuckled, then quickly sobered at Iphigenia's frown.

"I am twenty-seven, a spinster in society's eyes. You don't want a life like mine."

"But you won't be a spinster anymore, not after you marry Pa." Cassie added shyly, "And you'll be my . . . uh, *our* stepmother."

Iphigenia said nothing more and Carmen finished fitting the beautiful blue dress, pinning up the hem. Then Iphigenia suggested she and Cassie go to her room to pick out a petticoat. Cassie whirled around happily as she led the way down the corridor.

"I have so much fun with you," she told Iphigenia. "I love talking to you and learning new things."

"Though I'm not the only person you can learn from."

At this comment, the loneliness Cassie had felt ever since her mother died started creeping back up on her. She thought about what her pa had told her after the fancy dinner, after Iphigenia had gotten upset and the two of them had that talk in his office. He'd questioned that the city woman was really going to stay.

Cassie hadn't wanted to believe it. "You *are* going to stay here, marry Pa, aren't you?"

Iphigenia gave her a sidelong glance. "Why are you asking me that?"

"Because I would feel bad if you left." Cassie didn't think she could stand it. Her throat tightening, she babbled on. "Pa feels better with a lady around, too. He likes you."

"He loves *you*, Cassie. You can make him feel better by talking to him yourself."

Unsatisfied, Cassie was about to continue the discussion when they stopped short before Iphigenia's bedroom. The door was wide open. Cassie gaped at the sight of her twin standing in front of the bureau.

"What are you doing here?" Iphigenia asked.

Ginnie whipped around and her eyes flashed. "It's my house. I can be wherever I want."

Then, holding her vest to her side as if she were hiding something under it, she ran straight toward them, rudely pushing Cassie aside to bolt down the corridor.

Usually even-tempered, Cassie felt angry enough to punch her sister and was upset for Iphigenia. "I'm sorry, Miss Wentworth."

"*I'm* sorry. You're the one who has to live with her."

Once again, Cassie detected the hint that Iphigenia wouldn't be staying. Heart in her throat, she couldn't speak. And she hated her unruly sister, perhaps the reason Iphigenia had doubts about staying on with them.

But Iphigenia simply couldn't leave. Deep within, for some unknown reason, Cassie felt this woman was necessary to everyone's future.

As he'd promised, Stephen brought Iphigenia clumps of bluebonnets, as well as some pink flowers. On horseback, he handed down a whole bucketful to her.

"Lovely." Iphigenia hefted the wooden bucket. It was heavy, full of roots and soil, as well as flowers. "Thank you."

Cassie was equally enthusiastic. "Now we can plant them."

At the moment, Iphigenia wasn't in a hurry. Monte and several wranglers had ridden in with Stephen. The men were dirty and probably uncouth but quite colorful. Monte himself looked handsome despite the grime on his face and the sweat marks on his clothing. His features were generous but not coarse, his body fit and muscular. Not to mention that he sat his horse as if he belonged there.

Just looking at him, Iphigenia felt a thrill crawl along her spine and wondered if she had a fever. Surely no attraction to a man could make her feel so . . . unlike herself.

"Want some lemonade, boys?" Monte asked. "I'll get you some before you go back to the bunkhouse." Dismounting, he took off his revolver and holster, hanging them on a nail driven into a porch column.

Then, to Iphigenia's relief, he went inside.

Everyone had some lemonade before Carmen found a trowel. Anxious to get started, Cassie took the digging tool and the bucket to the big cottonwood. Iphigenia stuck around the men, listening to wild talk about rounding up wiley longhorns. Obviously highly aware of her presence—Monte had told them she was his fiancée—the cowboys were very polite. They called her "Ma'am" and refrained from swearing. As soon as they finished their drinks, they tipped their hats and strolled off toward the bunkhouse. Coming back outside, Monte went along with them.

Iphigenia found herself staring after him until she thought about Cassie. The girl was expecting her. Iphigenia hurried to the back of the house. The rocking chair still sat where Stephen had brought it yesterday. Reminded of the good time she'd had with the youngsters, she sighed. She'd tried in the nicest way to promote more independence in Cassie this morning and had failed miserably. The girl stuck like glue to her side. Someone's heart was going to be broken in this situation, no matter what.

Surveying the scene, Cassie glanced up with a smile for Iphigenia. "The best place for the flowers would be the east side of the tree, don't you think? That way, they'll get some morning rays but they won't be fried by the hot afternoon sun."

"Seems to be a good idea. How can I help?"

"I'll dig some holes in there." Cassie motioned to the soil inside the rock border. Most of the rocks were flattish stones two to three feet in length, some of them striated with earth tones. She knelt, trowel in hand. "Why don't you sort out the plants? They're all piled together in the bucket. They need the dirt around their roots but they have to be separated from each other."

Iphigenia picked up the bucket of flowers, admiring the blooms, noting some of them were wilted. She frowned, touched some petals, only to pause when she heard the sudden intake of Cassie's breath.

And was that a soft slithering sound?

She glanced up, stiffening when she saw a graceful, sinuous length of geometric pattern moving from beneath the stones near Cassie.

A serpent with a deadly triangular head.

A poisonous viper!

Before Iphigenia could even react, the snake coiled, affixing Cassie with a pitiless eye. The girl sat frozen, staring back, but the snake wasn't fooled. A dry rattle sounded as it shook its tail, getting ready to strike.

Heart in her throat, Iphigenia realized Cassie couldn't possibly get out of the way. In desperation, she hefted the bucket and threw it as hard as she could at her target. As it crashed into the snake, Iphigenia swooped down and grabbed Cassie. She dragged the girl backward, not pausing for breath until they were halfway to the house.

"My God, are you all right?" Iphigenia's pulse thrummed as she looked for wounds on the girl. "Did the creature strike you?"

"No," said Cassie, breathless herself. "I'm fine."

"Thank God!" Emotion surging, Iphigenia took the girl in her arms and held her for all she was worth. "I thought you were going to die!"

Cassie's voice was muffled. "Most rattlers don't kill you, if you get the venom out on time."

But the girl was shaking. Iphigenia knew she had been scared.

"Poor, sweet Cassie!" Iphigenia stroked her hair. "I don't know what I would have done if something had happened to you." When Cassie sniffled, she tried to be comforting. "There, there. It is all over."

"I can't help it. You actually care about me."

The girl doubted that? Iphigenia felt sharp emotional pain, as if a knife had pierced her heart. Tears pricked her eyes.

"Of course I care about you."

Though she realized that she herself hadn't known the depth of her own feelings. Cassie was the nicest child she had ever known, truly dear to her. How could she go off and leave her?

But she had to remember her baby. At least Cassie had one parent. Hope had none, unless Iphigenia retrieved her.

If only there were some way to work this out so everyone had what they wanted.

Torn, shaken to her core, Iphigenia gave Cassie one last squeeze and let the girl go. She turned her interest to the snake, trying to ignore Cassie's soulful gaze. "Has the rattler gone away, do you think?"

"If the bucket didn't hurt it too bad, it's probably still there. Or crawled under a rock again. We can get Pa or Stephen to shoot it."

"No need." Iphigenia remembered the revolver on the porch. "I shall shoot the damnable creature myself."

It was the least she could do. She could pay something for invading Cassie's life. She ran to the porch and slipped the Colt out of its holster, then headed back for the tree.

Cassie moved closer to watch.

Iphigenia fingered the butt of the gun, and placed her finger on the trigger. "For your own safety, you should go into the house."

"I won't get in your way."

Walking carefully, gun in hand, Iphigenia circled the cottonwood, sighting the rattler only a few feet away from the bucket. She shivered as the serpent flicked its tongue and flexed. It didn't even seem stunned.

"I hate snakes." Iphigenia took careful aim, anchoring the gun with two hands and squeezing the trigger.

Blam!

She thought the serpent's head went flying but she pulled the trigger again and again. Only when she was certain the beast was a twitching carcass did she relax her posture.

"It's dead." Cassie came up beside her to slip an arm around her waist. "You're wonderful!"

Iphigenia swallowed, turning as shouts and pounding footsteps heralded others approaching, undoubtedly having heard the shots.

Monte reached the two of them first, followed by Stephen. "What the hell's going on back here?"

The boy caught sight of what remained of the snake. "A diamondback, Pa. A big one."

"A rattler?" Taking a look for himself, Monte whistled.

"Guess you were telling the truth when you said you could shoot, Miss Iphigenia Wentworth."

"She took the head clean off," said Stephen, grinning. Picking up a long dead branch, he hefted the carcass and flung it as far away as he could.

Cassie frowned, letting go of Iphigenia. "That's the same stick I saw Ginnie playing with earlier."

Monte scowled. "Ginnie?"

"She had a burlap bag, too. She was scrabbling around in the rocks," Cassie went on, her face wreathed in anger. "Honest, I saw her."

"I believe you."

"There's hardly ever any snakes around here, Pa," added Stephen. "What with the wranglers having a rattler round-up every few months."

"Right." Monte took a deep breath, appearing pained as he roared, "Ginnie!"

The other twin appeared suddenly, nearly magically, seeming to slip out of the shadows behind the house. "You don't have to yell, Pa."

"What do you know about this rattlesnake?"

Ginnie shrugged. "I don't know anything."

"Oh, yeah? How did a big diamondback just happen to find its way down here? What did you have in the bag your sister saw you with?"

"Some sweet grass for my horse."

"Liar," said Cassie, sounding uncharacteristically cold and angry. "You wanted to kill Miss Wentworth, didn't you?"

Iphigenia was surprised, even more so when Ginnie made no denials. And before her dazed eyes, Cassie abruptly threw herself at her sister, knocking Ginnie to the ground.

"Leave me alone!" screamed Ginnie, striking out at her sister, though her punch failed to make contact.

"Murderer!" shrieked Cassie, kicking Ginnie and pulling her hair.

An open-mouthed Iphigenia gazed at Monte, relieved when he took action, wading into the fray to grab both girls by their collars.

"Stop it! Stop it right now! Nobody's gonna talk about murder around here but me."

Ginnie tried to squirm away from him. "Yeah, you!" she hissed. "I was only trying to scare that stupid city woman, not kill her or Cassie. But *you* murdered Ma!"

Monte appeared stunned.

"Ma didn't have to die!" Tears started to seep from Ginnie's usually hard and angry eyes. She positively quivered. "You could have gone to Pine Bluff and got what she wanted that day, Pa. But you didn't. You didn't care!"

Iphigenia couldn't help feeling as shocked as Monte appeared to be. He let go of both twins. Ginnie bolted. He glanced at Cassie, then walked off himself, leaving everyone standing there.

Stephen swung the stick back and forth, then threw it down.

Feeling badly for the children, Iphigenia tried to take charge. "Let's go in the house, clean up, and settle down. It'll soon be suppertime." She slid an arm around Cassie's rigid shoulders and handed the Colt to Stephen. "Would you replace this revolver, please? Your father will want to make sure it is safe in its holster when he returns."

Cassie went inside docilely, not objecting when Iphigenia also suggested she go to her room and rest. Looking confused, Stephen took the Colt and didn't come back into the house at all. Perhaps he wandered off.

Her nerves shot, Iphigenia longed to lie down and rest but couldn't bring herself to do so. Heading back out to the porch, she glanced around, not seeing either Ginnie or Monte. The sun sank in the west and blue-gray dusk crept across the land. She stepped off the porch and returned to the cottonwoods. The trees now cast deep shadows.

Shivering again as she thought about the snake, Iphigenia didn't fear there would be another one for her to happen upon. She believed Ginnie. The girl had known they would be planting flowers today and had wanted to scare her. Obviously still deeply upset over her mother's death, the girl hadn't considered the more serious repercussions.

Ginnie had revealed her sorrow and anger by screaming at her father. How strange, Iphigenia thought, for she herself had blamed Horace Wentworth for her mother's death.

When Iphigenia caught a flicker of movement beyond the cottonwoods, she stepped in that direction. Skirting some fencing and sidestepping bushes, she finally caught sight of Monte, his head bowed. As she came closer, she realized he stood before several graves. Three mounds of rocks marked with simple headstones. She hadn't realized anyone was buried on the property.

He didn't look up when she came up beside him.

She stood quietly for a moment, then asked, "Is your wife buried here?"

He nodded. "And my grandparents." His expression was brooding. "You must like wandering around, getting into places where you can stir up trouble. Haven't you had enough for one day?"

His hostility was unwarranted, but she wasn't angry in return. Instead, emotions brimming, she found herself somehow wanting to relieve his pain. By doing so, perhaps she could alleviate some of the suffering that had festered inside herself for years and years.

Though Amanda Ryerson couldn't help Monte, Iphigenia felt a surge of jealousy for the woman who lay in her grave.

She cleared her throat. "No, I suppose I have not had enough of trouble." Then she brought up the topic he could not, would not broach. "You didn't kill your wife."

A sharp expletive left Monte's mouth. "The accident wouldn't have happened if I'd done what she asked, just as Ginnie said."

"But it *was* an accident," Iphigenia assured him. "The buggy slid off the road. That could have happened anywhere. Life holds risks."

"Amanda and I argued before she left."

"Words don't kill."

He looked at her, held her gaze with his. "I don't know why you're doing this."

"I don't know why either."

Unless her guilt over leaving this family's tragic situation—children with no mother, a man anguished by loss—compelled her to do so. Or unless fate had brought her here to West Texas to teach her some sort of lesson.

Iphigenia didn't know why, but she reached out to Monte, to this hard man who buried his softer emotions and emphasized his hard ones like anger. She cradled his weather-rough cheek even knowing he might spurn her sympathy. But something happened between them. Her touch brought a gentler curve to his mouth, a gentler light to his eyes. He placed his hand around hers, and for a moment, they stood there in perfect harmony, sharing something she could not put a name to.

Then Monte took a deep breath and let go of her hand. "Let's go back to the house."

Taking a deep breath, Iphigenia nodded and tried to pretend that part of her hadn't longed for him to take her in his arms. Certainly not there, in front of his wife's grave. For heaven's sake, what was she thinking?

As they walked along, Monte shortened his stride, allowing her to keep up. She felt comfortable with his company, didn't mind his silence. He was so unlike the men she'd known in New York. Several feet separated them, yet she could imagine she felt warmth emanating from his powerful body. A responding heat flickered in her belly.

Iphigenia didn't know how it had happened, considering the bad start they'd gotten with each other, but she was attracted to this strange man. His unusual Indian-influenced beliefs and outlook intrigued her, even if she found some of them alien to her own. She respected his opinion, whether or not she agreed with it. She admired his unassuming intelligence, blunt integrity, and strength. Furthermore, he exuded a deep, dark sensuality that made her quiver inside.

As she mused on all that, the glow of kerosene light from the ranch house windows came far too quickly. Monte ambled to the porch and stopped to allow Iphigenia to ascend before him. The smell of food wafted outside.

He sniffed. "Smells good. Guess I'll eat and hit the pillow. I'm dead tired from working all day and I'll have the same load tomorrow."

"Everyone keeps saying you're short of men. Can I be of any help?"

"Not unless you can round up cattle."

That was actually a surprisingly appealing idea. "I'd be happy to try and work with you, Monte. I have the pants and the shirt Stephen gave me."

"Herding cattle is dirty, hard work."

"So? I'm willing." She bragged, "And I'm nearly as good with a horse as I am with a gun."

He frowned. "Are you serious?"

"Perfectly serious. So where are we taking the herd? Not to market?" She didn't want to think about what would happen to the animals once they got there.

"Nah, too early in the season for the long drive. Just moving some longhorns to a different part of the range where they can't have any more accidents."

Remembering Stephen's comment about rimrocking—someone purposely driving the cattle over a cliff—Iphigenia shuddered. Too bad they couldn't figure out who had done such a savage deed. Maybe then they could dispel some of the rumors about the R&Y being cursed.

"I'll be up at dawn," she assured Monte, in case they tried to sneak away without her. "So I'd better get to bed early. Good night."

"'Night."

Then she headed into the house, looking forward to the next day. She hoped Monte wouldn't try to stop her, for working on the range would serve many purposes. She could spare Cassie her presence for a day, get to know the land, and toughen up her riding skills. She needed to be fit, to have her wits about her before going after Hope. The thought of being reunited with her child soon set her heart to pounding.

Less important, she assured herself, was that working on the range would give her the opportunity to spend time with the most fascinating man she'd ever known in her life.

9

Mounted on a blood bay with a fine-looking head, Iphigenia felt excitement course through her as she traveled out onto the range with the R&Y cowboys. The country had looked only half as wild from the road. Exotic cactus sprouted among long, thin grasses and rocks seemed to be strewn about the brown earth as if by a giant hand.

She liked riding astride and maintaining close contact with the horse. As a girl, she had hoisted her skirts to ride from time to time, but had given in to convention and had taken to a sidesaddle when she reached womanhood. Then there'd been more interesting rules to flout.

Monte had kept close by since they'd left the ranch. "Those pants fit all right?" He eyed her behind and the outline of her thigh.

She tried to ignore her excitement at the personal attention he was paying her. "I love wearing trousers. They are fine."

The complete outfit—the denim trousers, a striped cotton shirt from Stephen, her own riding boots, and Cassie's wide-brimmed felt hat fastened under her chin with a cord—made her feel quite the wrangler even if she wasn't wearing chaps like most of the cowpunchers. Almost all wore spurs, as well, and a few even had canvas coats to keep the dust off their clothes.

Monte himself was wearing shotgun chaps, parallel tubes he'd had to climb into and had fastened around his waist. And on the backs of his boots he sported what he called OK spurs with rowels filed down to avoid scaring his horse's flanks.

He took off his red bandana and handed it to her. "Better tie this around your neck. Gonna be a lot of sun to deal with today. And when we get the herd moving, you can use it to cover your nose and mouth against the dust."

Her senses were stirred anew by the faint smell of him on the scarf. She did as he ordered.

"How far are we going?" she asked. "Not that I care about the distance. I am enjoying the ride."

"It's a few more miles up into these foothills. We should be seeing the chuckwagon soon and the ponies. The mounts we're riding are distance horses. We're gonna change to cutting ponies to round up cows."

Not having heard of cutting ponies, Iphigenia was intrigued. "That should be interesting."

"Real interesting," Monte laughed. "I bet you haven't so much as herded a milk cow, much less a longhorn."

"Are longhorns so different?" She'd seen the cattle with the great curving horns in some of the corrals.

"A Texas longhorn is clever, ornery and about as quick as a deer. You have to watch them every minute," Monte warned.

"If they're so difficult, why don't you stick to regular cattle?"

"Cause longhorns can graze on about anything and need very little water." He added, "I *do* have fewer full-blood longhorns than my grandfather. Started mixing them with Durhams some years back to put more meat on their bones. But it was mainly longhorns that survived that herd that went over the cliff. They were the only animals with enough sense to stop."

Iphigenia nodded. Bringing in the stragglers that remained from the catastrophe, to return them to pasturing closer to the ranch, was a smart move. There, more men were around to keep watch over them, to keep another "accident" from happening.

Stephen rode up to join her as they topped a rise. Below sat a wagon with a canvas cover and, nearby, the makeshift corral for the *remuda*, or remounts. The ponies were being kept fresh until the real work started.

"A couple of other men been staying out here the past couple of days," Stephen said with a grin. "You know that Pa has a lot of cowboys you've never seen, don't you? With a ranch this size, you've got to have linemen camped out every eight to ten miles. They don't normally come back to the main ranch for months."

"Guards for the borders?"

"Something like that. Pa doesn't want to put in barbed wire."

Monte snorted. "Leave the barbed wire to Jonah Barkley. I like my range open and free."

Barkley and his strange history as Monte's stepfather was another thing Iphigenia was curious about, along with the dire events Monte had said took place in Mexico, but she supposed this wasn't the best time to bring up such subjects.

"How about that little dun mare for Miss Wentworth?" Stephen asked his father when the whole crew dismounted at the wagon to choose saddle ponies.

"Sounds good. The horse is older and calmer."

Iphigenia objected to the special treatment. "I can handle any sort of animal. Why, I've ridden high-spirited thoroughbreds."

"But you aren't used to cutting ponies," said Monte. "You'll be flying through the air the first time your horse decides to make a turn."

"The horse decides?"

"Any cutting pony worth his hay can just about round up cattle on his own. They make a cowpuncher's life easier," Monte told her. "Besides, it's not as if you have to work yourself to death today. You could just get used to things, see how they're done. Why don't you stick by me and watch for a while?"

Was he trying to make things easier for her—or not taking her seriously? Iphigenia wondered, deciding it was up to her what and how much she wished to do.

Monte could tell that the dun mare didn't make a big impression on Iphigenia. The horse wasn't much to look at, kind of shaggy and bow-hocked, but she'd always been an excellent cow pony.

"Now when you get on her, remember that she'll respond to the lightest rein on her neck," he told her. "And when she puts her ears back, watch out, 'cause she's considering something. She may have caught sight of a steer and take it into her head to stop so fast and hard, your head will spin. Or she may take off and nearly dump you, heading him up."

"So you mean I have no control?"

"Don't fight the mare. Just stick with her. Try to

keep balanced and send her in the right direction once she's got the steer moving."

But Iphigenia remained irritable. "Perhaps you should be instructing the horse on how to deal with me. She seems to be the boss here."

Monte laughed and checked the dun's saddle girth to make sure it was tight. Iphigenia stood right by his side, obviously raring to go. She was mouthy and often prickly, but plenty daring, he had to admit.

Looking her over, noticing the fire in her eye and the pride of her posture, he felt a low thrum of excitement that went from his gut straight to his loins. But he told himself he was only making sure she was ready for a day in the sun. Her skin already had a golden cast to it, which meant she had tanned some, but she could stand even more protection.

"You tied that bandana I gave you the wrong way."

She fingered it. "Sorry, I am not familiar with cowboy fashion."

"I couldn't care less about fashion." He reached for the scarf and untied its knot, his fingers brushing against the skin of her throat and neck. It had been too long since he'd appreciated a woman's softness. "With your hair all braided and up under your hat, the back of your neck will be exposed unless you make a big triangle out of this."

Monte shook the bandana out and tied it back around her neck properly this time, noticing the covert way she watched him, listening to the slow intake of her breath. She was attracted to him. If he hadn't already figured that out, he'd be some kind of moron.

Too bad they couldn't do anything about the situation. But even with her attraction, Iphigenia kept distance between them. And Monte had plenty enough problems already. Women always seemed to create more for him. It was probably best that he forget about personal relationships and content himself with a casual roll in the hay from time to time. He knew places he could visit in El Paso.

Still, he couldn't take his eyes off Iphigenia as she mounted the dun. He admired her grace . . . and the sleek curve of her hip.

Damn! Was she ever going to leave his place to take care of the business she'd spoken of? Actually, he had mixed feelings about her departure. At times he wished she was long gone. At others, he knew he'd miss her something terrible. If he didn't watch out, his feelings would be hurt as well as Cassie's.

And he had a hunch that Miss Iphigenia Wentworth wasn't going to be so cold about taking off herself. She cared about his family, he could tell from how upset she'd been over the rattler nearly getting Cassie.

"Mr. Ryerson?" Shorty asked as he rode up, bringing Monte's mind back to business. "We gonna fan out like usual?"

"Sounds the best to me." Monte squatted down and drew a circle in the dirt, indicating landmarks at the circumference. Other wranglers gathered to look over his shoulder. "Ten miles should be good, with the chuckwagon and horse *remuda* at the center."

Each small group of cowboys would block off part of the range and weave their ponies back and forth, herding strays to the center like spokes of a wheel.

Monte noticed that Shorty chose a couple of cowpokes himself, heading off without Jake O'Brian. Not good news. Jake's former pal didn't want to work with him. The only one who seemed to let Jake's bad humor slide off his back was Norbert Tyler. If Jake didn't watch out, he was going to lose the men's cordiality and respect, making it difficult to do his job as foreman.

The wranglers might be self-reliant about their work, but they needed someone to decide what that work was to begin with.

For the first time, Monte actually thought about firing the man. He'd tried talking on numerous occasions, only to be met with a stone face. But he'd think about it later.

Monte himself was partnering Stephen, with Iphigenia riding along. He explained the round-up technique to her, again stressing that she should hang back and watch before she threw herself into the thick of things.

"I'm not too good at patching up broken bones," he warned.

"I am not going to have any broken bones."

Well, all he could do was hope she'd use some sense now that he'd brought her out here. He ordered her to stay back while he and his son rode up a rocky incline to flush some strays out of the brush. Stephen was the first to find one, a bawling scared old cow who probably wanted nothing more than to join back up with a herd. She took kindly to the driving and Monte motioned for Stephen to prod her toward Iphigenia.

As expected, the dun mare kicked into motion all by herself, with Iphigenia guiding the cow toward a spoke-line of the big circle they'd mapped out.

So far, so good.

Monte next came onto a couple of half-grown steers. One of them bolted, but was turned back by Stephen. They drove the animals down the incline toward Iphigenia, who again had no trouble herding the cattle in the right direction.

Everything was working out fine. Too fine, Monte thought, wondering why they hadn't encountered any problems. Even as he thought that, a problem met them head-on.

The brush right behind him suddenly came alive,

rattling and shaking as a big body burst through. The head that emerged was sporting at least six full feet of horns, proving their owner had lived long enough to know how to use them. The longhorn steer rolled his eyes when he saw Monte, twisting like a cat to take off in the opposite direction. Stephen's pony sidestepped, put his ears back and bared his teeth. Monte feared the steer was going to skewer his son and horse anyway, but the animal did a quick dash to the side at the last moment, crashing on down the incline.

Oh, Lord, Iphigenia!

"Watch out!" Monte yelled, but saw it was already too late to send her riding in another direction.

The steer hurtled onward and the little dun mare took action. Monte caught his breath as the horse swung in a fast circle, nearly unseating her rider.

Being thrown back and forth, Iphigenia clung to the saddle for all she was worth, finally leaning over and gripping the saddlehorn as the mare darted forward, bullied the steer, veered from one side to the other, and nearly sat on her haunches. The steer bawled his frustration and tried to feint. The dun mare came on again, trying to catch him before he escaped. The steer's long horns came directly for her.

That's when Monte noticed that Iphigenia had her lariat in hand. Leaning toward the steer, she smacked him good and hard right in the head.

"Hellish beast!" she screamed at the animal. "How dare you threaten my poor little horse!"

Monte couldn't help grinning, especially when the steer actually turned and bounded in the right direction, Iphigenia's dun on its heels. He heard Stephen laughing full out as the boy rode up to join him.

"Guess those ornery old steers better not mess with her, huh, Pa?"

"Guess not."

"She kept her seat awful good, too, don't you think?"

"Uh-huh." Monte lowered his voice. "Don't be praising her too much, though, or God knows what she'll want to do."

Or how full of herself she would get. Though he'd be damned if the crazy city woman wouldn't make a real wrangler if she wanted to. Monte had to add another dollop of grudging admiration to the attraction he felt for her.

By lunchtime, Iphigenia was quite sore from the hard riding, though she wasn't going to admit it to Monte. Finding a blanket, she wadded it up to put under her behind while she ate a plate of beans and corn bread alongside Stephen.

Monte was busy talking to the other wranglers. A small herd of cattle milled near the *remuda*, proof of the morning's work.

"So, are you enjoying yourself, Miss Wentworth?" Stephen asked, digging the gentle, star-shaped rowel of his work spur into the dusty earth.

"I always like honing my riding skills." Now if only she could get through the afternoon.

Reuben, the chuckwagon cook, came up with a pot. "Anybody want the rest of these beans?"

Stephen held out his plate but Iphigenia shook her head.

"Oughta eat hearty. Might get a bit wet this afternoon," Reuben said, gazing at the sky. "Look at them clouds over west."

"We've had quite a bit of rain this spring," Stephen told Iphigenia, "which is unusual. It's more likely to rain in the winter or summer here."

"When it rains a'tall." Reuben eased his creaky old frame down onto a barrel sitting nearby. His batwing chaps flapped out, the leather as old looking as he was. He had a face so wrinkled, the lines resembled a map. "But this spring, them *huecos* are gonna be full up."

"*Huecos*?" Iphigenia repeated.

"Waterholes." Stephen cleaned up his second serving of beans. "And some of the washes that run through this country are gonna be rivers, too."

Locating waterholes was one of Iphigenia's main challenges in getting to Fort Davis. "Is there any way to locate water when you're traveling?"

"It's best to have a map," said Stephen. "Pa has most of the *huecos* for this part of the country charted on the wall in his office. Blue circles."

Iphigenia had wondered what the circles were. She would add them to the crude map she'd already made out. One more step toward retrieving Hope.

Reuben rolled a cigarillo. "You kin also figger out where water is if you have a good eye. Look for birds flockin' at dusk and dawn, critter tracks, grasses getting all green sudden-like." He asked, "Who's thinkin' of travelin' anyway? Somebody you know?"

"I was merely curious." Iphigenia thought it best to be careful about what she revealed around Stephen. "Being from the east, I can see that travel is quite different out here."

"You bet your da . . . you bet," said Reuben, seeming to remember to watch his language around a lady. "Though travelin' today is a whole lot different than it was years ago. Nobody had maps with *huecos* marked out in them days." He took a big puff of the cigarillo. "Why, I had a pardner who rode all the way across Texas through New Mexico Territory on his own. Shot his own game and found his own water. Now that was travelin'."

"All on his own?" Just as she would have to do, Iphigenia thought. "Safely?"

"As safe as you could git with Injuns and hostile Mexicans and outlaws. The trick was not to build a fire at night and draw any attention to hisself."

"No fire? What about wild animals?"

Reuben let out a cloud of smoke. "Aw, wolves or coyotes ain't gonna bother you none. And bears're mainly in the mountains. It's the two-legged variety of animal that's most dangerous, and a campfire tells 'em where you be."

"Though you shouldn't camp near a pile of rocks," Stephen added. "Too much chance of rattlesnakes."

"And you gotta shake out your bedroll and your boots afore you use 'em," said Reuben. "Make sure you ain't picked up any scorpions or poison centipedes."

Though busy storing away the tidbits of information, Iphigenia shivered at the last piece of advice. The rattlesnake incident had been too close for comfort. She wouldn't mind avoiding anything that slithered or crawled for a long, long time.

"You gotta keep your hoss tethered nearby, in case he gets spooked," Reuben went on. "And keep your food wrapped and stored either in a tree or under a rock somewheres away from the camp. Don't want to attract any critters, if you don't have to. Now my pardner, he didn't carry any supplies a'tall. Ate light. Which is best for travelin' in the desert anyways. What you gotta have most of is water."

"Canteens?" asked Iphigenia.

"As many as you kin take. And fill 'em up at every *hueco* when you git the chance."

"As long as the water's good," said Stephen. "In the desert, there's a lot of alkali and minerals. Some waterholes go bad, turn to salt. Worse, some get polluted with arsenic."

"How can you tell if water is bad?"

Reuben cackled. "If you see animal bones nearby, that's how. Or if there ain't any plants growin' about."

There was so much to learn. Iphigenia only hoped she would remember everything or her own skeleton might become part of the desert landscape.

The older man was a font of information. With only a little prodding, he rambled on, talking about how a person shouldn't camp too near a waterhole, since animals will come there and spook one's mount. He also explained flashfloods, how dry washes could become torrents after a big rain. And he said a traveler should have several layers of clothes, since deserts were generally hot during the day but got cold at night.

Once Reuben started, however, he didn't want to stop. Iphigenia found herself politely listening to how to skin a jackrabbit, cut an armadillo out of its shell, and suck eggs that one found in birds' nests. Feeling queasy at the thought of gathering her own food, she swallowed hard, trying not to think of the stuff she'd just eaten.

Stephen had already gotten up and left. Iphigenia looked around and noticed him talking to Monte. The two Ryersons were walking toward her when they were accosted by Bill Harris, a wrangler who looked very upset.

"I ain't workin' for that bastard no longer!" the man said furiously. "He's got a mean streak a mile wide. He's gonna up and kill somebody if the rest of us don't kill him first!"

"Now, Bill," said Monte. "Let me talk to Jake. Maybe you misunderstood something."

So Jake O'Brian was causing problems again, Iphigenia thought.

"Misunderstood, hell. I thought he was gonna use that damned bullwhip on me. He already cut a few slices out of them cows. You're gonna have to doctor them wounds or they'll be drawin' flies."

Bill pulled a pouch of tobacco from his vest, but before he could put a wad into his mouth, Jake himself appeared. Iphigenia rose to get a clearer view. The man's face appeared florid, his eyes glittery.

"What's the matter with you?" Jake took hold of Bill and shook him until the pouch of tobacco dropped to the ground.

"Let go," Monte ordered, voice calm and low.

The foreman did so, but he turned on his boss. "Look, if you don't like what I'm doin', say so."

"All right. I don't like what you've been doing," said Monte straight out. "You were always pals with Bill here. You were friendly with most everybody else. What's eating you anyway?"

"Nothin'." Jake turned away. "I'm heading back to the ranch."

"Jake!" Monte shouted, but the foreman didn't so much as look back. "Damn it all, anyway!"

Iphigenia watched as the man took his horse, mounted, and rode off. In her opinion, Monte was better off without the troublemaker.

Trouble.

The rains Reuben had predicted came early in the afternoon. The crew had staked out another ten mile circle to work, Iphigenia's small group being joined by a fourth wrangler. When the clouds opened, she and Monte became separated from the other two. They found shelter beneath a rocky overhang.

Iphigenia would never admit it, but she was thrilled at the prospect of a rest. She'd ridden long at times, but never this hard. Her bottom felt as if she'd slid down a hundred yard rocky hill, while her legs fairly quivered when she dismounted. She cleared a space in the gravel beneath the overhang and sat down gingerly, back against the rock.

"Ah-h."

Monte squatted beside her. "A little tired?"

She wouldn't give him any satisfaction. "A little."

"I'd be surprised if you weren't. You're not used to this."

"But I'm not doing too badly." She took off her hat and held it in her lap.

"To tell the truth, you're doing damned well. Must have been a tomboy when you were growing up."

"Not exactly." When he glanced at her, she explained, "I always liked to ride and go out to the country, but part of the reason I did so was to escape the presence of my father."

"Never got along, huh? What about your mother?"

"She died before I was five."

That fact caught his interest, she thought, noting the gleam in his eye. "And your old man never got married again?"

"No, though I am certain his position in society attracted the attention of many women. He was always the stern, strict banker," Iphigenia said, the memory depressing her. "A difficult man, not one for small conversation."

"Or affection, either, I expect."

Now why was Monte bringing that up?

He stared out at the rain, heavy droplets that beat into the earth. "Have any brothers and sisters?"

"No, I'm an only child."

"Musta been even tougher on you then." He moved back and slid down to lean against the rock himself. "Your pa had no wife and only a little girl to deal with. He probably didn't know what to do."

Iphigenia felt her father deserved no excuses. "He would not care to do what he should, even if he knew it. Horace Wentworth is a mean-spirited man who expected me to take care of myself and stay out of his way. He only worried about appearances—how and when I was to appear at the table, dressed as I should be. When I was older, he cared only that I did not dishonor the family name."

Monte gave her a wry look. "Musta clashed all right, with your kind of personality."

Iphigenia said simply, "When I became older, I yelled back."

He nodded. "Shouting. Noticed that bothers you."

Somehow she was getting the feeling that Monte didn't have enough sympathy for her. Which hurt. But then, because of Ginnie, she'd begun to realize she'd been an angry child herself.

"I suppose I pushed the limits with my father," she admitted. "But I don't think the majority of our problems were caused by me. He falsely accused me of misdeeds on many occasions." After which she'd decided to live up to his mistrust. But she'd been the child, her father the adult. "I cannot remember his ever trying to understand. He simply reacted and punished me in various ways . . . locked me in my rooms, hired strict nannies, took away pets that I loved, sent me to the country . . . until he discovered I liked it there. And he withheld money if he thought I might use it for something I enjoyed."

Monte shook his head. "Sounds like a real sad situation."

Sad situation? Iphigenia continued to long for sympathy, but she tightened her jaw as Monte regarded her closely. If she broke down, she'd reveal everything.

"So now you've run away. Think your pa's looking for you?"

"I doubt that he cares enough to look very far," she said, hedging. "He told me he was sick of my annoying ways and would be only too happy to see me fend for myself."

"Think he wouldn't even worry that you're wandering around by yourself, without any money?"

Money?

Iphigenia started. Surely Monte wasn't fishing about to find out if she had claim to any. He didn't seem like the mercenary sort, though she knew his ranch was in trouble. But Monte had no more to say on the subject.

Iphigenia relaxed some when he finally directed his gaze out to the rain, his intriguing profile outlined against the gray, watery light. She liked the strength of his bold features, the way the tip of his nose hooked ever so slightly. He was definitely the most attractive man she had ever met.

"So you think your pa never wants to see you again?" he suddenly asked.

"I don't care if he wants to see me."

"Sure of that? He's your own blood. You don't think he has even one good bone in his body?"

Why was he hinting at reconciliation?

He went on, "There can be misunderstandings between parents and kids, you know. I yell sometimes."

"Though you don't seem truly mean-spirited. I believe you love your children."

"I hope *they* believe it. Me and Ginnie had a round yesterday. I'm confining her to the house until further notice. That rattler thing was serious business. Don't know what got into the girl."

So that was the reason for talk of reconciliation. Monte was worried about his own family problems. Iphigenia could relax even more if they would stop discussing her entirely.

"I know the girl seems troubled but she will very likely grow out of it. Especially when she realizes she has a parent who is concerned for her well-being." She thought of how disheartened Monte had seemed after Ginnie's accusations. "Don't let her blame about your wife stop you. She is simply angry, and you were a target for her."

"That's generous of you to say that, considering she had that snake earmarked for you."

"She was only trying to get attention." Iphigenia knew what that was like. Though she would never admit it, Ginny was longing for a mother's love every bit as much as Cassie was, even if the dark twin showed it in an opposite—and negative—way. "You should try to talk to her, tell her you care."

A comfortable silence enveloped them as they watched the rain. The sky seemed to be clearing and the drops came more slowly. A fresh sandy smell rose from the land.

"You do a good job at trying to understand my family," Monte said finally. "And you always seem real interested . . . why?"

Truthfully, "I don't know." She ran a finger along the seam of her denim trousers. "You seem to be asking many questions that I cannot answer of late." She grew warm under his steady gaze. "I am interested in understanding a family that has lost its mother, I suppose." She sighed. "I also see some of my past in Ginnie. I feel I am learning about myself." While at the same time practicing skills for handling a wild land and encountering strengths she'd never known she had, she thought. "Sometimes I think fate sent me here."

Did fate also demand that she use her skills and strengths to run away from the sometimes obliging, often vexing, yet always exciting man who sat beside her?

She couldn't help but grieve as she met his gaze, becoming mesmerized by the black depths of his eyes. She felt she would be losing something of importance before she even got to find out what it was. Then something imperceptible and instinctive passed between them, as if they were communicating without words.

Iphigenia caught her breath as Monte leaned closer and suddenly kissed her on the mouth. His lips were soft, his chin roughened by beard. She touched his face, her fingers welcoming the prickly sensation, and kissed him in return.

He groaned, sliding one arm about her back and the other beneath her knees to lift her into his lap. Heat spiraled from her core at the close contact. Having known a man's touch—as self-indulgent as Lamar's had been—she'd missed the closeness. She wound her arms about his neck.

"So sweet," he murmured, running his hands through her hair, freeing some of the braids.

Iphigenia didn't object.

She all but forgot where they were and what time of the day it was as she kissed Monte for all she was worth. She arched when he ran a hand along her spine . . . reveled in the strength of his chest and arms . . . made a soft noise as he turned her slightly to cup her breast. The crest hardened into a tight little bud. She pushed her breast into his palm and felt his fingers tighten around her tender flesh.

Her excitement grew tenfold when their tongues touched and she felt his arousal pressing against her hip. Iphigenia was certain that Monte Ryerson wanted to make love with her.

And she wanted him . . . in truth, not as a lark, the way it had been with Lamar . . .

Then Monte groaned again, breaking the kiss. She responded by pressing herself more tightly against him.

"This has got to stop." He released her, pulled back. "We're getting carried away."

Iphigenia said nothing as he scooped her out of his lap, then rose to his feet. Finally, deep embarrassment set in, followed by anger.

"I suppose you think I am a loose woman now."

"Not unless having some experience means loose."

That didn't help. "You think I foisted myself on you?"

"Not at all. I started things."

The rain had stopped and she could hear the snorting and stamping of their horses nearby. Frustrated that Monte had brought her back to the real world so quickly and thoroughly, she had a notion to take off.

"Don't get yourself in a tizzy," he told her, perhaps sensing her distress. "I haven't lost any respect for you. My view of women seems to be a whole lot more open-minded than the society you came from."

Her turmoil became somewhat assuaged. She supposed she could lie and claim innocence but why should she?

"You would marry a woman who was not . . . perfectly pure?" she asked.

"When you marry someone, you have to take that person's whole personality into consideration."

As if marriage were the issue, Iphigenia thought. They made their way out from the overhang and down a slope toward their mounts. Embarrassed over her show of passion, she was equally chagrined that she'd brought up matrimony on top of it. She shouldn't care about Monte's opinions. She shouldn't be so much as considering a possible alliance with the man.

Monte's liberal attitude toward women's behavior didn't mean he could accept an illegitimate child. She had to keep things in perspective, had to remember she'd come to West Texas for a serious reason—her daughter.

The last thing she needed was to get involved with another man who would make her lose her head.

"I need more money," Norbert Tyler told him. "You said it'd be worth my while."

Angry, he kept his temper as they stood in the deep shadow of one of Ryerson's barns. Though it was after dark, he'd been careful to choose a building that was some distance from the house and the wranglers' quarters.

Most of the R&Y crew had been delayed by the afternoon's rain anyhow. They'd be lucky if they returned by midnight.

"So what about the loot?"

Something the idiot had been whining on for days now, trying for blackmail.

"I have the money. I'll give it to you as soon as you do one more thing—a little job." He pointed to the barn. "Get up on the roof and mark some signs up there."

"Signs?"

"With blood." He handed Norbert a canteen he'd filled after butchering a cow. "Use the same ones you did for the chickens. It'll look like more witchcraft. Scare Ryerson good."

"This is gonna cost you even more."

"Done." He pointed again and watched the cowboy climb.

"Boards are loose," Norbert complained, cursing as he nearly lost a toehold while slapping on some blood.

"Don't fall." *Not yet.* "And be quiet." Now came the most important part. He tensed, smoothing the bull-whip he carried, securing his hold. "Climb over to the edge so's you can throw some blood on the front of the building."

Norbert cursed some more but managed to do as asked.

Those curses were the last words the cowpoke uttered as the man snapped the whip, expertly wrapping it tight around Norbert's throat. Then he jerked, pulled, probably breaking the idiot's neck even before Norbert fell.

The body landed face down in the dirt with a thud. He looked around, though surely no one had heard.

"Want more money, do you?" he growled, kicking the fallen man.

Then he grabbed the cowboy's lolling head and wrenched it around until Norbert's glassy eyes stared upward, his mouth sagging open.

"Looks like devilish witchcraft or spooks to me," he muttered, draining the rest of the canteen over Norbert's corpse.

When he sneaked away, he used a branch to cover what tracks his cloth-covered boots might leave behind.

He hated the savage blood that coursed through Monte Ryerson's veins . . . but he'd lived long enough in West Texas to learn some Indian tricks himself.

10

Darkness had long fallen by the time the last of the weary cowboys returned to the ranch. Iphigenia had thought her bottom would be relieved when she traveled in the chuckwagon rather than riding astride all the way in. She'd been wrong. The wagon's jolts sometimes made her teeth clench. The moon had slithered behind some clouds and she could hardly see where they were going. But Reuben guided the chuckwagon by instinct, stopping the team when he neared the bunkhouse.

He helped Iphigenia to the ground and asked, "You sure you're gonna make it back to the house, Miss Wentworth?"

"A leg stretch will do me just fine. Thanks for all your tips on branding."

That had been Iphigenia's earlier excuse for choosing the chuckwagon over her own horse . . . not that she figured she was really fooling anyone.

"Don't be steppin' into no snakeholes," Reuben called after her as she limped toward the back of the wagon.

She waved and, releasing her mount's reins, hobbled off, horse in tow. Those who'd preceded them—which included everyone on horseback, to her accounting—had left a few kerosene lanterns burning. A couple of tired-looking cowboys were moping toward their quarters.

Iphigenia went straight for the lit corral already filled with horses. She'd never been so sore and wasn't looking forward to the morning. Undoubtedly, she wouldn't be able to move to get herself out of bed. She felt like having vapors for the first time in her life.

Just as she thought it, she saw him. *Monte.* The only man still around. Leaning against a split rail, arms crossed over his broad chest, he seemed to be waiting for something. Her, no doubt, so he could gloat, Iphigenia thought testily. She shoved her embarrassment over the kiss and her idiotic question about marriage to the back of her mind, straightened her posture, and tried to walk naturally.

"I'll take the horse," Monte offered as she drew closer.

Iphigenia was too tired to argue. "Thank you." She chose to stand there for a moment until she regained her equilibrium after handing over the reins.

Monte took charge of the horse and undid the saddle leathers. "Feeling better after the ride home in the chuckwagon?"

"I was feeling fine to begin with," she lied.

"Sure you were," he said, sounding as if he were holding back a laugh. He slipped the saddle off and threw it over a rail. "Just like to walk funny, huh?"

"I have something in my boot," she insisted. "Probably a huge stone."

Monte couldn't hide the grin that softened his rugged features, making her heart thump strangely. More and more he was confusing her. She wanted to whack him on the head and kiss him at the same time.

"More'n likely you've gathered a goodly amount of dirt in that boot," he said, "judging by the rest of you."

He lowered his gaze. Slowly. All the way down to the boot in question. Warmth flooded her even as she realized how truly filthy she was.

Iphigenia murmured, "Oh, dear, I do need to bathe." Then remembered the hour. Carmen was long gone and she didn't have the energy to drag the water in from the well, heat it up, and carry it to the pantry herself. "I guess a quick splash with a little cold water will have to do until tomorrow."

"Not necessarily," Monte said. "The rainbarrels are full."

"The what?"

"The open barrels outside the kitchen. We've had so much rain, they're full. Water in 'em isn't nearly as cold as that from the well. It's been heated by the sun . . . at least enough to pour it over you if not sit in it. You can stand in the tub and use a pitcher to douse yourself."

The bathing technique sounded quick and very, very inviting. She felt as if dirt were choking every pore of her body. "What do I use to carry the water in?" She supposed she could manage a trip or two since it was so close.

"I'll do it," he told her. "Soon as I'm finished here. You set up the pantry and fetch your nightclothes, and I'll get the water."

Tired as she was, Iphigenia protested, "I can do it—"

"I'm sure you can. But I'm offering."

And she really didn't want to turn him down. "Thank you again," she said, backing away.

Standing there, horse reins in hand, Monte watched her, his expression strange. Iphigenia quickly grew uncomfortable. She turned her back on him and was relieved to hear the *clop-clop* of horse hooves, meaning he was tending to business instead of to her.

Once inside the house, she went straight to the kitchen where another lamp glowed softly. She laid the oilcloth over the pantry floor, pulled the tub in place, and set an empty pitcher for the water close by. She tiptoed to her bedroom so as not to wake Cassie or Stephen, who'd returned with the first group of men.

Her boots were the first to come off, then the hat and the bandanna Monte had forced on her. When she realized she was fondling the square of cloth—as if she could feel the man himself through it—she dropped the bandanna on the dresser as if it had burned her. Swallowing hard, she unpinned her hair, brushed and braided it over one shoulder.

Then she fetched a bar of scented soap, a towel, and a lace-trimmed cotton nightdress and wrapper, before limping back to the kitchen. She arrived as Monte wrestled a small rain barrel through the door, his shoulder and arm muscles tautly defined through the cloth of his shirt. Covered with as much dust as she, he was still something to look at. Enough to make a woman lose her good sense if she weren't careful, Iphigenia reminded herself. She was determined to be very careful, indeed.

Monte looked up from his maneuverings. "I figured I might as well bring a whole barrel in. No sense in doing things halfway. I'd appreciate your leaving me enough water to wash up, too. I'll take care of emptying the tub afterward."

There was something so personal about the thought of Monte's using the tub directly after she did, with water that had rolled off her naked body swirling around his feet . . .

Iphigenia avoided his gaze and nodded. "I'll only be a few minutes."

"Take your time. I'll wait on the porch until you're done."

"I'll let you know," she promised as he exited, closing the back door behind him.

Once inside the pantry, Iphigenia realized she couldn't close this door fully—the rain barrel stood in the way. She did her best, then checked to make certain Monte couldn't see her from his vantage on the porch. The windows weren't in her line of sight, so Iphigenia figured she was safe as long as Monte stayed put. Besides, the only lit lantern was in the kitchen itself, so she would bathe in shadow.

She removed her shirt and pants thick with dust and hung them on a peg, all the while aware of the man's disturbingly close proximity.

Naked, she stepped into the tub, filled the pitcher, and slowly poured some of the sun-warmed water over her. She'd never known such joy from such a small pleasure. Lathering herself with her bar of soap, she added water and spread the flower-scented bubbles all over her flesh. More water. More soap. More spreading.

A contented sigh passed through her lips and she indulged herself . . . until she remembered Monte was waiting for his turn.

She hurried, washing her face, then pouring another full pitcher of water over her flesh to clear away the soap. One last dousing of water, and she was refreshed and free of trail dust.

Iphigenia stepped out of the tub, toweled herself dry, and slipped into the nightdress. Pulling her wrapper around her, she left the pantry and paused at the back door where she tapped on the glass to signal Monte that she was done. The moment he rose from the stoop, she made for the dining room, leaving the kitchen as he entered it.

She was in the corridor and halfway to her own room before realizing she'd forgotten to take her clothes, towel, and soap with her. Hesitating only a moment, she turned around and hurried back for them before Monte started his own ablutions.

But upon reaching the kitchen, Iphigenia stopped short. Framed by the doorway of the pantry, his broad muscular back to her, Monte had already removed his boots and shirt. She rethought her mission. Perhaps it would be better to leave her riding clothes in the pantry until morning so as not to spread the range dust all over her bedroom.

She backed away from the kitchen . . . and yet could not make herself leave.

Monte was now stepping out of his lower apparel— chaps and pants and undergarments all together. She stood frozen, unable to move, fascinated by the way the golden light bronzed his strong male body. Muscular shoulders. Narrow waist. Tight buttocks.

While Lamar, the only other man she had seen totally naked, had been more conventionally handsome, he had been soft by comparison.

Monte was stepping into the tub now, and Iphigenia moved fast to swing the door between kitchen and dining room closed so he wouldn't see her when he turned to scoop a pitcherful of water from the rain barrel. She could still see him, though, through a wide crack.

As water rolled over his chest and stomach, followed by the bar of soap—*her* scented soap—Iphigenia's imagination began wandering, embellishing, then finally went totally out of control. She envisioned herself exploring Monte equally thoroughly, her hands smoothing his flesh . . . especially certain parts of his flesh.

Her stomach tightened, and her breasts yearned for the touch of his strong, callused hands. Breathing hard, mouth dry, Iphigenia licked her lips and backed off to run to her bedroom, unable to take another moment of the torture.

But once in bed, she couldn't sleep. She tossed,

turned, and when she heard him in the hall heading for his room, thought about Monte. About how she had come to Texas to marry a stranger, and had decided she could put up with his advances for the sake of her child until she could pay him off.

But Monte was no longer a stranger. And she longed for his advances. Burned for them.

So why shouldn't she have them?

Iphigenia tried to take hold of herself. The situation was so complicated. Monte had three nearly grown children, one of whom hated her, and she had a baby he didn't know about. Then again, all three of his children needed a mother . . . and she sorely suspected she needed them, too.

She needed love in her life, something she had never known.

Her thoughts drifted again to Hope, remembered the baby at her breast, remembered the love she'd felt, remembered feeling loved in return. Adding an infant to the household wouldn't put a burden on anyone. She suspected Cassie would take to Hope immediately, like a little mother hen with the baby. And that Stephen would be instantly protective. Maybe a baby would soften Ginnie, as well.

Perhaps things could be worked out so that everyone was happy.

Iphigenia knew she could be happy with Monte. He was a good man, and loving to his children. She wondered what it would take for him to be loving to her in the full sense of the word . . .

His kisses had inflamed her. She could only imagine what his caresses would be like. Then, again, she didn't have to imagine. She could find out once and for all. She'd never done anything so bold, of course, not even with Lamar. He'd been the one to seduce her.

But Monte was worth ten Lamars. Twenty. A hundred.

That settled it.

Before she lost her nerve, Iphigenia climbed out of bed. Blood rushing, breast heaving, she tiptoed to the door and opened it. Then, taking a deep breath, she took a dauntless step into the corridor . . .

And stopped, transfixed.

For there, just outside of Monte's bedroom, an apparition wavered. The form of an exotic beauty wearing a *camisa* and a peasant skirt, with long burnished hair spilling down her back to her waist. A form that was shimmering strangely, seemingly there . . . and yet not.

The ghost!

The phantom woman looked her way, and Iphigenia swore she heard laughter. The sound was hollow, like a wind whistling down the hall. Iphigenia shuddered at the unexpected chill that nipped at her bare toes.

Then she imagined hearing a woman's voice saying, *Monte belongs to me and always will*, before the wraith disappeared straight into his bedroom.

Heart pounding, Iphigenia backed into her own room, closed the door and leaned against the wooden panel. What did this mean? Who was the woman haunting this house?

She certainly didn't fit the description Carmen had once given of Amanda Ryerson—blue-eyed, fresh-faced pretty, curly brown hair—but the ghost simply *had to be* Monte's late wife. Something he obviously couldn't accept. Filled with grief and guilt, he wouldn't want to think he'd somehow kept the woman he'd loved for so many years from passing completely into the next world. He would want to think her safely ensconced in heaven . . . or wherever the Comanche side of him believed in.

At the same time, a part of himself that Monte had buried deep inside must want Amanda Ryerson to live for him.

And so she did.

Iphigenia refused to fight Monte's late wife for him—what an exercise in futility trying to compete with a ghost would prove. More bitterly disappointed than afraid, she slipped back into her lonely bed, tormented by thoughts of what might be going on in the bedroom at the other end of the corridor.

Tortured by nightmares, Monte tried to escape them in his sleep. He tossed, turned, fought his covers, but Xosi wouldn't go away.

Why do you turn from me, my beautiful man?

He felt cold fingers creep up his spine. He turned once more, flattening his back against the bed.

"Go away," he mumbled, refusing to open his eyes. "Back to whatever hell you came from."

The fingers were on his stomach now, smoothing, seducing, making him grow taut and hard even while part of him recoiled in distaste.

You see . . . you cannot resist me, came the voice in his head.

He sensed Xosi settling down along his side. His skin rippled with the cold.

Stop fighting what is between us. I can give you much pleasure. You remember this, do you not?

He remembered, all right. Their making love that last night. Xosi had been wild and abandoned and he'd taken everything she had to give. He remembered other things . . . his suggesting that she seduce Montgomery into letting the prisoners go . . . his inability to save her when Montgomery plunged his knife into her heaving breast.

His disgust and sickness at the human sacrifice.

Despite the chill of Xosi's palm, he throbbed. Ached. She manipulated him until his back arched. Sensation filled him as, seemingly without will, he imitated the thrusts of lovemaking. He wanted to stop . . . he couldn't. He'd gone so long without a woman that he was near to bursting. He was filled with the need for release.

And as he quickly drew closer to the edge, thoughts of a woman with long blond hair filled him, as well. "Iphigenia," he murmured.

The sensations stopped at once, leaving him suspended in frustration.

How dare you utter the name of that bitch when you are with me!

He couldn't help himself. "Iphigenia," he murmured again, suddenly devastated that he couldn't touch her, couldn't make love to her.

You will regret your decision to put this pale shadow of a woman above me, Xosi predicted. *For if I cannot have you . . .*

Hollow laughter filled him with a panicky sensation that drove him awake. Monte sat up in bed, shuddering, his skin pebbled. He swore he saw Xosi for a second before her shimmering silhouette disappeared like a candle extinguished.

His erection dissipated as quickly, leaving him frustrated, empty . . . and, yes, afraid.

Xosi was indeed haunting him. He had no illusions about her. She had been a beautiful and seductive woman, who'd chosen to believe she had true feelings for him. She had also been greedy and not above pettiness. And if he got too close to Iphigenia, who knew what wrath Xosi would wreak against the flesh-and-blood woman.

It was his fault. All his fault. Xosi would be alive if not for him. Cursing, Monte pressed a hand to his forehead. This was his punishment. To be haunted, possibly for the rest of his days.

And to have the one thing he was just now realizing he wanted more than anything—Iphigenia—threatened.

As much as he desired the beautiful woman, he wouldn't touch her, Monte vowed, not while Xosi walked the halls of his home. He'd been responsible for her death and that of his wife before her.

If anything happened to Iphigenia because of him, he would never forgive himself . . . and his soul would surely be damned for eternity.

The following morning, feeling damned on general principles—undoubtedly from not having enough sleep after a hard day on the range—Monte was downing his second mug of coffee in the kitchen when Iphigenia entered, her posture unnaturally stiff. Seeming startled by his presence, she straightened her back further and avoided his gaze.

"I'm here to get my things from the pantry," she told the housekeeper.

"I have already washed the clothing and hung it out to dry, Señorita Wentworth," Carmen said.

"Then you'll need help with the tub—"

"Taken care of," Monte growled at her, noticing the way her cheeks flushed at his attention.

"I see," she said, still refusing to look his way. "So then I'm not needed here, either."

Either?

Figuring he was missing something, Monte frowned into his coffee but kept his mouth shut. He didn't need an argument with her to start his day.

"Shall I bring you tea in the parlor?" Carmen asked Iphigenia.

"I can help myself."

Monte watched Iphigenia busy herself and wondered

if she'd even known what the kitchen in her fancy New York house looked like. No matter what challenge she was faced with, Iphigenia Wentworth was resourceful, he'd say that for her. She was also lovely, her beauty stirring him anew and reminding him of the nightmare.

Not that he'd exactly been asleep. As sure as the day was long, Xosi had been in his bed last night.

He shifted uncomfortably and wondered whether there could ever be anything more intimate between him and Iphigenia. Sure as hell not as long as Xosi's spirit stuck around. Something told him Iphigenia wouldn't be safe. But how could he get rid of the woman who haunted him?

Maybe if he found that damned mirror he'd have some control over what was what . . .

"Boss!" Shorty yelled, sticking his head through the doorway. "You gotta come quick. Trouble!"

"What sort of trouble?" Iphigenia demanded, even as Shorty took off and Monte set his mug down.

They headed for the door as one, brushing shoulders when they arrived at the opening. Leftover desire from the night before shot through Monte, and considering her flushed visage, he figured Iphigenia was feeling the attraction, too.

"Stay here," he ordered her, dashing out the door with little hope of her listening to him.

Shorty was running toward the barn farthest from the house. Monte caught up with him quickly, yelling, "What's going on?"

"Man's dead," the small man said, puffing. "Norbert Tyler."

Monte's gut clenched. "Dead how?"

"Dunno. Head's twisted around all funny like, and his body's covered with blood."

The word *curse* sang through Monte's mind. A curse

that Xosi had put on him in return for her death? He ran the rest of the way to the barn in tight-lipped silence.

Wranglers were gathered around the body, their low tones ominous. Monte pushed through the crowd, felt fear and hostility rumbling through his men. He took in the corpse . . . and the signs painted in blood on the barn. He knelt next to Norbert and turned the body over, his stomach clenching when the head lolled weirdly. Using his bandanna, Monte wiped away some of the blood from the throat and noticed an even bruising, as if something had tightened around the man's neck.

One of the men muttered, "Jake's right. This place is cursed for sure."

Monte whipped around to face him. "Yeah, by someone who doesn't like me."

"Look at the hex signs, Mr. Ryerson," the cowboy insisted, pointing at the upside down crosses and stars on the barn.

"You think some ghost painted those?" Monte demanded. "Or made this bruise on Norbert's neck?" He shook his head. "Another human being is responsible for this death."

"Weren't no footprints," Bill said. "I found Norbert first. I looked."

"No footprints at all?"

"No, sir. None."

"Then how did Norbert get here? Fly?"

A murmur went up through the growing crowd which now included a wide-eyed, pale-faced Iphigenia.

"I don't care what anyone says, this place is cursed, and I ain't staying no longer," one of the cowboys said.

"Me neither," another agreed. "First the horses, then the cattle, now a man. Ain't waitin' to be next in line to shake hands with the devil."

The two men stormed off. Monte rose and faced the

ones who remained. He looked closely at their expressions. He read fear in them, but how deep did it go?

"I tell you Norbert Tyler was killed by a man, not by a ghost, and not by some damned curse," Monte insisted. "Now are you with me?"

"I am," Shorty said without hesitation.

A murmur of reluctant agreement rippled through the rest of the men, easing Monte's mind some.

He didn't need to lose any more hands—too small a work force would put him in danger of not being able to run his spread or to bring his stock into market. One disaster could lead to another, and he was in financial straits as it was. Not that he could count on the rest of his wranglers to stick by him, Monte realized. Once word got out about Norbert Tyler, he expected he might have a few more defections.

"We can't leave Norbert here," he said, pushing the possibility of losing his ranch to the back of his mind and allowing sentiment to take over. "I need a couple of you men to carry him into the barn and cover him for the time being, another to ride into El Paso for an undertaker. We'll have to dig a grave and bury him in that little plot out north of the big pasture." He was referring not to the family graveyard but to the area alloted for the few strays who'd needed a final resting spot through the years. Norbert had no relatives as far as he knew.

He took a deep breath, gazing up at the bloody symbols. "Meantime, I also need someone to get that trash off of my barn."

He waited for volunteers. His men looked away from him. No matter that they were sticking with him, they believed what they wanted to. They feared having anything to do with Norbert's burial. They feared some vague curse that someone had planted in their heads. That someone undoubtedly being Jake O'Brian.

He assigned men to the task and waited for refusals. When none came, he was gladly relieved. Two men picked up the body, another took off to saddle up a horse, and the rest picked up shovels or went to see about getting the bloody symbols off the barn. A man had died, after all, a fact not to be taken lightly.

The rest of the small crowd drifted away, all but Iphigenia. "I'm sorry, Monte," she said, looking stricken. "Such a terrible thing for you . . . "

"Murder's not pleasant for anyone."

"Is there any way you can figure out who was responsible?"

"I can try." He was already inspecting the ground around his boots. "No guarantees. Maybe you oughta go back to the house."

"Yes." Seeming reluctant, she turned away.

Monte had to stop himself from asking her to stay, from comforting himself by taking her in his arms and resting his head on hers and inhaling her sweet scent. He had to remember that until he found a way to rid himself of Xosi's shadow, he couldn't make any advances toward Iphigenia. He couldn't possibly endanger her . . . or she could end up like Norbert Tyler.

The uninvited thought stunned him.

Even though he'd seen bruising indicating the cowboy had been killed by human means, deep inside Monte felt Xosi was ultimately responsible. If she hadn't shown up in the first place, there'd be no talk of curses . . .

The thought drifted off when his boot toe stirred something out of the dust where Norbert Tyler's body had been found. He crouched and picked up a piece of decorative braided leather—the kind that wound around a bullwhip's handle. He imagined a bullwhip would easily break a man's neck if the person who was wielding it knew what to do.

He glanced up at the barn, at the signs of the "curse," written in what probably was the same blood as covered the corpse. He wondered if Norbert had had anything to do with them.

It was too late to ask.

Fingering the soft hide, Monte only wished he knew whose bullwhip the leather had come from. Jake's? Barkley's? Or Luis Padilla's?

One of these men had it in for him, Monte knew, and until he figured out which, he was certain the R&Y would be plagued by more strange occurrences.

He only hoped that didn't include more deaths.

Sickened by the thought of a murderer being on the loose, Iphigenia was eager to take shelter in Carmen's safe kitchen, away from harsh reality. But upon entering, reality of another kind faced her. Ginnie was eating eggs and tortillas at the scarred table the housekeeper used for food preparation. Carmen herself was nowhere to be seen.

Iphigenia retrieved the pot of tea she'd brewed for herself and poured out a cup. The tea was tepid and bitter, but she sipped at it anyway and took a seat across from Ginnie. The girl shoved back her seat as if to break for the back door. Iphigenia darted out an arm to stop her.

"We have to talk."

Ginnie jumped as if burned by her touch. "Got nothing to say to you."

"Sit."

The girl glared at her but threw herself back into the chair. "So talk."

Thinking about the snake incident, added to all the other unpleasant encounters she'd had with Ginnie, Iphigenia calmly sipped at her tea until her equilibrium righted.

"You and I must come to an understanding. I am no threat to you."

Ginnie made a face. "Didn't think you were."

"Yes you do, or you wouldn't be so disagreeable. Your manner is troubling, not only to me, but to your family. Cassie in particular. She doesn't understand what's happened between the two of you. You've hurt her deeply."

A guilty expression flashed across the sullen young face, but only for a moment. "I'm not like Cassie. I don't need a new mother!"

Iphigenia heard the lie in the angry words. "I was very much like you not so long ago. I, too, know what it's like to be without a loving mother."

Ginnie looked at her suspiciously. "Your mother died?"

"When I was five. And I did all kinds of bad things to get attention from my father. But I didn't feel any better for it, not deep down where it counts. I always wanted something I couldn't have."

She thought she'd struck a chord in the girl until Ginnie cried out, "Well, I don't want you, and neither does Pa! You with your fancy ways . . . you're horrible . . . nothing like Ma was . . . and nothing like Xosi! She's perfect for Pa."

"Xosi?" Iphigenia had never heard of a woman by that name.

"Pa met her in Mexico," Ginnie explained, her smile triumphant. "She's beautiful, with long fiery hair. Xosi followed him back to the ranch. She loves Pa and she's not leaving. She would do anything for him."

Iphigenia gaped. Ginnie had just described the apparition she'd seen the night before—a phantom woman with long burnished hair and dressed in the attire of a Mexican peasant. But she'd never heard of ghosts that traveled from place to place.

She asked, "You say that this Xosi followed your father back to the ranch from Mexico?" Was this the "bad medicine" he'd referred to? He'd spoken of ritualistic deaths and a man who thought himself an Aztec god, but he must have left out some other names and details. "Where does Xosi live?"

Ginnie wore a cunning expression. "In a secret place."

"Within this house?"

The girl shrugged. "Maybe."

Iphigenia knew she'd seen a vision the night before, not a living presence. The specter apparently hadn't been Amanda Ryerson. Her skin prickled.

"Did Xosi die here? After following your father from Mexico?" Death on the premises being the only explanation Iphigenia had ever heard of for hauntings. Furthermore, it must have been a recent death, since everyone said the eerie incidents had started not long ago.

"It's none of your business." Ginnie rose, face still sullen, obviously straining at the bit to get away. "Can I go now?"

The girl knew about the ghost, was obviously attached to it. Cassie had said that Ginnie changed several months before. Was the girl's attachment to a spirit the reason for that? Was this Xosi influencing Ginnie to do bad things like placing rattlesnakes where people would encounter them?

And what else might the girl be led to do?

Ginnie had been sneaking around the house the other night. She'd lost interest in working with the men because she had more important things to do. Somehow, this was all tied in with the ghost, Iphigenia was certain of it.

"Be careful, Ginnie." The girl's thinking was clearly not straight. More important at the moment, however, was physical threat. "A man was killed here last night. Don't go off by yourself, all right?"

"That all?"

Iphigenia nodded.

Ginnie flew by her and out the door, muttering to herself, "Not my Ma. Can't tell me what to do."

Iphigenia sighed and only hoped Ginnie wouldn't find more trouble than she could handle.

Alone, she tried to think of ways she could help the girl, her mind wandering back to Xosi. Since Monte told her that, if there was a ghost, it wasn't his wife, he was undoubtedly aware of the wraith's identity. And yet he hadn't spoken of any woman who'd died the past few months. Why? Was he hiding something? Or merely sparing her unpleasant details? The latter seemed more likely, considering the integrity of his character.

Iphigenia should have gone to him the night before. She could have helped him face the bizarre situation. Most of all she shouldn't have let some apparition keep her from the man she loved.

Man she loved?

Shocked, Iphigenia realized she did love Monte. She desired him physically, yes, but her attraction went far deeper. Despite his unusual background and beliefs, despite his dark moods, he was the most decent and straightforward man she'd ever known, a refreshing change from a society where people rarely expressed their true opinions or feelings. And he was a family man who loved his children and let them know it, so unlike her own father. But most important, Monte was the kind of man she needed—strong enough to take her on, strong enough to love her despite the fact that she could be difficult.

But *did* Monte love her?

He desired her, of that she was certain. His embraces had revealed his passion. But he'd also been holding himself back from taking what he wanted . . . what she would have gladly given. Why?

Because he cared?

Because they were not married?

The conclusions she'd drawn in bed the night before about being able to work things out so that everyone was happy came back to her. She was thinking it could work when heavy footsteps on the stoop alerted Iphigenia to Monte's arrival. Knowing she had to talk to him about it, her heart thundered with anticipation. She waited to see what his mood would be. Surprisingly, his expression was not nearly as dour as she had expected.

"Are you all right?" he asked.

Warmed by his concern, when it was he who had been most affected by the death, she said, "A cup of tea helped. Would you like one?"

He shook his head. "Tea won't fix my problems. I need to look for something."

She followed him through the dining room and into the corridor leading to his study. If she put this off, she might not find the courage later. He hardly noticed her presence, so intent was he on searching through shelves and drawers. He even removed the cushion on his chair.

"Monte, may I speak to you a moment?"

"I'm sure I couldn't stop you from speaking your mind," he said, sounding distracted.

"I've been thinking about how I came to be here—"

"You've decided to leave."

"No, not that. This is very difficult." And very unconventional, but then she had never let that stop her before. "I, uh, would like to stay."

He stared at her uncomprehendingly.

She felt her palms sweat as she stated, "I came to marry you and I am willing to go through with my part of the bargain." Troubled daughter and haunted house or not.

His expression relayed shock and something else . . . but still he said nothing.

"Your children do need a mother," she went on, her confidence shaken. "And, uh, we are attracted to one another." She thought about mentioning the difference her trust fund could make for the ranch, but she didn't want him to think she was trying to bribe him. "Other people have gone into marriage with less."

She was trying to think of how to introduce Hope into the conversation when he finally spoke up.

"No."

"No? You don't want to marry me?"

"Marriage shouldn't be some kind of damn bargain." He was glowering at her, making her insides quake. "Marriage is for two people who love each other."

Iphigenia swallowed hard. She loved Monte, so that must mean he didn't love her . . . or didn't think he could. What else had she expected? Her own father hadn't loved her. Aunt Gertrude hadn't loved her. The father of her child hadn't even loved her.

Why should Monte be any different? She wondered if she was such a terrible person that no one but an innocent like Cassie could love her.

"I see," she finally managed to say.

She could also see that Monte was stiff with tension. Something akin to fury distorted his bronzed features. Was he so enraged with her merely for bringing up the subject? Devastated that Monte had dismissed her proposal so very thoroughly, Iphigenia backed toward the door.

Eyelids stinging, she ran to her own room before he could see her cry, knowing that whatever she did, wherever she went, she would always be haunted by his rejection.

11

In a foul mood over Iphigenia's bloodless suggestion that they marry, Monte managed to avoid her for the rest of the day. In addition to overseeing the normal work, he had the arrangements for Norbert Tyler's burial to attend to. Late in the afternoon, an undertaker and a coffin arrived. Norbert was laid out for the proper Christian service to take place the following morning. Some of the wranglers claimed that Norbert had once said he'd been baptized Protestant, so a man had volunteered to escort the minister from the scruffy little church in Pine Bluff for the occasion.

Monte stayed with the cowpokes all day, ate supper with them at the bunkhouse, and waited until late at night after everyone had retired to return to the house.

Once in his lonely bed, Monte's thoughts were filled with Iphigenia. Her beauty, her passion, his need for her. He didn't know why he let her proposal get to him deep in his gut. Any other man would have jumped at the chance to call a woman of beauty and breeding his own. Even a particularly difficult woman like Iphigenia Wentworth. But Monte had known Amanda's love, and he wasn't about to accept less from any woman he would consider marrying.

Besides, even if he were tempted to marry Iphigenia in the hopes that love would come—which he wasn't, Monte assured himself—he couldn't take such a chance with her life.

He hadn't forgotten about Xosi.

More certain than ever that the key to her phantom existence lay in the little mirror Xosi had given him in Mexico, he'd made a renewed effort to find the damned thing, nearly tearing up his office in the effort. No luck. Someone had stolen it from his desk. He'd asked his kids about it. They'd all denied ever seeing it. He'd believed Stephen and Cassie implicitly. He'd hoped Ginnie was telling the truth.

And he wondered about Jake O'Brian.

His foreman had easy access to the house. Less than a year before, Monte wouldn't have thought the man capable of developing thieving ways. But Mexico had changed Jake for the worse, maybe not only in temperament. Had the foreman searched the study and stolen the mirror, thinking it was valuable? Had he somehow released Xosi in doing so?

Xosi.

Not in the mood for another bout with her, and needing a good night's sleep, Monte rose and went to the trunk sitting beneath the window. Lifting the lid, he rummaged blindly, his hands finding that which he sought—a leather thong holding a bear claw decorated with feathers and stones. His Comanche father had the piece made for him, and Monte had faithfully worn the symbol of good medicine for many years.

Until he'd returned from Mexico.

Thinking the bear claw hadn't protected him or those he would have saved, he'd stopped wearing it. His mistake. At least he hoped so.

Monte slipped the thong over his neck, hoping that it would keep Xosi away and allow him a good night's sleep. Hoping that it would somehow reverse the burden of the curse. For Monte was beginning to believe that he was cursed in truth and that it had to do with his being there when Montgomery released the dormant Aztec gods in Mexico.

A doomed feeling haunting him, Monte figured that unless he did some fancy thinking, he was going to pay with the things he held dearest.

A tense Iphigenia watched the next morning unfold through her bedroom window. Some distance from the outbuildings, Monte, Stephen, and the men were gathering to give the dead cowpoke a proper burial.

She let the curtain drop, then went back to her task of packing the smallest of her bags. At last she was going to Fort Davis to rescue Hope. One horse couldn't carry much—and containers of water were most important—so she had to content herself to take only a single change of women's clothing. Her jewels were still secreted in the folds of the petticoat she'd worn the day she arrived. In addition, she packed a few personal items, nearly panicking when she couldn't find her mother's music box.

She searched not only the dresser, but the whole room. No use. The music box was gone.

Ginnie!

Furious with the girl, Iphigenia thought to seek Ginnie out and shake her until she returned the precious item, her only tangible reminder of the mother she lost. But doing so would lose her precious time. And perhaps having the music box would bring Ginnie some kind of comfort that she desperately needed. So Iphigenia decided to let it go, realizing that the music box was merely an object, that she would always hold dear what little memory she had of her mother.

Monte's rejection had pushed her into action. In her heart, she'd known all along she didn't belong on the R&Y. Living there entailed hard work and enough dust to choke a horse, not to mention a mysterious ghost. Monte Ryerson could keep it all for himself.

With that in mind, Iphigenia added to her bag the map she'd copied from the one in Monte's office and went in search of breakfast, knowing she would have to eat enough to keep her going all day. As it was, she would have to spend the night on the trail—Fort Davis was too far for a tenderfoot to reach without stopping to rest. She didn't want to worry about having to spend more than one night in the wild merely because a demanding stomach made her stop for meals, as well.

Her heart lurched when she found Cassie and Carmen in the kitchen together. For some reason, she'd thought she would be alone this morning.

"Morning, Miss Wentworth," Cassie said, her smile only a bit dimmer than usual.

"Cassie." Unnerved, Iphigenia glanced at the food on the stove. "Carmen, I'm ravenous. I would like a big breakfast—several eggs, tortillas, rice, beans."

The housekeeper gave her a surprised look, for Iphigenia usually ate little in the morning, but said, "*Si, Señorita Wentworth.*"

Iphigenia was edgy at the unexpected company. She had planned to find several canteens and fill them with water—remembering Rueben's warning that water was the most important item in the desert. Also, she needed to pack extra food for when she camped out. While Carmen cracked an egg into a frying pan, Iphigenia poured herself coffee. She sat at the kitchen table with Cassie, wondering how she would manage gathering the needed supplies now.

"You're planning on working with the men again?" Cassie asked.

"No," Iphigenia said, then realized the girl was staring at the man's shirt and trousers she was wearing. "I mean, not immediately, of course. Because of Mr. Tyler. But later." She forced a smile and hoped Cassie would buy it.

The girl nodded, her expression sober. "It's terrible someone was killed here. It's terrible to have a curse on you." She sounded as if she were about to cry.

Iphigenia's throat suddenly felt as if she'd swallowed a lump the size of Texas when she said, "This curse business is ridiculous. You have had bad luck, but your father thinks the source is human. Someone who wants to pay him back for some grievance."

"You believe that?" Cassie asked.

"Definitely."

And Iphigenia felt a pang of guilt that she was going off and leaving them all before the situation was settled. Poor Cassie . . .

No, she had to stop thinking like that. There was nothing for her here, she reminded herself, while her own daughter waited for her at Fort Davis. Still, she could hardly look at the girl without longing filling her. She would miss Cassie most of all. Well, maybe not *most*. But most after Monte.

Carmen slid a full plate before Iphigenia. She'd asked for a lot of food and she'd certainly gotten it. She supposed she could roll any leftovers in tortillas to bring along for her journey.

Trying to figure out how she was going to sneak away under Cassie's nose, she asked, "So what are you going to do with your morning?"

"I don't know. Pa said I didn't have to go to the burial, but . . ."

"Do you want to go?"

"I think Pa needs me."

Tears struck the back of Iphigenia's eyelids. "He does need you, Cassie. He loves you so much." *She* loved the girl, as well, though she didn't dare say so. If Cassie broke down, Iphigenia might not be able to leave her. "Though a burial isn't a pleasant event for anyone."

"But maybe I *should* go."

Iphigenia didn't argue, and in the end Cassie did go, and Carmen insisted on accompanying her. The two left the house and set off across the grounds, the housekeeper's arm around the girl's waist.

Watching them, Iphigenia put a last forkful of eggs in her mouth and washed it down with coffee.

Then, refusing to think about the people she was leaving, she made her final preparations.

Even after the first good night's sleep he'd had in weeks, Monte couldn't shake the doomed feeling as he stood before Norbert Tyler's grave. The cowboys gathered round, hats in hand. Nearby, Stephen put a protective arm around Cassie, while Carmen pulled a shawl over her head and crossed herself.

"We are gathered here to pay our last respects to Norbert Tyler," the minister began.

Monte's mind drifted, weaving along the path of troubles that had plagued him for months now . . .

. . . until the sound of hooves flashing against the hard earth jolted him back to the present.

Riding straight for the small group gathered around the grave was Luis Padilla. He was accompanied by several men, one of whom used to work for Monte. The minister's words faltered and everyone looked to the newcomers. Luis stopped his horse mere yards from where Monte stood.

"So there has been yet another death," the Mexican said.

Monte knew he referred to his brother Roberto as being the first. "You know something about the details, Luis?" he asked, staring at the bullwhip strung to the man's saddle.

"Only what I hear." The Mexican glanced back at the barn where tracings of the bloody signs still stained the wood. "You are cursed . . . if not by God, then by someone with a great hatred."

"Like you?" Could the man have done this terrible thing, then come to gloat? Monte wondered.

Not answering directly, Luis once again said, "I am a God-fearing man, a good Catholic." He pointed at the minister. "You have brought a heretic to bury the dead. Find a priest to bless the dead man's immortal soul . . . and to remove the curse from this place before it spreads."

A murmur rumbled through the crowd.

"Afraid for your own skin?" Monte asked, his temper building.

"Roberto should have been so cautious. You handed him over to demons, then did not even return his body so he could be buried properly in consecrated ground. Now Roberto's soul has no rest. Nor do I."

Wanting a closer look at the bullwhip—he still had the piece of leather in his pocket and hoped to see if it was a match—Monte moved in on Luis. "Revenge gives no rest."

He shot a hand out to grab the leather, but Luis's mount shied. The Mexican's eyes burned fire at Monte as he backed his horse away from the gravesite.

"Do not touch me or mine!" Luis warned. "Or there will be another grave for your men to dig!"

Another rumble through the crowd, this time louder.

Cassie screamed, "You leave Pa alone!" while running to her father's defense, and startling the observers.

"Cassie, stop!" Stephen yelled, chasing after her.

Not fast enough. As his daughter whipped by, Monte caught her around the waist and yanked her to him. Cassie squirmed in his arms, as if she wanted to get at Luis Padilla as she had at Ginnie a few days before.

"Calm down, girl," he ordered.

Cassie soon settled down, but she was sobbing quietly. Luis's burning, hate-filled stare settled on her. The hairs on Monte's neck rose at the unspoken threat.

"You get off my land now, Luis Padilla. I've never hurt you or yours intentionally, and I never will. Not unless you give me good reason."

The Mexican remained where he was for a moment, as if he would defy Monte, then, without another word, sharply reined his horse and rode off. Like good little soldiers, his men did the same.

Monte stared after them until the cloud of dust faded in the distance.

Realizing he was still crushing Cassie to him, he eased his hold on the girl and turned to the silent men surrounding the grave. He could feel a wave of unease roll over them. The minister stood at their head, his prayerbook folded closed, his head bowed.

"Reverend," Monte said, "sorry about the interruption . . . and about what was said here. Luis Padilla has the right to his own beliefs but not to insult you. I apologize."

"No need, Mr. Ryerson," the minister said. "I am used to intolerance."

As was Monte, if for a reason of race rather than religion. He nodded. "If you'd go ahead and finish your service, I'd be mighty grateful."

And while the minister prayed over the dead man, Monte thought about Luis Padilla's suggestion that he have the curse removed from his spread. Couldn't hurt. Besides, he was ready to try just about anything to improve his luck—not that he would use a priest to do so. But he might consult a Comanche medicine man who would know how to reverse curses and banish ghosts.

In the meantime, surely his bad luck had been used up for a while. For the life of him, Monte couldn't imagine what else could go wrong.

Iphigenia slashed away her tears as she took one last look back at the Ryerson spread. She'd been riding uphill and had reached the summit. Once over the top, the familiar landscape and buildings would be a thing of her past.

Over by the far pasture, the burial was just ending, the tiny, insect-sized cowboys scattering to do their day's work. How tragic that a murdered man couldn't be mourned properly with even one day off. How lucky that she'd left when she had, giving her time to ride far enough away so that no one would notice her and try to stop her.

Iphigenia noted four figures walking together toward the house. A lump filled her throat. The woman and girl were Cassie and Carmen, and no doubt the men were Stephen and Monte. *Monte.* Her heart surged painfully when she thought of leaving the man just when she'd discovered she loved him. But if he didn't at least care for her enough to consider marrying her, her departure was for the best.

Eyes filling with tears once more, she turned the little dun mare and headed away from the only place that had ever felt like a real home to her.

"You and I are going to do just fine together," she told the mare, patting her neck. "Even if you aren't considered a distance horse." Still getting used to riding astride, she didn't care to travel too fast, anyway.

She'd chosen to take the cutting pony because the dun was spirited and smart, if not particularly impressive. Never before having considered doing anything so daring in her life as setting out alone across the wilds of Texas, Iphigenia figured she could use all the help she could get. Besides, she had a connection to the cutting pony that she wouldn't have with another horse. She was even going to make sure to pay someone to return the mare to Monte, who treated animals decently.

"You'll need a name if we're to be companions," she told the dun. "Something pretty, so you'll feel special." Everyone should feel special sometime, even animals, she thought. After a moment's consideration she said, "Belinda." Beautiful in Spanish. "That's what I shall call you."

She would talk to the mare until the animal was sick of the human voice, Iphigenia decided. Doing so would help her get through two days of scary riding. She didn't want to think about the night ahead. She didn't want to think about Monte, either, but she couldn't shake the memory of his harsh visage.

"I cannot help wondering what Monte's reaction will be when he discovers we have left," she said to the mare. "Relief, most likely. I was an inconvenience, you know, Belinda. I turned his life upside down." She sighed. "I even made his daughter Ginnie turn against him openly." A fact she bitterly regretted. "No doubt he'll be glad to see the last of us," she sadly admitted.

The little mare bobbed her head and snorted, as if in agreement. Tears sprang to Iphigenia's eyes once more.

"None of this," she muttered, blinking the moisture away. "We have to keep our wits about us so that we do not get lost or attacked by wild creatures."

For the land before her was intimidating. Beyond the profusion of grasses and cacti, yucca and mesquite, beyond the dry washes, rose rock walls. Erosion and weathering had produced dazzling formations that were beautiful . . . and could be equally deadly.

"We are going to make it, Belinda," Iphigenia assured the mare, patting her neck. "You and I make a splendid team, as we already showed everyone."

As they'd showed Monte.

Memories of him plaguing her, Iphigenia goosed her mount into an easy lope along the trail and focused all her energies on the journey.

"She left, Pa!" Cassie yelled at Monte the moment he stuck a boot on the back stoop. "Miss Wentworth up and left us!"

Monte's heart plummeted, but he quickly got hold of himself and demanded, "What are you talking about?"

"She's gone."

"Gone where, for a walk? Or a ride?"

He looked around as if he could spot her through the gloom of dusk. He didn't like the idea of her being away from the ranch house alone after sunset, whether on foot or horse.

"No, you don't understand," Cassie said, pulling at his arm. "She took her things."

"Are you sure about that?" he asked, already pushing past his daughter through the kitchen and to the corridor.

He raced down the hall to Iphigenia's bedroom, Cassie directly behind him. He threw the door open. The room seemed neat and tidy as usual, and when Monte crossed to the armoire and opened it, a multitude of her fancy Eastern outfits popped out at him.

That helped him simmer down some. "Cassie, look, her clothes are still here."

"I did look. Miss Wentworth didn't take much, but her traveling suit that she wore on the train is gone. And her mother's music box."

Monte still didn't want to believe this. "Maybe she put them elsewhere."

"I looked. Her hairbrush and mirror are gone, too. And the stuff she uses on her skin to keep it pretty."

Something cold and hard settled in his gut. "When?"

"I haven't seen her all day, not since we left for Mr. Tyler's burial. I thought maybe she was so upset by the murder and maybe so tired from helping you and the men that she was getting extra rest. I didn't start worrying and trying to find her till an hour or so ago."

"She's finally gone?" Ginnie asked from the doorway. Neither of them had even heard her approach.

"And it's all your fault!" Cassie accused her twin.

Monte glanced toward Ginnie. She seemed happier than he'd seen her in weeks. Fearing Cassie was right about Ginnie having something to do with Iphigenia's departure, he asked, "Have you seen her today?"

Monte didn't like Ginnie's sly smile when she said, "I say good riddance."

"You shut up!" Cassie yelled.

"What're you so upset about?" Ginnie wanted to know, her taunting tone getting under Monte's skin. "We don't need her!"

"I do so!" Cassie countered. "I love her!"

Monte stepped between his daughters. "The two of

you don't always have to agree, but it would be nice if you tried getting along better."

"Yes, Pa," Ginnie said, giving him a look of innocence that made him want to take her out to the woodshed and smack her.

Not that he ever had.

But then his emotions were in turmoil. No denying it, Iphigenia was gone. But for how long? And to where?

"She doesn't know this country," he said more to himself than to the girls. "What does she think she's about?"

"She's been using us, Pa," Ginnie told him, voicing a fear he himself had. "Now that she doesn't need us any more, she's taken off. Maybe with another man."

Monte clenched his jaw and gritted out, "Not another word, Ginnie."

"You gotta find her, Pa," Cassie said, clinging to his arm desperately. "Bring her back before something bad happens to her."

Though he'd been out working the herd all day, meaning that Iphigenia probably had an eight or ten hour head start, he didn't hesitate. Already rushing out to tack up a fresh horse, he said, "I'll find her."

But whether he would bring her back was another question. He couldn't force Iphigenia to do anything against her will. He didn't think she'd gone off with another man, but Ginnie had been right about Iphigenia's using them in some way. He'd sensed it all along. Her and her secret . . .

No matter. He had to see that Iphigenia was safe. When she'd asked him to marry her, he'd been defensive because she hadn't said anything about love. But then, neither had he.

Love? Was he really in love with the irritating and stubborn Miss Iphigenia Wentworth?

Monte couldn't find any other explanation for the gut-wrenching feeling he had around her. How else could she have gotten inside his skin when he was least expecting it? He had to be in love with the woman.

Which made everything worse. He hadn't dealt with Xosi yet. What in the blue blazes *was* he going to do about Iphigenia when he found her?

Peering through the dusk, Iphigenia searched for a place to camp before darkness descended like a blanket across the land. She'd passed through craggy canyons, across a shrub-dotted desert trail, and down into a dry arroyo. She'd checked her map and knew she should be finding fresh water somewhere close by.

"Smell any water, Belinda?" she asked, finding comfort in the sound of her own voice.

The dun whickered in response.

"Well, never fear," she said with more assurance than she was feeling. "We shall find it."

They moved up the arroyo into thickening vegetation. She recognized prickly pear cactus, sumac bushes and low-growing oaks. Then Iphigenia picked out the most dulcet sound in the wilderness—the melodious ripple of running water.

Relieved, she squeezed her heels into Belinda's sides and turned the mare toward the sound. Minutes before darkness swallowed them whole, she spotted the thin spray of water trickling down a tiered wall of rock. At the bottom, a small pool drained into a shallow creek that flowed for a dozen or so yards before being guzzled by the thirsty soil.

Belinda must have smelled the water, for the dun's head came up and she increased her pace as she made a direct path for the pool. Arriving at its edge, the mare stopped and snorted, her flesh vibrating with eagerness.

Iphigenia gladly dismounted, groaning when she tried to straighten her legs, which felt as if they might be permanently as bowed as the dun's. While gingerly flexing her limbs, she allowed the mare to drink. She herself finished the water in the last of her three canteens, then refilled them all and looped them back over the saddle horn.

"Better make camp while we can still see what we're doing," she murmured, leading her mount to a flat area about a hundred yards away from the water.

After tying a lead to a bush, Iphigenia removed the horse's bridle. Next she set the canteens, her bedroll, and her bags down, then deftly undid the saddle leathers. But when she removed the saddle itself, the weight made her stagger and nearly fall. She saved herself only by dropping it with a loud *thud*. The dun edged away at the disturbance and eyed her balefully.

"Let's hope I have enough energy in the morning to lift the damned thing," Iphigenia told the horse. "I do not fancy riding bareback."

Belinda snorted, as if agreeing.

Fortunately, the area was luxurious with grass, so Belinda settled right in, munching away. Iphigenia's stomach growled, reminding her she'd only had a bit of left-over breakfast all day. By the light of a half moon and a sky sprinkled with stars, she unpacked her saddle bags, lit a small lantern, then gathered dried grasses and twigs and made a fire, despite Reuben's warning about not drawing attention to one's self. She would smother the flames and douse the lantern as soon as she'd cooked herself a meal.

Into a small pot, she poured water and beans that Carmen had been soaking, enough for tonight and the morning. Then she added a few chunks of salt pork for flavoring. As the water bubbled, the aroma made her mouth water.

This startled Iphigenia.

"Good heavens, Belinda," she said, now automatically sharing her thoughts with the mare, "a short while ago I would have been satisfied with nothing less than a proper meal with the proper number of courses, served in a proper manner. Now here I am looking forward to beans and pork that I shall eat out of a cooking pot."

Had her tastes changed so?

Or was it she herself who had changed?

Iphigenia thought about the possibility as she continued to feed the small fire and stirred the contents of the pot.

She had been very demanding when growing up, she admitted to herself. Though she'd never craved all those expensive gowns and jewels, or fine foods and wines, she'd yearned for what they stood for, the one thing that had been withheld from her: love. Since she couldn't have her own father's love, she'd demanded he spend his precious money on her.

In contrast, she had found few material things, but had seen much love on a West Texas ranch. And she had even felt the warmth of Cassie's and Stephen's love for herself. They had made her feel special. So had Monte, though obviously his attraction had been to her body rather than her heart.

Yet again burying the debacle of her proposal, Iphigenia turned her thoughts to her daughter.

"Hopefully, tomorrow or the next day, we shall reclaim Hope from the Fricketts." Iphigenia couldn't wait. "I intend to lavish every emotion on my daughter that my father withheld from me. No little girl will ever feel so wanted and so loved."

And, unless she were as cursed as Monte, Hope would love her equally in return.

Spirits rising, Iphigenia tested the beans and pronounced them done. She unwrapped a chunk of corn bread that Carmen had meant for that evening's meal. She saved half for the morning, then took a bite, following the corn bread with a big spoonful of beans.

"Mm, delicious," she told Belinda, "though I doubt you would have the proper appreciation for human food." Unless it was an apple or carrot, neither of which Iphigenia had been able to bring.

She continued eating with enthusiasm. When she was satiated, she wrapped the remainder of her food and took it a dozen yards or so from her camp, then placed rocks on top of the small pile.

After a hug for Belinda, who was still grazing, Iphigenia was ready to sleep if she could. She smothered the fire, climbed into her bedroll, and reluctantly doused the lantern's flame. Exhausted, feeling far older than her years, she settled down, hoping for a good night's rest.

Visions of Monte danced through her head, and she drifted . . .

. . . until several jagged howls caused her eyes to pop open and made the blood rush through her veins.

Coyotes or wolves in the distance bayed at the half moon. *In the distance* was what she needed to remember. No reason a wild animal would get anywhere near her.

But as Iphigenia settled once more, the surrounding desert suddenly sounded alive. A faint noise in some bushes. Twigs and leaves being brushed. A snort. A gentle pronghorn or a dangerous bobcat? How could she tell?

Her chest twisted with building anxiety.

Then she realized that Belinda with her honed animal instincts would be the gauge by which she could judge their danger. She listened intently. The little mare whickered softly and the hoot of a nearby owl mocked her.

Iphigenia laughed aloud at herself.

Much more relaxed, she closed her eyes and let the night sounds lull her. Scrabbling. Low chattering. Then a screech that made Belinda snort and dance, and Iphigenia shoot up, the hairs on the back of her neck raised.

"Go away!" she whispered.

More screeching, the angry sounds distinctly familiar.

Now irritated that her rest was disturbed, Iphigenia found a match and lit her lantern. Sure enough, there by her food supply, she caught a glimpse of glowing eyes surrounded by black masks. Two guilty-looking raccoons had dragged out a few morsels of her food and were trying to decide whether or not to continue. Iphigenia picked up some stones and tossed them toward the raccoons—aiming to miss, of course. One striped-tailed animal nearly did a back flip in its haste to flee, while the other snatched a final piece of corn bread and stuffed it in its mouth before scampering away.

Iphigenia didn't know whether to be angry or to laugh at the antics. She glanced over at the dun, who was staring at her. "Can you imagine the nerve, Belinda?"

In answer, the mare blew softly through her nose.

Tension relieved, Iphigenia lay back and snickered, wondering what Monte would have to say if he could see her now.

Monte.

Why did her thoughts always gravitate to the man who'd rejected her?

Iphigenia could see Monte in her mind's eye as clearly as if he stood before her. Her heart pounded as if he were stretched out next to her . . . kissing her . . . touching her. She closed her eyes, willing him away.

But she feared that Monte Ryerson would be a part of her forever.

*   *   *

Xosi sensed Ginnie's triumph the moment the girl called to her. Such strong emotion made it easy for Xosi to escape her prison. She fled gladly.

"Chica, what is it?"

Sitting cross-legged on her bedding, Ginnie grinned at her. "We did it, Xosi, you and me!"

"What exactly did we do?"

"Rid ourselves of Miss Iphigenia Wentworth," the girl said, her voice low as if she feared someone might be listening. "The pouch I made with the hair from her brush and that music box she loved worked exactly as you said it would!"

Xosi experienced a thrill of triumph. "So your father told her to leave?"

"No. She up and went herself." Ginnie's grin died. "I just hope Pa doesn't find her."

A triumph that was short-lived. "Your father went after her?"

"He was afraid she might hurt herself. But she got a good head start, enough to get to a town for sure. Hopefully she'll lose Pa along the way. Or at least refuse to come back with him."

Xosi was worried. "But what if he does find her?"

"Then we'll put another spell on her."

Xosi hoped it wouldn't come to that—she wasn't certain exactly how the first one had worked. But she didn't want Ginnie to doubt her, so she merely said, "Perhaps you are worrying for nothing, chica."

"I hope so. If I never see Iphigenia Wentworth again it'll be too soon."

"Sleep and dream that she stays away."

"I'll try. Xosi . . ."

"Si, chica?"

"Once she's gone for good, does that mean you'll be around all the time?"

"We'll see."

If only she could promise that. Xosi wanted nothing more than to walk the halls of this house as a living, breathing, flesh and blood woman. Having experienced Montgomery summoning up the old Aztec gods, she believed anything was possible. However, she also firmly believed that Monte would have to desire her, to feed life into her cold body to make her transference possible, to make her live again. And so far, even though she'd been able to tempt him, he had resisted the darker side of his nature.

"Remember, dream the blond gringa away," she instructed in the motherly tone that Ginnie so liked. She understood even as she used the girl, having grown up motherless herself. Motherless and fatherless. Her brother Tezco had been her only family. "Think on what you want most, chica, hope and desire with all your being."

Ginnie's emotions would feed her, keep her in this shadow world, possibly until daybreak. If only Monte hadn't gone after the gringa! Monte was clearly weakening to Xosi'a seductive charms.

Seeing that Ginnie's eyes were closed, her breathing deepening, Xosi fled the room, bitter that she would be held captive in the mirror once more by morning.

Would this torture never end?

12

After steadily climbing up into the mountains for better than half of her second day on the road, Iphigenia was exhausted and feeling a bit woozy when she finally got to the top of a rise and spied Fort Davis.

Excited, she patted the little mare's neck.

The sun had set and dusk was gathering. Too late to seek out her mother's people until morning, she realized with mixed feelings. At least she wouldn't have to spend another night in open country. Her cash was limited, but she had enough to stable her horse that night, plus obtain a hot meal and soft bed with a roof over it for herself.

Most important, she would be able to prepare herself for the emotional reunion ahead.

First thing in the morning, she would track down the Fricketts and relieve them of Hope. She only hoped they wouldn't be too sad at losing her baby after having her for three months. She remembered Aunt Gertrude's maid saying they had several children of their own, so surely they would be able to part with one who was not.

"Come, Belinda, only a short while longer until you have oats, a nice change from wild grass," Iphigenia said, urging the mare forward.

In the settlement the buildings were of stone or adobe and had peaked tin or cedar shingle roofs. Davis was an open fort, with no walls surrounding it or separating it from the adjoining town to its south, so she followed the winding road past officers' quarters and soldiers' barracks.

More than one uniformed man spoke to her, undoubtedly because she was alone and dressed so unconventionally. God only knew what they thought of her.

Drawing on her finely honed upper-crust manner, she sat stiffly and stared straight forward until the uniforms became scarce and a few women appeared. She drew close to one who trod the board sidewalk.

"Excuse me, ma'am, but I'm looking for a place to stay the night. Do you know of anyone who might rent a room to me?"

Dressed in a proper—if too hot for the climate— high-necked dress and hat, the woman sniffed and said, "No one who would want your sort under their roof. Try Murphy's Saloon."

The rebuff stung, but Iphigenia swallowed the cutting remark she would have liked to make in return. She would find the stables and ask the owner for assistance.

Halfway through town, she spotted a sign that guided her to McCaffrey's Corral back on a sidestreet. She passed a carriage coming out of the corral. A man with a shock of white hair latched the gate behind them and headed for the barn.

"Excuse me," Iphigenia called. "I need a stall for my mount."

The elderly man slowed and squinted up at her. "No problem long as you got cash up front."

"I have money."

The man took the reins from her and stroked Belinda's nose while Iphigenia dismounted with a groan.

"Been traveling hard?"

"Two days. Added to which, I am still getting used to riding astride."

He merely grunted, giving her clothing a speculative once over. "So how long you plan on being in Fort Davis?"

"Only until tomorrow, I hope," Iphigenia told him, retrieving her bag. "I'm in search of some distant relatives. Do you know of Abner and Naomi Frickett?"

"Nope. Might have better luck at the general store. Mail goes out from there."

"And of course the store is closed."

"Until morning."

Good thing she'd already planned on waiting until morning to find them.

"Belinda isn't the only one who needs to be put up for the night. Can you tell me where I can find a room?"

"We got hotels. Try the Lempert or the Texas Star."

The Texas Star was closer, and Iphigenia was relieved to find that the establishment had a dining room, so she wouldn't have to go in search of food. A quick wash and a brush through her hair and she was ready for the thick steak advertised on the dining room's chalkboard.

After a good meal and a good night's sleep she would be ready to face anything.

*   *   *

Monte didn't want to face the truth that he was in quite a quandary. Staring into his campfire, he knew that when he found Iphigenia—and he would, for she'd left a trail straight to Fort Davis that a greenhorn could follow—he wouldn't be able to let her go.

He needed her. His whole family needed her, even Ginnie, though it would be as hard as pulling teeth to get the girl to admit to such.

An even better reason was that he loved the woman—he was still mourning the fact that she didn't feel likewise.

So what was he going to do once he caught up to her?

All along he'd known Iphigenia was in some kind of desperate situation to have left New York in the first place. Maybe it was something he could fix. Then he could send her back home or to some other city where she would fit in.

And leave him with a broken heart.

But what else could he do? He couldn't force her to love him. He hadn't yet taken care of Xosi, but he'd scare up that medicine man first thing when he returned to the R&Y. He only hoped it wouldn't be too late to protect everything he held dear.

And he only hoped he would be able to find the right words to keep Iphigenia from disappearing from his life forever.

The first thing Iphigenia noted when she drove her rental buggy to the Frickett ranch the next morning were half a dozen thin, barefoot children playing tag in the dirt road leading up to a shabby adobe house. There were six of them, the oldest being nine or ten, the youngest a mere toddler. No sign of a baby, though.

And beyond the children was a pasture where several horses grazed. None of the creatures looked tended to. Coats were dull, manes and tails lumpy as if loaded with burrs.

A sense of unease washed over her. These people looked to be too downtrodden to take on another's child. She prayed Hope had been better cared for than the Frickett's children or livestock.

She stopped the buggy and descended. The noisy children quit their game and gathered round as she slapped the dust from her traveling suit. After her encounter with the woman in Fort Davis, she'd decided she needed to be presentable.

"Who're you?" a small boy, filthy from top to toe, asked.

A girl a mere inch taller and equally dirty, her simple dress tattered, added, "We never get no visitors."

Iphigenia looked to the oldest of the brood. "I'm here to see your parents."

"What for?" he asked, expression surly.

"I am Hope's mother."

"Who?"

Wondering if she'd taken a wrong fork on the way out—indeed, hoping she had—Iphigenia said, "I'm looking for the Frickett place."

"You found it," he assured her.

Giving Iphigenia an unpleasant jolt.

"You do have a baby here, don't you?" she asked, her stomach tightening. "Hope Wentworth?"

When he shook his head in the negative, her heart plummeted, but then he said, "We got a Dinah, though."

"Your little sister?"

"Nah. She don't belong to us. Don't know why Ma took her in."

"Oh, then she is here." Iphigenia took a deep breath. No doubt Aunt Gertrude had given them the baby without bothering to tell them her name . . . if she'd even remembered it. "Can you take care of my horse and buggy for me while I speak with your parents?"

"I guess."

A jittery sensation filling her, Iphigenia approached the house and noticed the adobe walls were crumbling. The door was open. She glanced into the dark, bleak kitchen and saw a thin woman with straggly brown hair at the stove.

"Excuse me. Naomi Frickett?"

"The same." The woman turned, eyeing her clothing speculatively, enviously. She herself was wearing a wash-worn shapeless gingham. "What can I do for you?"

"I am Iphigenia Wentworth." She looked around for signs of a baby, but there was no cradle in the kitchen. "My mother was your mother's second cousin." Surely Hope was here somewhere, she thought frantically, as she informed the woman. "I've come for my child."

Naomi's mouth dropped open, but she quickly covered her surprise. "Abner! Better get in here."

"Where is Hope? I'd like to see her."

Naomi Frickett stared down into her stew. "You'll have to talk to Abner about that."

Which made Iphigenia even more nervous.

"What're you squalling about now, woman?"

The man who came through the doorway nearly filled it. He was wearing a wrinkled suit and a ruffled shirt, the garments totally incongruous with the setting. His heavy-jowled face needed a shave, and his bloodshot eyes were having trouble focusing on the scene in the kitchen.

Naomi wiped her reddened hands on her skirts.

"Abner, this lady is Iphigenia Wentworth from New York City. Dinah's real Mama."

"Actually, her name is Hope," Iphigenia said pleasantly, trying to keep a positive attitude when warning signals were going off inside her. "I assume Aunt Gertrude's solicitor didn't tell you that."

Naomi Frickett didn't blink, and merely said, "Abner, she's come for the baby," in a fear-filled tone.

Her husband turned his sour gaze on Iphigenia. "Oh, you have, have you?"

Iphigenia licked her lips and forced a smile. "Yes. She's mine and I had no say about giving her up. I was in my sickbed when she was taken away without my permission. But I do want her." Heart pounding, she appealed to Naomi. "As a mother, you can understand how I feel. I've been frantic about my baby and determined to get her back. The whole thing was a terrible mistake, one I've come to rectify."

Abner grabbed a bottle from a shelf near the stove. "An' how much do you propose to pay to rectify it?"

"Pardon me?"

"How much are you going to pay us to get the brat back."

Pay?

Brat?

Iphigenia felt sick.

"I am certain Aunt Gertrude compensated you quite well to take care of my child—"

"It's all used up," Abner said, taking a swig straight out of the bottle that no doubt contained tequila or some similar spirits. "I need more."

Used up how? Certainly not on his children or on his wife or on his property. Undoubtedly he was hording the money, other than buying himself fancy clothes and enough liquor to keep him drunk. Though appalled,

Iphigenia knew she needed to be very careful as to how she handled the situation.

"May I see Hope?"

Abner belched. "Name's Dinah."

"May I see Dinah, then?"

"Get the damn brat!"

Naomi scurried to do her husband's bidding. And for the moment that she was in the kitchen alone with Abner Frickett, Iphigenia sweated with fear. She thought the man capable not only of greed but of great cruelty, and prayed that he hadn't turned on her baby.

Dear God, please let Hope be all right . . .

Naomi returned, carrying the little girl, who was naked but for a rag wrapped around her bottom. Though appalled that they hadn't even clothed Hope properly, Iphigenia realized that she would at least be able to see any signs of neglect or cruelty. No bruises. An adequate amount of flesh on her little bones . . . unlike the other children. She was even clean, thank goodness, and therefore hopefully free of disease.

"Here she is," Naomi said, bouncing Hope on her hip, her expression softened.

Iphigenia recognized the woman's fondness for the baby, which assuaged more of her fears. Naomi, at least, thought of Hope as more than a *damn brat*.

Telling herself she must keep her head if she wanted to get out of there with her daughter, Iphigenia held out her arms. "Please."

The woman looked to her husband for permission. He took another swig of drink and grinned, showing her his rotten teeth.

"Let her hold the brat so's she knows what she's missing."

Iphigenia was hard pressed not to cry when Naomi handed over her child. "Hope," she cooed, trying to keep her voice from trembling. The little girl put a hand in her face and smiled. "You're so beautiful."

More beautiful than she had remembered. The red wrinkled skin had smoothed out to creamy firmness. The fine whisps of fair hair had thickened. And her eyes were a brilliant blue that reminded Iphigenia of a clear sky on a fine summer day. Hope blinked at her and let out a squeal of pleasure.

"Oh!" Overwhelmed by the emotions that swept through her, Iphigenia placed her cheek atop Hope's head, inhaled her scent, and held her baby as if she would never let her go again. "I've missed you so."

"That's enough!" Abner barked. "Take her back, woman!"

"No, please, not yet," Iphigenia said, her heart breaking anew even at the thought of having Hope removed from her arms. "I've hardly had time to look at her."

"Time enough."

Naomi's expression looked fearful. Iphigenia expected the woman might bear the brunt of her husband's displeasure if she didn't respond immediately. Worse, Abner might take out his anger on Hope, and he was big, too powerful for Iphigenia to fight. She forced herself to hand the baby over, prepared to negotiate for her release.

"What do you want?" she asked the man.

"Money." He waved the now half-empty bottle at her. "I thought I said money."

Iphigenia refused to flinch. How could anyone place a price on a child? Rage coursed through her but she managed to ask calmly, "How much?"

Abner scrunched up his face. "Now let me see. For all the good care we've taken of the brat . . . uh, the angel that I've grown to love like one of my own . . ."

"How much?" she repeated.

He grinned, took a gulp of liquor, and wiped his mouth with the sleeve of his suit. "I'd say a thousand U.S. will do me right fine."

Iphigenia gaped. "A thousand dollars?"

"I weren't talkin' about no pesos."

"You're out of your mind," she said, her anger surfacing. "She's my child. I'll have the law on you!"

Abner guffawed. "You jest do that, missy. I have a piece of paper drawn up by that solicitor of your aunt's that says the baby's ours. It's all legal like. Some judge friend of hers signed it and everything. So bring on the law if that's what you want, but it won't do you no good."

Seeing the futility of that action, Iphigenia cried, "But I don't have a thousand dollars!" appalled anew at her aunt's heartless actions.

Abner drained the bottle. "Then I guess we'll jest keep this here angel until you figure out where to get it." He turned to Naomi and snapped, "Woman, git the brat outta here."

Without waiting for another word, Naomi scurried out of the room with the baby.

Her breathing nearly stopped. Yet somehow, Iphigenia got hold of herself in the midst of her panic. He wanted money, she knew where she could get it.

The jewelry sewn into the hem of her petticoats.

She'd intended to support herself and Hope on the money from their sale until she could figure out what to do. But there was no question that she would have to sell them immediately merely to regain custody of her child. Then she and Hope would be required to live frugally until she could come up with some plan for their support.

Anything to get her baby away from this monster . . .

She straightened. "I shall see what I can do."

"I bet you *shall*," he said, mimicking her.

Clenching her jaw so that she wouldn't cry, Iphigenia stormed out of the decrepit house. The children were looking over the livery horse.

"He's so much prettier than our horses," the older of the girls said.

Only because her father did nothing to tend to his own, Iphigenia thought, though she didn't say so. "Thank you." She took the reins and stepped up into the buggy. "And thank you all for taking such good care of him."

The children smiled and waved, and Iphigenia felt her heart break anew, this time for them. No one should have to live in such squalor. She pasted on a smile and waved in return, then drove off to a chorus of friendly shouts, knowing that, while she might be able to buy her baby's freedom, these poor children would remain under the thumb of a father more horrible than she could ever have imagined.

By midafternoon, Iphigenia saw the desperation of her situation when, after having every other shopkeeper in town turn her away, her last chance said, "A hundred dollars is the best I kin offer you."

Iphigenia stared at the diamonds, rubies, and emeralds in gold settings that she'd spread out on the counter. "But they're worth thousands."

"Yeah, maybe in some fancy city like New York or San Francisco. But we don't have much call for jewels out here. I'd have to give them to one of the traders who comes through every coupla months. He'd have to bring them elsewhere—maybe San Antonio or El Paso—to even sell them to someone who could turn us a profit. Meanwhile, I'd be waiting until the trader came back this way for a return on my money."

"You do not understand. This is for my daughter. So I can rescue her from a horrible man who demands I pay him one thousand dollars for her safe return."

"Sounds like a matter for the law. Or the army." When she didn't respond, the man's expression turned truly regretful. "A hundred's the best I can do," he repeated.

"Then it is no use."

Too numb to cry, Iphigenia swept the jewelry up and into the velvet pouch she'd brought the pieces in. They had begun as her future with her baby. Then they'd become Hope's salvation. Now it seemed they were worthless, at least here.

What was she to do?

Despondent, Iphigenia realized she would have to go elsewhere, to a city where she could get more for the jewels, at least enough to free Hope.

"Which is closer?" she asked the shopkeeper. "El Paso or San Antonio?"

"El Paso."

It would be a long ride, though, and not one she had any desire to make alone. "I suppose Fort Davis has no train depot."

"No, but Marfa does. That's a good twenty-mile ride south of here. The Southern Pacific'll take you straight to El Paso."

He gave her directions and she thanked him with as much warmth as she could muster. Then she returned to her hotel, changed into her man's clothing once more, checked out, and fetched Belinda.

Iphigenia left Fort Davis the way she'd come, through the military area. Again she ignored the stares and too-friendly calls from some of the uniformed men. She backtracked a bit, so intent on finding the crossroad that would lead her to Marfa, that a rider was practically upon her before she realized she wasn't alone.

"Iphigenia!" came a familiar demanding voice.

"Monte?"

Stunned, Iphigenia whipped around in her saddle and spotted Monte charging for her, hell-bent-for-leather. She brought Belinda to a halt. Dear Lord, what had brought him so far from the ranch? Realizing he must have come after *her*, a rush of emotion filled her and she could no longer hold herself back. Tears trailed down her cheeks and she began to cry even as Monte drew his mount up next to hers.

"What the hell, Iphigenia, are you hurt?"

She shook her head and cried harder, unable to stifle the sobs that shook her.

Monte dismounted in a flash and was by her side, dragging her out of the saddle. She clung to him, too distraught to fight or even to be embarrassed. His warmth was an oasis in the midst of her grief.

"What's wrong?" he asked when the sobs subsided some. She tried to wriggle free, but he held fast. "You're not going anywhere until you tell me what's going on."

She needed to tell someone. She *had* to tell someone. Staring up into the rugged face she knew as well as her own, she began, "I came to West Texas for a very personal reason."

"Really?" he said in a sarcastic tone.

Her cheeks colored. What would he think of her once he knew? It took all her courage to go on.

"A little more than a year ago, I met a charming man. I thought I was in love." She paused and bit her lip. Only now did she have a sense of what love really was like. "One thing led to another . . ." She couldn't look at him. ". . . and I bore his daughter."

Iphigenia felt Monte's arms stiffen around her. A

lump grew in her throat. Now he would condemn her as had everyone else she'd ever cared for.

But all he said was, "You had a child? What happened to her?"

Iphigenia licked her lips, willing her voice not to tremble. "My Aunt Gertrude—not wanting scandal to be connected to the Wentworth name—bribed some distant relatives to take her as far away from New York as was possible."

"Relatives in West Texas," he said with certainty.

She nodded. "On a ranch not too far from here."

For a moment, Monte remained silent, making her continue to fear the worst. Then he said, "Well, why the hell didn't you tell me about this in the first place?" He loosened his hold on her so he could cup her shoulders and push her far enough away that he was looking into her face. "You didn't have to sneak around like some kind of criminal."

Did that mean he accepted the situation? Hope bloomed in Iphigenia's heart.

"I was treated like a criminal in New York. My father banished me to my aunt's cottage in the Adirondacks so that I would not embarrass him before his friends or business aquaintances. He cut off my allowance so I had no funds to do otherwise." Her eyes prickled as she felt more tears start to form. She blinked at them. "My aunt gave my baby away, even knowing the doctor said I would never have another—"

Monte frowned. "This isn't New York, Iphigenia. And folks have done a lot worse than loving someone and bearing him a child."

My God, he *was* accepting the situation. He accepted *her*!

Dazed and touched, she had to request that he repeat himself when she realized he was asking a question.

"Where's the baby's father?"

"I could not tell you. Lamar Blake up and left the moment I told him I was carrying his child."

"Bastard." Monte said even worse under his breath. "So you answered the advertisement for a wife to get you to West Texas, thinking you would have the opportunity to get your daughter back."

She nodded, meeting his dark gaze, again thanking God he wasn't judging her.

"Your people—you didn't find them?"

"Oh, I found them, all right. I thought they would be understanding when I came to claim Hope, though I expected they might be sad at losing her." Her chest tightened. If she didn't watch out, she would be sobbing again. She took a deep breath. "The truth is, the Fricketts didn't want Hope for anything other than the money Aunt Gertrude offered as a bribe." Remembering the fond way Naomi looked at the baby, she amended, "Or at least that's what Abner Frickett was interested in. And now he wants more. If I am to rescue Hope from that dismal existence, I first must find one thousand dollars to line his pockets."

Monte's eyes went wide. "He wants to sell you your own child?"

"Exactly."

"Let me at the bastard—I'll teach him a thing or two about being civilized!" He was already going for his horse. "How far is it? We'll have your baby back in no time."

"No, Monte!" Iphigenia ran to catch his arm and stop him, feeling the warmth of him through his shirt, a warmth she'd despaired of sharing. "Aunt Gertrude had her solicitor prepare a document granting Abner legal guardianship. If you do anything so foolish as to take Hope, he will have you jailed." Something that would break her heart as surely as had the loss of her child. "Then what would happen to your own family and ranch?"

The fight went out of him. "I don't know what would happen to the kids. Jonah Barkley would get his hands on the ranch for certain."

"Your stepfather?"

"He has some legal rights to the place." But Monte dismissed the subject with, "It's a long story." Then he took her in his arms.

She felt her knees grow weak, now that she had the chance to lean against him.

"Listen, I want you to know that if I had the money, I'd give it to you so you could get your daughter back." He stroked her shoulders, gazing down at her. "I may be land and cattle rich, but I'm cash poor. And with this curse business, I could lose everything."

"You would give me the money if you had it?"

"Any decent person would."

If she hadn't already fallen in love with him, she would have offered him her heart and soul now.

If only he would take them.

"You are wrong about anyone being willing to give away money for the retrieval of a bastard child. Only a special person would be so generous—a man of courage and strength and decency."

Seeming embarrassed, he let go of her and turned away. Finally, he took up the reins and mounted his horse. "Guess we'd better get a move on. We got a good hour or two left until dark before we have to stop for the night."

It made Iphigenia realize he thought she'd been returning to the ranch. She didn't know whether to be hopeful about that or not. "I wasn't planning on going back to the R&Y."

"Oh, yeah? Then where do you think you're headed?" His brow furrowed. "New York?"

"I have to catch the train that goes to El Paso. I have some jewelry, which I tried to sell in Fort Davis. My best offer was a hundred dollars. Perhaps in El Paso—"

"You're not going traipsing around the country alone." His tone brooked no argument. "We'll go back to the ranch and figure this thing out. Together."

Together.

The way he said the word stirred Iphigenia, touched her heart. Perhaps Monte did have some feelings for her, after all. And she didn't really want to do this alone. It seemed that even surrounded by people, she'd been alone all her life.

She wanted to touch Monte, to make certain this wonderful man was real, but she merely said, "All right."

Patting Belinda's nose, she mounted the mare. Monte backtracked and she followed. To her embarrassment, she felt tears trying to surge forth again and fought to hold them back. But how could she not feel emotional?

To distract herself as they rode along, she decided to try to forget about her own problems and make conversation. She remembered the reference to Jonah Barkley and how he'd get his hands on the land if something happened to Monte. She wasn't the only one with serious problems.

"So what is behind Barkley's feud with you?"

For a moment, she didn't think Monte would open up to her. Then, with a big sigh, he admitted, "Barkley has some reason to think he deserves the land."

"Tell me about it."

They were riding into the sunset. The rugged vista around them glowed with a harsh beauty that sparked something inside of Iphigenia, drawing her in.

"When she was just sixteen," Monte began, "Ma met this Comanche named Red Knife and fell in love with him. Grandpa Will would never have stood for her taking up with a redskin, so she up and ran away with him. 'Course old Will sent men after her. They dragged her back and he ignored the fact that she'd married Red Knife. Said some Injun ceremony didn't mean nothing in the white world. But he couldn't ignore her belly."

"She was pregnant with you." No wonder he was more open and accepting than most people.

"Grandpa Will didn't want shame brought upon the family, so he bribed his nearest neighbor Jonah Barkley to marry her and be my father."

"Your grandfather paid Barkley?" Just as Aunt Gertrude had paid Abner Frickett.

"Not with cash money, but with promises of more land when he died."

"The R&Y?"

"So Barkley thought, though I don't think the old man ever intended him to get everything. Barkley married Ma, but he treated her rough, me rougher."

"He actually beat you?"

Her own father had put her off with indifference, but Horace Wentworth had never raised a hand to her.

Monte nodded. "Whenever he had a mind to it. When I was ten, I'd had enough. I ran away, found Red Knife's camp. I rode with the Comanche for nearly five years, until Red Knife was killed. Didn't know what else to do so I came back to the R&Y, but Ma was already gone. She'd waited for me to come back . . . then one day, she'd just run off."

"She couldn't take Barkley's cruelty anymore, either."

"Or she went looking for me," Monte said, sounding guilty.

"You can't blame yourself. You were only a child and she loved you."

"Anyhow, there was nothing left for me. Grandpa Will would hardly speak to me. And I knew that if Barkley tried raising a hand to me again, I would split him open and skin his hide. So I left again, joined the Confederate Army. But West Texas and the land were too strong to resist. After the war, I came home to stay and got a big surprise. Grandpa Will said I was brave to serve the Confederacy and actually welcomed me back like some kind of hero. He left me the best part of the ranch when he died. He willed Barkley land, too, as promised, but not the part with the creek that he expected."

Hence Jonah Barkley's hatred of Monte. No matter that he hadn't gotten what he'd wanted, Iphigenia still thought Barkley had gotten more than he deserved. As far as she was concerned, any man who raised a hand to a woman or child should be shot.

"You never found out what happened to your mother?" she asked.

"We got a letter saying she died."

She heard the guilt in his voice again.

And Monte kicked his horse and moved ahead of her, a lonely silhouette against the growing dusk of the desert.

13

Monte ached as he watched Iphigenia set up her bedroll near his as if nothing were wrong. Throughout dinner, she had acted equally stoic, pretending her heart wasn't breaking, even when giving him a full account of her visit with the Fricketts. But he could hear the emotion in her voice, could sense her grief and longing lurking just beneath the surface. Whatever he had to do, he was going to see to it that she would have her baby in her arms, and soon.

"You don't plan on keeping the fire going, do you?" she asked worriedly.

"For a while."

"Reuben told me it could be dangerous."

Monte smiled at her. "*I* can be dangerous. I'd like to see some hombre ride up and try to pick a fight tonight." To try to mess with the woman he loved even more than when he'd set out to bring her back. "Come sit with me."

He was on his own bedroll, his saddle propped behind

him as a backrest. Iphigenia did as he asked but was careful to keep a bit of a distance between them. Monte was tempted to move closer, to put an arm around her and draw her to him, but he chose to bide his time.

"The warmth does feel good and the light is comforting at night," Iphigenia admitted.

"Being able to see is always comforting," Monte said, not meaning the fire. "I'm glad I finally know what's been on your chest."

"Pardon me?"

"What's been troubling you," he explained.

"Oh. And what about you?"

"Me? You mean this curse business?" More and more he was believing in it himself. "Actually, I've been thinking about scaring up a medicine man, though that may take some time, considering the government has moved the Comanche to Oklahoma Territory."

"If you do find one, will he be able to rid you of your ghost, as well?"

He gave her a sharp look. "You make it sound personal."

"Isn't it?"

Monte felt certain she knew more about Xosi than he'd ever told her. "You've seen her."

"The other night," Iphigenia admitted. "She is very beautiful."

"*Was*," he corrected. "She's dead. Xosi's haunting me is part of the curse."

For he was now certain that, even though the terrible things that had been happening had been executed by a human hand, the events were somehow linked with what happened in Mexico. And that meant with Xosi.

"How are the two connected?"

"I told you about going into Mexico to get back our men taken for that madman, Montgomery. Xosi and her brother Tezco were the bandits responsible for the actual abduction. They went along with the madman's schemes for the money. They thought Montgomery would find the lost treasure he told them about, and they would steal it. They didn't realize people would be sacrificed to the Aztec gods along the way."

"You mentioned that before," Iphigenia said. "That Montgomery thought he was the incarnation of Quetzalcoatl. Do *you* believe that?"

Monte didn't have to think about it. "I would swear that ancient death spirits breathed through him and his followers, yes." He could see the doubt written across Iphigenia's beautiful aristocratic face, though. "And in trying to trick Montgomery, Xosi brought his wrath down on her—a wrath that still haunts her in the grave."

She seemed startled at that, and quickly asked, "Then Xosi was not killed here in West Texas?"

"No. Why would you assume that?"

"Ghosts do not usually travel," Iphigenia said, her brow furrowing in thought. "What on earth happened?"

He sensed in her a war between disbelief and acceptance. He didn't blame her. Despite the Comanche mysticism he'd been raised with, he'd felt something of the same himself.

"Xosi and I shared her last living night together."

Monte felt weird telling her, but then she'd admitted to him that she'd had a lover, the father of her child. Both were in their pasts, after all.

"I convinced Xosi that since Montgomery was fascinated by her, she could do something to help us all," he went on. "We were planning an escape the next day. She seduced him, then foolishly decided she could control him. In the morning, Xosi—rather than the man assigned to the task—took the place of the woman to be sacrificed. My half sister, Louisa," he added. "I'm sure Xosi didn't think Montgomery would kill her. She must have had some plan for that damned gold wheel on the altar. An Aztec calendar of sorts, the wheel of time."

"So Montgomery cut out her heart?"

"And placed it in the wheel's center. That's when the rumbles started getting louder. Terrible earthquakes swallowed that damned site whole."

"And you think that the sacrifice and the earthquakes were connected, that there was a connection between the two?"

"Maybe you just had to be there."

He could see her trying to accept the concept as she said, "And you feel guilty over Xosi's death because you suggested she distract Montgomery. But you didn't tell her to put herself in such danger."

"I feel guilty because I had the drop on Montgomery. I could have shot him, stopped him from killing Xosi. Only I didn't." He paused, recalling that awful moment all over again. "I hesitated too long. Montgomery had been an officer in the Confederate Army. He saved my life." And then Monte had watched him go mad, and cut out the Union officer's beating heart. "There's too much unexplained, including the fate that brought me to Montgomery and united me with a half sister I didn't know. You wouldn't believe the way all the details came together. I would have to be plain stupid not to believe higher forces were at work."

Iphigenia looked thoughtful. "I suppose it would be hard to deny," she finally admitted. "Even if it does test one's entire belief system. But what about Xosi? Ghosts usually haunt the place where they died. How did she get here?"

"I suspect she came along with the mirror."

"A mirror?"

"Xosi always wore a mirror pendant. It hung on a silver chain and looked just like a little hand mirror. She gave it to me the night before she died, claimed to see things in it she couldn't explain. She said the mirror was magical, and through it, a part of her would always be with me. I guess she was right. She musta come back with me."

Against his will, Iphigenia figured, and possibly against Xosi's will, as well. The woman had merely been selfish, not evil. She should be resting in peace.

"Now if only I could find the damned thing," he muttered, "Maybe I could figure out how to set her free."

"You lost it?"

"I left the trinket in a drawer of my desk, but it's not there now. Someone stole it."

Iphigenia didn't hesitate. "Ginnie."

Though Monte wasn't exactly surprised, he asked, "You've seen her with it?"

"No, but she's the one who told me about Xosi. And other things have been missing, from Carmen's kitchen knife which was with Ginnie's things, to my mother's music box."

"She stole from you?"

"I caught her in my room a few days ago. She practically ran Cassie down getting out of there. I suspect that's when she took the music box."

Monte swore a blue streak. "When I get home . . . "

Iphigenia moved closer, and put a hand on his arm. "Monte, Ginnie needs your understanding."

"She needs to be pinned up by her ears."

"She misses her mother just as much as Cassie does, only she acts differently."

Acts differently. Monte didn't like the sound of that.

"She'd better not be responsible for what's been going on around the ranch," he muttered.

For if Ginnie had the mirror, she had control over Xosi. Or was it the other way around?

Monte had a cold feeling inside. Either way, his daughter was somehow involved.

Iphigenia thought of herself as a practical woman, one not given to flights of fancy. Her beliefs in the way the universe worked had been instilled in her as a child and she had never doubted them. But listening to Monte, she couldn't deny the power of his story. The possibilities. She'd always believed a person's spirit could be trapped in the perpetual present. But Xosi broke the rules. She hadn't died on the R&Y as Iphigenia had first assumed.

And if one rule were broken . . .

"You don't think Xosi was somehow responsible for Norbert's death, do you?"

Monte shook his head. "A flesh and blood person killed him." He added, "But that person could have been influenced by Xosi."

From his grim expression, she realized who he meant. "Ginnie?" Remembering the snake incident, Iphigenia shuddered. Even so, she didn't think the girl had tried to kill her, merely to scare her. "I don't think Ginnie could go so far as murder."

"I hope you're right. I don't know what to believe."

Iphigenia's heart went out to Monte. He shouldn't have to doubt his own daughter.

She moved closer and settled her back against the saddle as he'd done. Laying her head on his shoulder seemed like the most natural act in the world. And when he wrapped an arm around her, she shuddered with longing. He needed her for the moment, even though he didn't love her. She closed her eyes and dared to allow herself to pretend.

He shifted and she accommodated him, finding her right breast pressed against his chest. Beneath the man's shirt, her woman's flesh responded, the tender nipple tightening and aching for his touch.

"Iphigenia," he murmured, his serious features bronzed by the fire's glow.

"Yes, Monte?" she whispered.

His answer was silent, uttered in a brush of his mouth against hers. Her lips parted and a long sigh escaped them. He surrounded the sigh, surrounded her—his mouth over hers, his limbs wrapping around her body until she no longer knew where she ended and he started. His kisses soon became more demanding. Their tongues danced.

His hand was tangled in her hair, his fingers busy at undoing the knot she'd twisted to keep it up under her hat. Soon he released the strands to let them spill over her neck. He smoothed the hair over her shoulder and down her breast, and she pressed into his hand and moaned into his mouth. The hand traveled to her middle and she felt him unfastening the buttons of her shirt.

Iphigenia did likewise. She wanted to feel his flesh against the pads of her fingers. She wanted to explore him, taste him, make love with him. Her few experiences with Lamar had been pleasant adventures, but had not produced this mind-shattering need that began in her center and filled all of her.

Monte crushed her back against the saddle and lifted himself a moment to open the man's shirt she was wearing. Staring at her breasts that tightened and tingled under the intensity of his gaze, he removed his own shirt and vest in one clean swoop. His beauty took her breath away. The firelight laved his skin with a sensual glow, bringing each muscle into relief against the dark night.

Iphigenia reached up and touched him, for how could she not, the temptation was so great. His flesh quivered under the brush of her fingers. Then, her eagerness driving her, she began using both hands, exploring the very solidity of his taut flesh in the most intimate way she knew how. He was hot to the touch, but no hotter than she.

Monte braced himself over her, as if waiting for her invitation to go further.

Trailing her hands to his waist, Iphigenia gave it to him. She unbuckled his gun belt, for he still wore his weapons. The leather and metal hit the ground with a resounding thud that startled her.

Noises suddenly seemed louder, smells sharper, emotions more intense.

I love you, Monte, she thought, only wishing she could say the words and that he would echo them.

Her fingers shook slightly as they unbuttoned his denims. She'd never removed a man's clothing before, for Lamar had always come to her naked from behind the screen where he'd undressed. Anticipation made her breath come hard. Monte seemed to be breathing harder, especially when she slid a hand beneath the layers of cloth and found him hot and turgid.

He sucked in his breath and pressed his weight against her palm. She moved her hand slightly. He adjusted and pressed again and instinctively, she followed. She thrilled to feel him grow longer and harder as she took up the rhythm, her own hips naturally following the movement of her hand.

He lowered his head, suckled first at one breast, then the other, until her nipples were stiff little points and her back was arched. When he bit the tender tip, then sucked it deep into his mouth, a wanton cry escaped her.

With a growl, Monte worked at the buttons on her

trousers, popping one in the process. It shot away and hit a nearby rock with a ping.

They both laughed, the combined sound husky and breathless.

Then Monte plunged a hand through her trousers' opening and down to the joining of her thighs. Iphigenia sobered. He found her, his work-roughened fingers opening her to his more intimate exploration. Her thighs spread, her bottom tightened and the next thing she knew, Iphigenia was filled.

Then she was moving against him as he was against her, sensation after sensation nearly overwhelming her. She sought something that had heretofore eluded her. A pinnacle of pleasure that she had never before reached with Lamar. Monte's fingers worked magic, spreading, smoothing, seeking. Suddenly the intensity was too much for her. She arched and gasped as her world splintered into bright lights. She clutched at him and heard his groan as if from a distance. He jerked within her hand and a wet warmth told her he had reached ecstacy.

Before she could drift down to earth, Monte settled back and started removing her boots. Her pants came next. Then his. Finally, even as her world righted, he removed her shirt completely and began stroking her, starting at her breasts and trailing his hands back down her belly to her thighs and the center of her desire. She moved restlessly as she felt the anticipation grow in her once more.

"Monte?" she whispered, trying to grab onto his elusive hands.

He sat there for a moment, smiling. "Don't worry, we're not done. I just wanted to take a minute to admire you."

Actually, she *had* thought they were done, for she had never before experienced the fulfillment he'd just given her. That they weren't done, that something else was to come, filled her with heat. She lay before him naked, vulnerable, aroused, her hair spread out about her in gold tangles.

Monte's deep dark eyes narrowed with desire. She'd never felt so beautiful in her life . . . bone-deep beautiful, earthy beautiful, woman beautiful.

She sat up and reached for him. He groaned and moved over her, letting her use her hands and mouth to please him. She explored every inch of his body, and when she reached the flesh between his thighs, she knew she was doing something right, for he was hot and hard. She thrilled to the knowledge.

And to the way he chose to gratify her. Kissing her knees. Nipping the insides of her thighs. Exploring with his tongue what he had previously done with his fingers.

Fisting his long raven black hair in both hands, she arched harder into his mouth, spreading her legs wider, urging him on with little cries. But as she approached the pinnacle for a second time, he suddenly stopped. In one smooth movement, he hooked one of her thighs with his arm, raising her leg so that her knee was bent over his shoulder even as he entered her.

Startled, Iphigenia thought to object, but the protest sounded liked approval, she realized, as, indeed, it was. This felt different from what she'd experienced, but like everything else Monte had done to her . . . wonderful.

She curved her free leg around his back and settled in for the ride. Her gaze touched his face, his chest, the joining between their bodies that she could barely make out by firelight. The sight of him entering her, then pulling out, hard and gleaming of her essence, inflamed her. She reached down to touch him, reveling in the thrusts that began in her fingertips and ended deep inside.

She explored him more fully, her fingers circling, teasing, enticing. In return, she grew more eager for fulfillment. His slow movements quickened along with his breath. She, too, was ready. She strained against him and once more felt the universe expand. He grew rigid for a moment, then cried out, her voice joining his, together shattering the desert quiet.

Monte groaned and, releasing her raised leg, covered her with his damp body. Iphigenia clung to him, wishing she would never have to let him go. Wishing she would never have to return to reality.

Reality.

Thinking about the failed mission he'd distracted her from for a glorious if too short time, she sighed deeply.

Monte shifted to the side so he could see her. "What's wrong?" he asked, stroking the hair from her face. His thigh still wrapped around her hip possessively.

"I feel a little guilty."

"About making love to me?"

"No. I meant . . . forgetting Hope."

"Iphigenia, I swear to you we'll get your baby back, no matter how."

"Not through force," she said anxiously, horrified more than ever at the thought of Monte behind bars.

"Then we'll find some other way. I promise."

She settled her head on his shoulder and wound an arm across his chest, content that he meant what he said. But how? While Monte was the type of man to keep his promises, he didn't have means to the cash Abner demanded.

But she did, Iphigenia realized, wondering how to bring up the subject.

Before she could figure it out, Monte was nuzzling at her neck, and renewed sensations were swamping her.

Feeling very voluptuous and downright carnal, she hung back her head and closed her eyes, for the time being finding solace in Monte's lovemaking.

At daybreak, Iphigenia awoke tangled in a bedroll and around Monte. Blinking, she realized she was staring straight into his beloved face with its sharp nose and sensual mouth. His dark hair swept along his cheek, teasing her fingers to brush it away. As if Monte sensed her watching him, he opened his eyes, allowing her to lose herself in their very blackness.

"Morning," she murmured, reaching out to brush away the hair and to cup his cheek.

He kissed her palm, then nipped at the tender flesh below her thumb. A now familiar sensation zinging through her, Iphigenia wiggled her bottom and realized other flesh was tender, as well. Monte had been truly savage, untamed, keeping her awake with his erotic demands for hours.

She smiled at the sensual memories that even now stirred her. "I was thinking."

"So early?"

"Mm-m."

"Really?" he asked, his tone suggestive.

"No, not that!" She felt heat rise to her cheeks. Though she'd abandoned herself to his lovemaking in the dark, she couldn't quite do the same now. "It's broad daylight, for heaven's sake."

"So I can see you even better."

Iphigenia blushed furiously.

And Monte gave her an expression that undoubtedly was meant to convey his disappointment. Instead, he merely looked comical, making Iphigenia laugh.

"So what were you thinking about?" he asked.

"About that marriage proposal of mine," she blurted without preamble, not quite the way she'd imagined bringing up the subject. "Perhaps you turned me down too quickly."

Anxiously she stared into his face, praying not to see anger. She didn't, though his expression changed to something more cautious. Swallowing hard, she asked, "Did you mean it when you said you would do anything to help me get Hope back?"

"You know I did."

Not certain of how he would react, Iphigenia fussed with the blanket and took a big breath. "My mother left me a trust fund, payable upon the date of my marriage. It's a lot of money, more than I need to pay off Abner Frickett. The rest can be used on the ranch."

Monte's mouth firmed. "No."

"Oh."

His immediate rejection crushed her. She rolled away and sat up, taking the blanket with her. Blankly, she looked for her scattered clothing until she felt Monte's hand on her arm. Swallowing, she faced him.

"I won't take your money," he told her. "But I do want to see Hope in your arms."

Did he mean . . .

"What are you saying?"

"That I'll marry you . . . under one condition."

Stunned, she stared at him until his agreement registered. Monte was willing to marry her, after all. Only— "What condition?"

"That we don't tell anyone at the ranch. We sleep in our own bedrooms."

"But why?"

Had he been disappointed in her as a lover? Or did he think she would not be an adequate mother to his children?

"Xosi never liked competition when she was alive," Monte told her. "I doubt she'll like it any better now."

Though part of her believed Monte's tale, a practical part protested. "But what can a ghost do to us?"

"I don't know," Monte admitted in all seriousness. "And that's what I'm afraid of."

A few hours later, having returned to Fort Davis, Monte had made all the arrangements. The fort's chaplain had agreed to do the deed in the small chapel at the edge of the military base. Iphigenia had insisted on changing back into her more feminine attire, and so he was waiting for her to return from where she'd disappeared into a back room.

A young lieutenant named Hap Morely and his wife Aggie had agreed to witness the marriage. The husband was quietly talking with the chaplain, while the wife was helping Iphigenia.

This gave Monte plenty of time to think about the step he was about to take. He hoped he hadn't made a mistake. A marriage was a lifetime commitment, one difficult enough to keep when two people loved each other. He knew Iphigenia found him desirable, but he had no illusions as to why she was marrying him—only for Hope's sake. She'd already telegraphed her father to transfer her trust fund to the First Bank of Fort Davis.

Maybe his love for her would be enough for the present, Monte thought. He could only pray that the future would hold a return of his affections.

"We're ready," the chaplain announced.

Monte looked to the door where Iphigenia had disappeared. Aggie stood there, waving him to his spot.

Then Aggie joined Hap, and Iphigenia entered the chapel, her eyes locked with Monte's as she slowly made her way toward him. Her traveling outfit was fancied up with some of her jewelry. Around her neck, she wore a single row of diamonds and emeralds. Matching earbobs shone among the silky strands of her blond hair that was pinned up in a soft, flattering style. Her smile was at once tremulous, as if she wasn't certain that she was doing the right thing, and radiant, as if she was.

Iphigenia stopped short before him. Monte couldn't tear his gaze away. To his eyes, she'd never looked so beautiful . . . or so alive. Her ivory skin had been touched with gold from the sun since she'd come to Texas and there was a spark in her green eyes, a vitality to her entire manner. His heart pounded knowing she would soon be his. As the chaplain cleared his throat, Monte wished their union would shove away the dark shadow in his life.

"We are gathered here for a joyous occasion, the union of Monte Ryerson and Iphigenia Wentworth," the man began. "The beginning of a lifelong commitment . . ."

Lifelong.

The shadow stirred, alarming Monte, reminding him that women who got involved with him didn't fare well. His mother. Amanda. Xosi. All women who had loved him . . . all women who had died before their time.

But Iphigenia didn't love him, he reminded himself, oddly comforted by the realization.

And it would be to her advantage and continued good health that she never did.

14

When they arrived back at the R&Y late that night, after a long hard ride direct from Fort Davis, Iphigenia was so exhausted she imagined Monte might have to pick her up and carry her into the house. She decided the idea was only fitting since they were newly-weds.

Then she remembered the threat of Xosi and the fact that no one could know about their marriage.

Sobered, she dismounted, groaning when the lack of control over her legs nearly landed her in a heap on the ground. She caught herself on the saddlehorn and fell against the mare. Belinda snorted but didn't dance away. The cutting pony was probably too tired, not being used to traveling long distances any more than Iphigenia was.

"I can take care of the horse," Monte told her, trying to remove the reins from her hand.

Hanging onto the leather, she straightened. "As can I."

"You're in no shape—"

"I shall do it anyway!"

Her snapping at him was stupid, she knew, for he was merely being considerate. But ever since they had left the chapel as man and wife, a silence had come between them.

"Suit yourself."

He turned his back on her and tears stung Iphigenia's eyelids. She could hardly believe they'd been so close only the night before. On the journey back today, he'd kept them riding hard and fast, had rarely spoken, and had acted like she was a stranger.

Steeling herself, she set about relieving Belinda of her burden, and feeding her. Though Iphigenia was hungry herself—they'd stopped twice only long enough to ingest some wretched thing called jerky—she decided she'd settle for her nice, soft bed and worry about food in the morning.

But when she and Monte walked back to the house side by side a bit later, she felt the tension between them mount. Was he thinking about bed, as well, one they wouldn't be sharing?

"You got our story straight?" Monte asked, his expression unreadable.

This irritated her anew. "I left the ranch in a pique because of a disagreement and you brought me back. A difficult concept to remember."

Iphigenia swore she heard Monte gritting his teeth. She marched ahead of him, pausing only when she saw two horses tied up near the house.

"Company," she said, hoping Jonah Barkley hadn't come calling again.

Monte slid a hand over the horse closest to them. "Still warm. Whoever it is hasn't been here long."

Iphigenia was already racing up the porch steps. She'd barely gotten inside the front door when she froze at the sight before her—Cassie and Stephen entertaining two men who were strangers to this house. A bottle of spirits and two glasses sat on a small stool one of the children had placed directly in front of the sofa.

The one who was not a stranger to Iphigenia looked up. His eyes widened. "Iphigenia? What in heaven's name have you been about?" Horace Wentworth demanded, coming to his feet, his white mustache twitching. "And those clothes!"

Iphigenia heard Monte enter behind her. "Father. How could you have gotten here so soon?"

She glanced at her father's companion, a man who wore a fancy two-gunned holster with his dusty black coat and pants. A hired guard?

"What do you mean so soon?" her father asked.

"I just sent the telegram this morning."

"What telegram? You mean you came to your senses?"

Realizing Horace Wentworth didn't know what she was talking about, she asked, "Uh, why are you here?"

"Maybe you'd better take him into my study to talk things over," Monte suggested, still directly behind her.

"And just who might you be?" Horace asked, bristling. "The man who lured my daughter into the wilderness with false promises of marriage?"

"No, that was me," Cassie said. "I put the notice in the newspaper without Pa knowing."

Iphigenia noted both the girl's and Stephen's interested expressions. "Uh, Father, would you please follow me to some place more private?"

Without waiting, she turned on her heel. Her father followed, saying, "Graves, you wait for me here."

"Yessir."

"Cassie," Iphigenia heard Monte saying. "Where's your sister?"

"Up in the attic. Alone as usual."

"Not for long."

Iphigenia knew he wanted to get down to the mirror business with his daughter. She only wondered what business her own father had with her . . . if it wasn't her trust fund.

Once inside the study, she wasted no time. "How did you find me, Father? And what are you doing here?"

Anger reddened his features. "I had detectives on your trail the day after you disappeared. And I have come to bring you back to New York, of course."

"Why?"

His white eyebrows arched. "You are my daughter."

"An interesting time for you to remember that."

"Do not be insolent with me, or I shall—"

"What? Cut me off? You already did that. Except for my mother's trust fund, of course. And I shall be needing that money as soon as possible."

"That trust fund only comes to you after you marry."

"Yes, it does."

Realization hit him hard. His white hair seemed to bristle. "You wedded that . . . that cowboy."

Iphigenia knew that what really appalled him was that his daughter had taken up with what seemed to be a full-blood Indian. Most conservative Easterners would be prejudiced.

"I would prefer you keep your voice down. The children do not yet know about our marriage, and Monte and I would like to tell them in our own time. Now, about my money—how soon can I have it?"

Her father began pacing. "So Ryerson's a fortune hunter, eh?"

"He doesn't want the money. I do. It is mine."

"Only if I approve of the man you marry," he informed her. "And I certainly do not."

He was doing it again. Controlling her life. "Do you really hate me so?"

He stopped short, appearing surprised. "You're my daughter." He paused. "I love you, of course."

"There's no *of course* about it. You never treated me with love. You even gave my child away."

The accusation made her father squirm, she noted with satisfaction.

"So the child *is* the cause of this foolishness. Sending her here to your mother's relations was your Aunt Gertrude's doing, not mine."

"You didn't stop her."

"I didn't know until the fact was accomplished." He sighed. "But perhaps it was for the best."

"The best?" Iphigenia was more outraged than she'd ever been in her life. Her chest tightened. "You think it's best for Hope—that is your granddaughter's name, by the way—to be living in squalor with a man who neglects his own children? A man whose wife fears rather than respects him?"

"Your Aunt Gertrude provided enough money—"

"To keep Abner Frickett drunk for a good long time. Though perhaps he drinks faster than most men, for he wants more—a thousand dollars that I do not have." Feeling tears well up in her eyes once more, she steeled herself so that she would not cry before this cold, harsh man who had sired her. "You think on that, Father, before you withhold money that is rightfully mine. You think of the life to which you would be condemning your own grandchild!"

With that, she ran out of the study and into her bedroom where she slammed the door and threw herself across the bed for a good cry. Her father's presence brought home how small his regard was for her.

Why should she be surprised that he thought even less of *her* daughter?

But worry that he wouldn't release the trust fund

caused Iphigenia to dry her tears and do some quick thinking. She turned over in her bed, and stared up at the ceiling. She could still try to sell the jewelry elsewhere. But if that plan failed, if she couldn't raise the thousand dollars, what then? She couldn't, absolutely *wouldn't* leave Hope in the hands of Abner Frickett any longer than she had to.

Perhaps she wasn't willing to allow Monte to steal her child for her in fear that he would land in jail and possibly lose his ranch . . . but the only thing *she* had to lose was her freedom. If it came down to it, Iphigenia promised herself, she would risk everything. She would buy a few good distance horses and weapons with whatever money she could get for her jewelry. Then she would return to the Frickett ranch, take her child, and disappear into the wilderness, riding as far away from West Texas as she could get.

For Hope's sake, she couldn't consider the heartache she would suffer if she never again saw the man she loved.

"Mirror?" Ginnie repeated. "What mirror?"

Monte stared into the face of his daughter and wondered how she had drifted so far from him, Cassie, and Stephen. "A pendant in the shape of a hand mirror on a silver chain. It's very important to me, Ginnie. I gotta have it back."

"Pa, I don't know what you're talking about."

"I think you do." He could see it in her eyes. His kids could never lie to him without his knowing. "I think you found it in my desk."

Her expression went from innocence to anger as she hopped out from under her covers fully dressed. "You're calling me a liar and a thief!"

"Are you?" he asked, even more sad than he was angry.

"At least I'm not a damned murderer!" she yelled.

"You watch your mouth!" Monte warned her, his temper flaring at the reminder of Amanda's death.

But before he could stop her, Ginnie raced out of the room. Monte thought to go after his daughter, then realized he had something more important to attend to.

Finding the mirror.

He stripped back the makeshift bed and searched it. Nothing. He continued sorting through the things that Ginnie had brought from her old room and had piled everywhere, but it was no use. Either she'd hidden the mirror outside the house . . . or she was wearing it around her neck as Xosi used to.

Monte cursed himself for not handling the situation better. Until he found the pendant and could do something about Xosi, none of them would be safe, especially not Iphigenia. And until she was, he could never be a real husband to the woman he loved, not in this house where shadows dwelled.

He only hoped no other disaster would occur before he convinced Ginnie to hand over the accursed mirror.

He rode in on the late night wind chasing the clouds across the moon. His horse's hooves were covered with soft cloth so they would not make noise, so that Ryerson would not be able to examine his tracks and name him.

He checked the house. All dark.

He hated doing his own dirty work, but there was no help for it. Norbert Tyler had been too greedy for his own good. Trusting anyone else would be too dangerous— even the two gunmen he'd brought in to protect him didn't know about this.

A noise alerted him. Already at the corral, he drew up his mount and gazed around. Another odd sound. A skittering, but no movement. Perhaps a small animal scurrying across the grounds in search of food.

After dismounting, he tied his horse to a post, took the sack of grain from his saddlehorn, and slipped through the slats of the fence. Time for the curse to strike again. Horses whickered and huddled away from him. He grinned. They were a greedy bunch. They'd change their minds when he offered the grain. He'd only let a few eat the moldy contents. Then those horses would sicken, maybe die, and the curse would be blamed. And more men would desert Ryerson.

It was only a matter of time before the bastard was ruined for good.

He heard another noise, closer this time. The animals stamped and snorted, a few breaking free of the herd and racing across the corral. The hair on the back of his neck stood straight up. He had the weirdest sensation . . . like the time he'd ransacked Ryerson's desk and found that damn little mirror that had seemed to be alive.

Still, he fought his response—he could see nothing despite the moon now shining once more. He moved toward the animals while opening the grain sack.

"Stop right there!" a voice ordered him.

Easing his arm down, he turned and looked into the muzzle of a rifle trained on him hardly more than a yard away. A cowboy had the drop on him.

"What the hell you think you are doing sneaking around in here in the middle of the night?" Pablo demanded.

A horse neighed, followed by another. The herd was restless, making him doubly nervous.

"Nothing," he said, surreptitiously dropping the bag behind him, hoping the cowboy hadn't seen it. "I'll be going now." Only far enough to get the drop on Pablo, of course.

But the man waved his rifle. "Not until we visit Mr. Ryerson, let him figure out what you were up to."

"Look, I'll leave this minute. No harm done."

"I don't think so."

Another tactic might work better. "How much do you want to keep your mouth shut?"

"I don't . . . "

Pablo's words trailed off as a greenish glow some way outside the corral caught their attention. An irregular orb, it pulsed, floating some feet from the ground.

"*Dios*!" breathed Pablo.

It was just like that night on the range when rumors of the curse had begun to spread. His flesh crawled. But he couldn't let the bizarre situation stop him from lunging at the cowboy and grabbing the barrel of his rifle. Remembering himself too late, Pablo fought back. But the other man was considerably smaller and no match for him.

He struck the cowboy in the neck with his elbow and tore the rifle free, then without hesitating, whacked him in the head with the metal barrel. Pablo went down, just like the sack of grain. And he knew that he couldn't let the little bastard live to talk. But how to kill the man? He had to make it seem like the curse at work.

A curse that seemed too real. The horses circled restlessly, already half spooked. Ready to run. He gazed over his shoulder. The greenish glow wavered in another spot now.

Swallowing hard, cold sweat beading his brow, he climbed the lower rung of the fence and reached through to fetch the bullwhip from his saddle. Then, unwinding it, he lunged at a couple of horses. One neighed and shied, the other raced across the corral. He threatened others with his bullwhip, making certain that he only hit them hard enough to scare them, not scar them. Once they were milling about, he forced them toward the center of the corral, where Pablo lay groaning.

The downed cowboy cursed in Spanish when the first horse clipped him in the back. He tried to protect his head with his arms when another came racing straight at him. But when several of the terrorized animals rushed him at once, Pablo didn't have a chance. Several tons crushed the life out of him.

His death gurgle was almost lost among the pounding of the hooves.

Triumphant, he threw the man's rifle on the ground near his body, then slipped back through the fence where his own mount danced and snorted. As the moon sneaked under cover of the clouds once more, he drew himself up in the saddle, taking one last look for that elusive spook light.

Then he slid away into the night under cover of darkness.

Monte had his hands full trying to keep his men calm the next morning when they found what was left of Pablo.

"It's that damn curse!" one muttered darkly. "The herd up and killed one of us. What's gonna protect the rest of us from another accident?"

"Leaving, that's what," said another.

"Now hold on a dang minute. This accident don't make no sense!" Shorty yelled. "Pablo, he were expert with them cayuses. They'd never get the drop on him."

Monte agreed fully. He was checking out a bloody lash across a horse's flanks.

"*Dios*," a Mexican said, crossing himself. "We should have left long ago."

"I'm telling you, this is the work of a human hand just like Norbert's death," Monte said. "Look here. Someone used a whip on this horse."

A muttering went up among the dozen cowboys gathered round in the corral. Tense, Monte could do nothing more but wait for the outcome.

"Sure looks like some varmint has it in fer you, boss," Shorty said. He gazed around at his fellow wranglers and raised his voice. "Someone who wants us to think the R&Y is cursed so we'll abandon Mr. Ryerson likes rats off'n a sinking ship! Are we gonna let someone mess with us like that?"

"Not me."

"Me neither."

Only the Mexican refused to join in support of Monte. Crossing himself again, he backed out of the corral, then ran as if the devil himself was on his heels.

At the same time, Iphigenia was running across the grounds from the house, the skirts of her rose-colored dress gathered in both hands.

Monte returned his attention to the wranglers who chose to stand by him. He gave a couple of the men instructions to bring the dead man into the barn and lay him out respectfully. He asked another to ride into Pine Bluff where Pablo's family ran the blacksmith shop, for Monte was certain the dead man's relatives would want to see to the burial themselves.

Iphigenia entered the corral as Pablo was being carried out. Eyes wide, expression stricken, she asked, "What happened this time?"

"I'm not certain. Someone spooked the horses last night." Rather than taking her in his arms to comfort them both as he wanted to, Monte kept hold of himself. He began circling the corral, trying to find something that would tell him who was responsible. "Pablo's dead."

"Another death . . ."

A piece of rough cloth practically buried in the earth between two horses caught Monte's eye. He slapped their rumps to get the animals out of his way, then crouched to pick at the material.

"Well, now, what have we here," he murmured, lifting a grain sack that had been pounded into the ground. Some of its moldy contents spilled out.

"What is it?" Iphigenia asked, drawing closer.

He looked up at her, but couldn't avoid admiring the soft curve of the breasts he'd memorized only two nights before. Even in the midst of turmoil, he wanted her. He rose to his full height, and without taking his eyes off her, plunged his hand into the sack and pulled out a bit of the contents.

"Moldy grain." He held it out for her to see. "Someone wanted the horses to sicken mysteriously. Then anyone with a superstitious bone in his body—probably every cowboy in these parts—would put it to the curse."

Iphigenia's expression changed as understanding dawned. "Pablo must have tried stopping the man."

"And died for his effort."

They stared at each other in silence for a moment. Iphigenia went pale and Monte could tell how horrified she was. He, too, was horrified that someone could kill another man simply because he was in the way.

"How are you ever going to figure out who did this?" she asked.

"I don't know, Iphigenia. Without more to go on than I have, I surely don't know." He glanced down at the rough-woven sack in his hands and noticed the markings. "Dreyer Grain," he said. "Half the county buys grain from Matt Dreyer, including me."

One of his own men could have done this, he realized, Jake O'Brian immediately coming to mind. As usual when there was trouble lately, the foreman was nowhere around.

Another name came to him, but he didn't want to think Ginnie might have had anything to do with Pablo's death. Still, he remembered another grain sack, one Cassie had accused Ginnie of using to move that rattler to the rocks near the cottonwood. And he'd had that go-round with her the night before. Surely she hadn't done something so horrible to get even with him.

As the thought of Ginnie being involved brought him to a new low, Monte was glad when Iphigenia changed the subject, saying, "I need to speak to my father again. Where did he sleep last night?"

"On the trail, no doubt."

"You kicked him out?"

He noted her tone wasn't accusing. He shook his head. "By the time I had that talk with Ginnie and searched her things for the mirror, he and that gunman of his were gone. Stephen said they had a private talk and left in a hurry."

All the remaining color left her face. "I should have known. He came to get me, but I was not important enough to fight for. The story of my life," she said. "Father could not even stay long enough to try to convince me to go back to New York with him."

"New York?" Monte didn't know why he should be surprised that she might want to return to her familiar life. Not that he would try to stop her, he thought, even as his gut tightened.

"And he refused to release my trust fund," she said, her forehead wrinkling. "I am so sorry, Monte, and after I promised I could help ease the problems around here."

"Don't be sorry for me," he said stiffly. "I told you I didn't want your money. But it would've been nice if you could've used the money to get Hope back."

"I shall get my daughter from that awful man," Iphigenia vowed. "One way or the other."

Figuring she meant the sale of her jewelry, Monte nodded. They might have to go a piece to get the money she needed, maybe all the way up to Albuquerque or Santa Fe, but the trip would be worth it. If only he could leave the ranch this minute. But Monte knew that was impossible, not until he could finger the person who'd been causing all the trouble.

He didn't want yet another death on his conscience, for though he hadn't killed Norbert or Pablo, he felt responsible.

Especially if his daughter had anything to do with it.

Late that night, Ginnie thrashed in her bed, mumbling, sweating, the little mirror next to her heated skin. Xosi fed on the emotion, knew the girl was having a terrible dream, released herself from her prison.

For a moment, she thought to abandon the girl, wander the halls and try again to seduce her beautiful man. But something made her stop. A feeling she hadn't had since she'd last seen her brother Tezco just before . . .

"Chica," she called, touching the girl's arm. She didn't want to dwell on Mexico. "Awake, little one."

"Aah!" Ginnie sat straight up in bed, eyes opened wide with fright. She was shaking.

Xosi tried to soothe Ginnie's sweaty brow, even knowing her touch was cold. She felt more drawn to the poor little girl than she ever had before. "You were having a terrible dream."

"About the murder."

The murder they had both witnessed the night before.

"It has nothing to do with you. Let us concentrate on something more productive." Though Monte and

the blonde woman were sleeping separately, Xosi had sensed the closeness between them and was certain they had become lovers. "We must find a way to make this Iphigenia Wentworth go back to New York as she should have done with her father."

"No. I'm not doing anything more to her," Ginnie said, hopping out of her bed. "The snake was enough. I could have killed her . . . or Cassie."

Her power growing with the intensity of the girl's agitation, Xosi nevertheless tried coaxing. "I only meant we should scare her—"

"No! We gotta fix the man who's trying to ruin Pa." Hugging herself tightly, Ginnie paced. "He's a damned killer and he's gotta be stopped!"

True. Xosi hadn't minded when Ginnie had claimed someone was spreading rumors of the supposed curse—she didn't mind being responsible for putting a little fear in people's hearts—but murder was a different story. She didn't want to be blamed for the deaths of men who had never done anything to her, men she had not even known. Then Monte would never soften toward her, and she would be trapped in this hell of her own making forever.

"Maybe the bastard needs a taste of his own bad medicine," Xosi finally said.

"But how?"

She wished she knew. As usual, not admitting her limitations to the girl, she asked, "What would most hurt him?"

Ginnie sighed. "It'd be dangerous. I could cut some of his precious barbed wire."

"Wire?" Xosi was unfamiliar with the word.

But Ginnie's dark eyes were alight with purpose. "Fencing. I'll cut his wire so his cattle can wander away, maybe even across the Rio Grande into Mexico!" She grinned. "Xosi, what would I do without you?"

Xosi was more than willing to take responsibility. She was proud of her young protégé. With the proper tutelage, Ginnie was becoming as clever and resourceful as she herself had been forced to be at that age.

It was her only consolation until she found a way to free herself of this prison permanently.

Having found it impossible to sleep, Iphigenia wandered outside. Though she had prayed her father would act like a human being, release her trust fund so that she could rescue Hope—*his own flesh and blood*—he'd deserted them both.

Now she would have to desert Monte Ryerson, she thought, her heart heavy.

As if thinking his name had conjured him, she spotted Monte standing in the moonlight just outside the little graveyard. Knowing she shouldn't—that she should make a clean break as soon as possible for her own sake if not for his—she went to join him, unable to help herself. She would never be able to forget her love for him, or to erase their night of passion. She didn't want to. She feared that she would never find a love so intense again, and that their one night together would have to last her whole life.

Coming closer, she realized he was standing in front of his late wife's grave, his head bowed as if he were praying. About the situation in general, or Ginnie in particular? She hesitated, unwilling to interrupt. A moment later, he lifted his head and stepped back. Then he turned and saw her.

"I could not sleep," she told him.

"Me, neither. Too much on my mind."

She nodded. He had not only his family and ranch to think about, but the people who worked for him.

"I'm gonna have to stop the killer, whoever it is. I only hope to God it's Jake or Padilla or Barkley. That's what I've been figuring."

She knew he was again dreading Ginnie being involved. "How will you ever know?"

"By facing them down. Tomorrow won't be too soon. I won't be able to close my eyes till then."

Sensing his growing tension, she drew closer. "Perhaps a walk would help."

"The way things are going, one of us is bound to step in a snakehole and break a leg."

She reached up and touched his face, wishing she could smooth away the worry, the anguish, the guilt. She knew he blamed himself for the deaths. The wind soughed through the nearby cottonwoods, the sound eerie in the night.

Monte kissed her palm, wrapped his arms around her back, and pulled her close. "I need you, Iphigenia," he whispered into her hair. "You have no idea of how much."

Her heart beat rapidly at the words. And her own guilt was almost unbearable. She would have to leave him in his most desperate hour, perhaps the very next day. She couldn't stand the loss to herself . . . yet she had to for Hope's sake. Tears filled her eyes and she clung to Monte, not knowing how she ever would make the break and keep her heart intact.

"Hold me," she murmured into his shoulder. "Just hold me tight."

Never let me go, she wanted to add.

"Iphigenia."

With one arm he crushed her to him. The other hand he tangled in her loose hair and pulled back her head. The moon was bright and she could see compassion softening his harsh features. He knew what she was feeling if not why. A tear slipped down her cheek. He lowered his head, kissed the tear, licked the trail of salt from her skin. She shuddered.

Inexorably, their mouths drew closer, their lips sought each other, their tongues twined and clung together desperately, as if for the very last time.

Heat spread beneath the thin nightgown and wrapper, and Iphigenia yearned for a more intimate contact. As if Monte sensed her restlessness, he stroked her shoulder and ran his hand over it and between their bodies. He slipped beneath the outer wrapper and found her breast covered only by the thin nightgown.

His kiss deepened, his tongue thrusts imitating the rhythm of two bodies joining. He picked up the same rhythm with his thumb on her breast and with his hips. Fire burning deep inside her, Iphigenia responded in kind even as her knees went weak. Monte held her upright, and continued his exploration through the thin batiste. He smoothed his hand between them, down her belly. Shifting slightly, he invaded her most sensitive flesh, still through the thin material of her nightgown.

Iphigenia yearned for him, making her nearly lose control. Still, she had some presence of mind left and thought to find someplace more private, for they were within sight of several windows.

And they were an even shorter distance from Amanda Ryerson's grave.

Shuddering with the realization as if hit with a good dousing of cold water, Iphigenia pulled her mouth free and pushed at Monte's chest.

"Someone might see us."

"You're right," he said. "Let's find someplace private."

But when he took her wrist and tried to pull her away from the graveyard, she held her ground. "No."

He stopped short, gave her a puzzled look. "Why not? We're man and wife now. And as long as we don't let on—"

"I just . . . wouldn't feel right."

They hadn't yet consummated the marriage—at least she didn't think making love the night before the wedding counted. Perhaps Monte could get an annulment when she disappeared. Then he would be free to marry again.

Crushed by the thought of him with another woman, she turned away and faced the house. What she saw took a moment for her to register. Then her eyes widened.

"Monte, look . . . the attic."

His soft curse told her he saw it, too—a greenish glow moving around the room. "Xosi!" he growled.

Monte was off in a shot, Iphigenia following, checking the attic windows as she ran. The glow suddenly faded into nothing well before Monte reached the house. Wondering if he was aware of that, Iphigenia ran faster, sides heaving, breath coming harsh. Still a distance before her, he threw open the front door and ran into the parlor, pausing only to take a lit kerosene lantern with him. Slowing, she followed, even knowing what they would find upon reaching the attic.

"Nothing!" Monte cried when she came up behind him. He was holding the lantern high. The bed was a tangle of covers. A nightgown lay in a heap on the floor. "Ginnie's gone!"

Iphigenia wondered how much he knew about his daughter's nighttime activities. "She can't have gotten far. She's probably out back."

Even as Monte started down the stairs, the beat of hooves nearby told them they were too late. "Damn!" he cursed, continuing back to the parlor.

By the time they stood staring out the window, the horse and rider were tiny figures in the distance. Iphigenia felt Monte's frustration.

"We could wait up for her," she suggested.

"She could be out all night. I'd go after her now if I thought I had a chance of catching her. She's as slick and fast and clever as a Comanche warrior when she wants to be. If anybody inherited my Pa's blood in this family, it's her."

"Then what are you going to do?"

"Wait till morning, I guess. Then she'll give me the truth and the damned mirror or I'll shake both out of her!"

His intensity was frightening, yet Iphigenia instinctively knew he wouldn't hurt his daughter. She put out a hand to comfort him, but he avoided her touch.

"Go to bed," he told her gruffly. "No use both of us losing sleep over this."

Sensing he wanted to be alone with his thoughts, Iphigenia nodded. "Good night, then."

Monte didn't answer, merely turned his back and stared out the window. With a lump in her throat, Iphigenia returned to her room and went to bed, feeling the weight of the situation on her own shoulders. Monte had sworn he would help her get Hope, but he was in bigger and more immediate trouble.

Could she really live with herself if she left him to deal with this mess alone?

She was still searching for the answer when, as dawn lit the sky, sleep finally claimed her.

15

Ginnie had been cutting fence for hours by the time the sky lightened. Xosi had kept her company for most of that time, but eventually she'd faded—before daybreak, as was her habit. Ginnie had put all her fear and her fury into her work and now she was exhausted.

Stuffing the wire-cutters into a pocket of her denims, she swiped hair from her forehead with a gloved hand. For the moment she was satisfied just watching cattle wander off their own territory now that there was nothing to stop them.

If only she could tell Pa about what she'd done . . . but she couldn't. No doubt he wouldn't like it. To his way of thinking, she hadn't been able to do anything right in a long time. And maybe she hadn't. Something inside her had busted when Ma died, and she'd gone a little crazy. She hadn't even been able to talk to Cassie about it. Her only solace had come along with the mirror she'd found under a chair in Pa's office, the one he'd brought back from Mexico. Xosi understood how bad she felt.

To her shame, Pa already knew she was a liar and a thief. That's why she hadn't been able to tell him about the murder. He wouldn't believe her. But she'd had to do something to make up for keeping quiet.

Hardly able to keep her eyes open, she figured she'd better get back to the R&Y before anyone realized she was missing or Pa said more mean things.

She turned around . . . right into a hard chest.

A grizzled man grabbed her shirt front. "Well, looky what we have here, Dandy," he said to his companion, who still sat his horse. "As I live and breathe, a little Ryerson troublemaker!"

Ginnie struggled to free herself. "Let go of me!"

Her captor grinned, showing off several gold teeth. "I don't think so, darlin'. Not until you explain yourself to the boss."

His boss was a murderer!

Panicked, Ginnie kicked the man's shin. He yelped and let go of her, but when she turned to run, he yanked her by the hair and spun her around. Fingers clawed, she went for his face, but before she could make contact, he did. A clip to her chin stopped her short and left her dazed. Her world spun and the fight went out of her.

"A real little spitfire," the man named Dandy said.

The one with gold teeth ducked and butted his shoulder into her stomach. Ginnie couldn't fight him. The next thing she knew, he'd lifted her and the ground was moving below her. And then she was being handed up to the other man.

"The boss is going to be real happy with us," Dandy said.

"Yeah, we may even get us a nice reward."

Ginnie tried not to panic. She would have to keep her head if she was going to get out of this scrape alive.

*   *   *

"Are you going to leave us again?" Cassie asked.

Ensconced in the rocking chair beneath the cotton-wood, Iphigenia stared out in the direction that Monte and his men had gone earlier that afternoon. Then her gaze dropped to the bluebonnets Stephen had picked for her. They were healthy and blooming, probably because Cassie had made certain they were watered. The girl would do anything for her.

And the least Iphigenia could do was give Cassie an honest answer in return. "I might have to."

"I thought maybe . . . you liked being with us at least a little."

A lump grew in Iphigenia's throat as she caught the girl's distraught expression. "I do, Cassie, honey. More than a little. Sometimes we can't do what's easiest."

"Is it the baby?"

Iphigenia started. "How do you know about Hope?"

"I overheard something your father said to that man Graves before they left—about you wanting him to get your baby back. Why did you let her go in the first place?"

Shoving vile thoughts about her father to the back of her mind, Iphigenia explained. "The choice was taken from me by my aunt. I fell in love with Hope the moment I held her, so I knew I had to get her back."

"That's why you answered my notice for a wife for Pa? Because your baby is in Texas?"

The girl had tears in her eyes and obviously felt betrayed. Iphigenia felt her own lids sting. She rose and brushed an errant strand of hair from Cassie's eyes.

"I'm afraid so. My father had cut off my funds and I was desperate. But once here, I learned to love you all very quickly."

"All of us? Pa and Stephen and Ginnie?"

Iphigenia knew Cassie was really asking if she loved her. She circled the girl with her arms. "I care about your whole family, Cassie. Loving Ginnie isn't as easy as loving you, but that's because she's troubled." Something Iphigenia understood. "But I have feelings even for her."

"Then why would you ever leave us?" Cassie looked stricken. "Go get your baby and bring her back here," she pleaded. "I can help you take care of her . . ."

Cassie's voice faded off under the pounding of hoofbeats. Iphigenia let go of her and stared out toward the oncoming horses. Her instincts warned her trouble was at hand. As far as she knew, the R&Y wranglers had ridden off with Monte.

"Cassie, get in the house."

"I'm not leaving you!"

But Iphigenia determinedly pushed the girl toward the door even as two men rode up and stopped yards from them.

"Where's Ryerson?"

"What's it to you?"

The man revealed gold teeth. "We got his girl."

"Ginnie?" Cassie shrieked, making an about-face. "Where's my sister?"

She lunged toward the mounted man, but Iphigenia grabbed her and held her fast. "How do I know you have Ginnie?"

The man removed something from his pocket and held it out for her to see. It was a silver chain with a small hand mirror attached to it. Iphigenia's heart pounded as she stepped forward just far enough to take it from him. This was the mirror Monte had described. The mirror that held the key to the curse. But Ginnie must had the mirror when she rode off the night before.

Iphigenia felt sick inside. Ginnie was in big trouble.

Heart pounding, she asked, "What is it you want?"

"The boss wants a pow-wow with Ryerson. Tell him to come where the creek runs near Flood Canyon at dusk. And to bring the deed to the R&Y if he wants to get the brat back."

Iphigenia didn't even know what time Monte and his men would return. Likely it would be after dark. "What if he can't make it?"

"Then the girl'll die," said the other man, who until now had been silent.

"You leave my sister alone!" Cassie screamed, darting forward before Iphigenia could stop her.

The gold-toothed man removed his gun from his holster and pointed it at her. Wanting to kill the man, Iphigenia grabbed Cassie and held her protectively.

"My God, Cassie, don't be foolish."

A white-faced Cassie nodded.

Iphigenia gave the bastard her most furious expression. "How dare you threaten a child?" she cried, wishing she had a gun so she could shoot the smirk off his ugly face.

"I dare a lot more, missy."

"Maybe we should show 'em, huh, Murdock? The blonde looks pretty tasty."

Even as Iphigenia's eyes widened in renewed shock, the other man said, "Keep your fly buttoned, Dandy. We're not here for that. Remember, tell Ryerson to bring the deed to Flood Canyon, at dusk, alone." He had the audacity to tip his hat at her as if he'd come for a social call, then turned his horse and rode off.

The man named Dandy gave her a searing look before following.

And Iphigenia realized she was gripping the mirror so tightly that her hand began to hurt. Oddly, the pendant seemed hot as if her anger had transferred to it.

Still in Iphigenia's arms, Cassie began sobbing. "If they hurt Ginnie, it's my fault."

"What?"

"After she let that snake loose, I wanted something bad to happen to her, to punish her, and now it has."

"Cassie, honey, being angry with someone can't make bad things happen to them. Ginnie's being in trouble isn't your fault. It isn't even hers." Though if the girl hadn't ridden out in the middle of the night, she would still be safe. "Blame those men and whoever they work for."

Suddenly a flustered and red-faced Carmen came running outside. "I was upstairs when those men rode up. I saw that one point a gun at my Cassita."

"I'm all right," Cassie said.

"You must come inside and sit. I will get something soothing for you to drink."

Cassie didn't protest being fussed over. Though she was thirteen, in love with pretty dresses and manners, nearly ready to go to social events, she was still a little girl, Iphigenia realized.

As was Ginnie.

Iphigenia spent the next few hours in turmoil, wondering about the girl's fate. Ginnie had been through so much already. Remembering Dandy's leer, Iphigenia prayed the men would do nothing to push Ginnie over the edge. Worrying that they might, she couldn't concentrate on anything but wishing Monte home. If she knew where the men had headed, she would ride out to find them. But the range was a big place, and surely she would miss him.

The later it got, the more agitated she became. She didn't doubt the men's claim that they would kill Ginnie if Monte didn't show up at the appointed spot by dusk.

But what if he wasn't in time?

Someone had to be.

She could be, though she hadn't the faintest idea of where the deed might be.

Knowing what she must do, Iphigenia rushed to her bedroom where she changed into her men's clothes. She braided her hair and stuffed it under her hat. About to leave the room, she noticed the haunted pendant that she'd left on the dresser. On impulse, she picked it up and hung it around her neck, so nothing could happen to it. The mirror felt cold against her breast.

Next, she went in search of weapons. A locked cabinet in Monte's study gave up a knife and revolver, both of which she tucked into her belt. For good measure, she took a rifle and extra ammunition. Then she searched the desk, but found nothing resembling a legal document. She'd have to go without it. Before leaving the study, however, she examined Monte's map of the R&Y, found the spot where the creek swept close by a canyon. Flood Canyon, Murdock had called it. Undoubtedly it filled with water when the creek overflowed. And she knew the rains had continued up north, leaving the creek swollen, its current swift and dangerous.

Finally, she went in search of Cassie, who was sitting in the kitchen vacantly watching Carmen cook dinner. The girl was pale and quiet, and it was obvious that she'd been crying some more.

"I am off to find Ginnie," Iphigenia announced.

"No!" Cassie jumped up and wrapped her arms around Iphigenia's waist as if she could physically stop her. "They'll hurt you, too."

"Someone has to go, and I fear your father will not be back in time. I shall be all right, Cassie. I must be." Or there would be no one to rescue Hope. "Carmen, you will stay with Cassie?"

The housekeeper's expression was grave. "Every moment, Señorita Wentworth. But please, let me get my husband. He will go with you."

"There is no time to waste. Besides, he has a bad limp."

"One woman against men. And such dangerous ones." Carmen's eyes showed her worry.

"I shall prevail." She had to. And before either Cassie or Carmen could stop her, she headed for the door, then turned back to say, "If Monte returns, tell him to bring his men to Flood Canyon as fast as he can."

The girl made a motion to follow, but Carmen enfolded her in a strong no-nonsense embrace.

Even after saddling up Belinda and setting out for the rendezvous, Iphigenia couldn't erase the vision of Cassie in Carmen's arms, watching forlornly as she left the house. Iphigenia only hoped that she could carry through with her promise.

Along the way, she kept an eye out for Monte or any of his men. "Pray that we find them, Belinda. Or that they head home early and find us before we get into trouble."

Soon the sun sank low on the western horizon, but the only life she saw was a lizard slinking under a rock and a bird fluttering onto a branch of a cottonwood.

As she progressed, the pendant around her neck seemed to grow heavier.

But it wasn't until they approached a small wash with a ribbon of water a few feet wide that she imagined the mirror shuddered . . . as if it really were haunted. Iphigenia mused on the tales of ghosts she'd heard and thought she remembered hearing that spirits couldn't cross a body of water on their own. Then crossing water, even carried by a live person, would give a ghost reason to be afraid.

Iphigenia lifted the mirror and stared into it.

A pale and angry face stared back for a moment before fading out slightly as Belinda stepped into the water. Iphigenia's heart pounded and she gave a little cry. But she steeled herself, staring into the mirror even harder, noting the spook seemed to be struggling and frightened. Her image wavered, and only when they had crossed the shallow wash did it become distinct again. The woman was beautiful and obviously Mexican, with long, fiery mahogany hair.

Iphigenia's hand shook. "Xosi? Is that you?"

How is this you know my name?

Iphigenia started at the voice that seemed to come from within her own head. "You are real!"

Who cares what you think? Where is Monte Ryerson? Why is he not going after his daughter himself?

"You sound worried," Iphigenia said, wondering if she should be worried about herself talking to a mirror. In the desperate situation, however, nothing seemed too bizarre.

Of course I am worried. The chica *might be hurt by that murderer!*

"What murderer?" Iphigenia asked, suddenly pulling on Belinda's reins. "What is his name?"

I have no idea. Ginnie did not tell me. Where are you taking me?

"To find Ginnie."

You? Dios, she is doomed.

"And if she is, you wouldn't have access to the outside world, would you?" Iphigenia figured that to be the real reason a ghost would be so upset.

To her surprise, Xosi appeared furious at the accusation. And the mirror grew uncomfortably warm. Iphigenia laid it against her sleeve.

You think I am so heartless? Ginnie and I share

*more than you can imagine. She has chosen me to
replace the mother who died. I would not see her hurt.*

"But you have hurt her by using her! Since she found
your mirror, she's changed for the worse, always getting herself in trouble."

This is not my fault!

"Isn't it? I suppose you had nothing to do with her
feelings about me, either."

A moment of silence was followed by Xosi's saying,
Even so, you ride to help her?

"She is an innocent young girl, haunted by her
mother's death just as I was by mine. I understand her,
and I care about her. I must get on with it," she added,
giving Belinda a kick. "The sun is setting fast. Dusk will
soon be upon us."

Then perhaps I will be able to help you.

Iphigenia couldn't help but wonder, what could a
ghost do against a flesh and blood murderer?

Midway through the afternoon, Monte rode with Stephen
and his men into Luis Padilla's barnyard. Pablo's death
had been eating at him since the day before, and he
decided he couldn't let it pass. Luis's hate seemed to have
a life of its own. Monte hadn't forgotten the man's timely
visit during Norbert's burial, his insistence that Monte
get a priest to exorcise the curse. Had he taken advantage of the fact that Monte had not followed his orders?

Luis must have had a sentry posted, because when he
came out under the *portal*, he was armed with a rifle in
one hand, his bullwhip in the other. And several men,
similarly armed, moved in from different directions.

Aware that they were surrounded, Monte glared at
the Mexican. "Expecting a visit, Luis?"

"I heard about Pablo."

"News travels fast." Monte indicated the armed men. "You nervous about something?"

"I am nervous about you, Ryerson."

"That because you have reason? How long have you known about Pablo's death?" He worded the accusation carefully. Luis could take it as he wanted.

Luis understood his meaning exactly. "I am tired of being persecuted!" he said, his dark eyes flashing. "I am ready to face you like a man."

Monte glanced around at the armed cowboys. "With plenty of backup, of course."

"I will instruct my men to do nothing to interfere."

Fair enough. A cold anger filling him, Monte was about to dismount when Jake pushed up next to him.

"Now hold on, Monte," the foreman said. "What's another death going to prove?"

Sinking back into his saddle for the moment, Monte returned, "Maybe it'll finish the curse."

"More killing is senseless!" Jake insisted, his eyes wild. "I'm tired of living this way. Haunted. Seeing demons in my dreams is enough. I don't need to see them awake, too."

Wondering if Xosi had been messing with Jake in addition to him, Monte asked, "You've been haunted?"

"Cursed, just like you. We'll never forget what we saw." Jake's voice trembled. "How could you even think about taking a life after seeing what that butcher did?"

And Monte realized Jake wasn't talking about Xosi, but about Beaufort Montgomery. "Someone's been taking lives."

"But I don't think it's been Padilla," the foreman insisted. "And it ain't me, neither."

Monte thought he might be a fool, but he believed Jake, even as his gaze dropped to the bullwhip attached to the foreman's saddle. He stared for a moment, then realized Jake's bullwhip had been made from leather that had been stained dark, unlike the braided piece of natural leather he'd found after Norbert's death. He looked more closely at Luis Padilla's bullwhip. Natural leather. Then at the handle. The trim had been tied into an intricate series of knots rather than braided.

A sense of certainty filling him that Jake was right, that Luis was not the one, Monte had to be sure. "Who supplies your grain, Padilla?"

Though Luis's brow furrowed in puzzlement, he didn't hesitate. "Hernando Santiago."

Monte looked around for the grain sacks. A few were stacked in front of the near barn. Even from the short distance, he could tell the markings were different from the ones Matt Dreyer used. Then certainty filled him. Luis wasn't the killer, either.

Cursing himself for being a fool, Monte said, "Looks like I owe you an apology, Luis."

The Mexican stared at him suspiciously. "Because you are afraid of me?"

"Because I finally figured out who's been stirring up all this trouble," Monte said, whirling his horse around. "Shoulda known it all along."

And on some level, he probably had.

Monte charged away from Luis, aware that his men followed. How could he have been so stupid thinking the curse was Luis's or Jake's way of getting revenge over what happened in Mexico, when Jonah Barkley had never forgiven him for inheriting the best part of the R&Y?

Somehow, Xosi's appearance was tied up with Barkley's sudden desperate bid to ruin him. Had the cruel old man actually had a run-in with the ghost, or was he merely using Xosi just as he had Monte's mother all those years ago?

*   *   *

Escorted by his new hired gunmen, Murdock and Dandy, Jonah Barkley had the pleasure of personally squiring Ryerson's whelp to their rendezvous site. Her horse was tied on a short lead that was attached to his saddle. She'd fought him at first—had tried to get away—but after he'd put the fear of God in her with dire threats she sat silently, staring straight ahead as though she were dead already.

Jonah smiled grimly. *Dead.* That's the way he wanted to see all the Ryersons after the way the old man had tricked him into marrying his whiny, sniveling daughter Sarah, who'd run the moment his back was turned. The old bastard had left him land, all right, the part of the R&Y without water. He'd tried everything over the years to get his due. Legal maneuvers. Scare tactics. Nothing had worked.

Not even killing Amanda Ryerson.

He hadn't meant to, of course. He'd merely been out to scare her into wanting to move far away from West Texas. He thought she could influence her besotted husband to sell. But as he'd threatened her with a few shots well-aimed to miss, her horse had spooked and her carriage had overturned. Amanda Ryerson's neck had snapped like a dry twig, and he'd felt not one ounce of remorse. He hadn't felt anything.

He'd realized then that killing came naturally to him.

And they would all have to die eventually, Jonah thought—after he got the deed to the remaining R&Y land, of course. More unfortunate accidents. If he left even one Ryerson alive, he or she was bound to exact revenge eventually. Jonah had no interest in watching his back every second of every day for the rest of his life. That's why he'd hired Murdock and Dandy—

strangers who would help him, then disappear. No local would ever know he'd been involved.

A rush of water alerted him to their position. They were coming on the creek, swollen with rains further north. He stared at the water, at the entire length of raging, roaring water that he could see, and felt his life's blood pulse.

"Looks like we beat Ryerson here," Murdock said.

Jonah scanned the small shadow-limned canyon on the other side. Empty. He'd chosen this location both because the rock walls would provide safety for their backs, and because the creek that he so desperately wanted crossed its path. Even now, a quarter of the canyon was awash with flood water.

"If Ryerson doesn't show by dark, what do we get to do to the girl?" Dandy asked.

"Mind your business," Jonah told him. "The girl's mine to kill, at my own pleasure."

Ginnie suddenly came to life, her fingers clawing at his face as she screeched, "I'll kill *you*!"

Chuckling, Jonah ducked. "And I thought all the fight was gone out of you." He removed his sidearm from its holster, and still smiling, shoved it square between the girl's frightened eyes. "Bam!" He mimicked the gun's kick as if he'd actually used it. Ginnie's reddened face went all white. Then kicking his horse toward the rickety-looking bridge, he said, "Give me another reason, and I'll do it for real. Wouldn't that be a nice sight for your pa—your head busted open like ripe fruit, your brains splattered all over his land?"

The girl finally broke down and sobbed, her chest heaving.

Jonah laughed with triumph as they crossed the bridge that creaked and swayed under them. He avoided what looked like the worst of the loose and rotted boards and trotted out through the shallow water spreading along the canyon floor. To commemorate the momentous occasion, he would have the bridge fixed up right, first thing when the land was officially his.

But his rumination was short-lived when Murdock said, "Hey, Mr. Barkley, you got company, but not the kind you expected."

Jonah glanced back to see the blonde bitch of Ryerson's coming their way, hell-bent-for-leather, wearing men's clothing and armed with a rifle. Wondering if Monte had even heard about his threat, he cursed in frustration. "One of you boys go get the lady."

Dandy whirled his horse around and sped back across the bridge. One of the boards gave way, and slanted toward the water.

For the woman's sake, Jonah made an elaborate show of his power, pulling the girl out of her saddle so that she was dangling against his leg, and once more pressing the gun to her forehead. "Don't do anything foolish, or the girl is dead!" he shouted.

That brought the woman to heel. Her expression horrified, she let Dandy ride right up to her. He slipped the rifle from her saddle, and she came peaceably across the bridge. The gunman followed, so involved in watching the woman that he didn't watch where he was going. His horse stepped on the rotted wood that had already half given. The horse screamed as its leg went through. Mount and rider seemed suspended for a moment before toppling over and being sucked into the roiling water below.

16

Dusk fingered the ranch's buildings as Monte dismounted and gave his reins to Stephen. He was intent on telling Iphigenia about his discovery and eager to discuss the situation with her. Perhaps between the two of them, they could come up with some sort of plan to trap Barkley at his own game . . . before he killed again.

But he was only halfway to the house when Cassie came flying out of the kitchen and into his arms. "Pa!" she sobbed. "It can't be too late! It just can't."

"Too late? For what?" He looked to Carmen, who stood in the kitchen doorway, equally stricken.

The housekeeper crossed herself. "Two men came for you earlier."

His heart pounded. "Whose men?"

"I do not know. They only said if you wanted to see Ginnie alive, you must meet them with the deed to your land at Flood Canyon."

"Damn that Jonah Barkley!" Monte said, certain his stepfather was responsible. "When am I supposed to meet them?"

"Now. Dusk. And they said you must come alone. Only . . . Señorita Wentworth . . ."

"What about Iphigenia?"

Cassie sniffed and looked up at him through tear-filled eyes. "Miss Wentworth took your weapons and went after Ginnie herself."

"Dear God. Stephen!" he shouted.

The boy was already halfway to the corral. He glanced back. "Yeah, Pa?"

"Get me a fresh mount. A fast one. And hurry! I gotta move fast to save Ginnie and Iphigenia."

Flood Canyon was nearly half an hour's hard ride from the ranch. He only prayed he could get there before dark. Before another death shattered their lives.

He wouldn't think that Iphigenia—foolish, brave woman that she was—might already have met some terrible fate.

"Pa, what are you gonna do?" Cassie asked, running after him as he rushed toward the house.

"Give them what they want."

"I'm going with you!"

"No! You'll stay here with Carmen."

Cassie grabbed his vest to stop him. "But Ginnie's scared and hurt," she insisted. "I've been feeling it all day. She needs me."

Monte shuddered. Neither of the twins had been wrong when they'd had these feelings before. They'd grown up with some sort of intangible connection that most people didn't have, but all that had seemed to go awry about the time he returned from Mexico.

About the time he'd brought Xosi into his home, Monte realized now.

"I'm sorry, Cassie, but you have to stay here where you'll be safe."

With that, Monte rushed to his study. Having feared

Barkley would try to get his hands on the deed when he wasn't around, Monte had buried it beneath one of the floorboards. He flipped the colorful woven rug aside, and using his knife, pried the loose board free and retrieved the deed.

He would do anything to see his girl safe . . . just as Iphigenia had tried to do for hers.

He would also do anything to see the woman he loved safe.

The land wasn't as important as their lives, he thought as he stuffed the deed into his pocket. He'd give up the damn deed if he had to and worry later about getting the land back legally—or any other way he could. His immediate concern was that neither Ginnie nor Iphigenia get hurt.

Still, as he raced through the house, Monte slipped his revolver from its holster, made certain it was fully loaded. He had a bad feeling himself.

Outside, he came face to face with Stephen, who was holding two fresh mounts. Pride filled him when he noted the determination in the boy's eyes. But he couldn't let him come with him.

"I was told to go alone. Besides, if I don't come back, son, someone has to take care of Cassie."

Stephen's facial muscles worked as if he were trying not to cry. "Don't talk like that Pa. You gotta come back. You and Ginnie and Miss Wentworth."

Monte did something Stephen hadn't tolerated in years. He hugged the boy and got a squeeze in return. Then he was off.

Even as the gunman screamed with terror, Iphigenia felt the bridge beneath Belinda's hooves give. She urged the little mare faster and realized the rotting boards had

given out behind them. The lighter combined weight of
her and her horse probably saved them from joining
Dandy and his, who were swept downstream as she and
Belinda touched solid ground.

Iphigenia thought quickly. Dandy had relieved her of
her rifle, but he hadn't checked her person. She still had
both her sheathed knife and her revolver tucked into
her waistband, hidden by the man's vest that rode low
on her hips.

And she wore the mirror pendant tucked beneath
her shirt. Xosi was still shuddering against Iphigenia's
breast in reaction to the creek.

Watching back from the mouth of the canyon where
the land was dry, Jonah Barkley grinned as if he'd
enjoyed the spectacle. He must be truly cruel, Iphigenia
thought, or else insane. He was still aiming his gun at
Ginnie, though no longer at her head.

"Thank you for joining us, Miss Wentworth. Ryerson
is certain to give me what I want now."

Iphigenia observed Ginnie worriedly. Even in the
fading light, she could see the girl's face was white, her
eyes swollen from crying. "Are you all right?"

Ginnie took a shaky breath and nodded.

"Might as well stretch our legs," Barkley announced.
"Murdock, help the lady down."

"Do not trouble yourself!" Iphigenia told the gunman sharply as he rode up next to her.

She'd never gotten off a horse so fast—other than
unintentional falls when she'd taken reckless jumps. She
noted Ginnie was allowed to dismount, as well. Murdock
was right beside her, taking the reins from her and leading Belinda to a twisted tree that was trying to grow from
the rock-strewn canyon floor. He tied up the mare and
his own gelding, then did the same with the other horses.

Ginnie stood where she'd gotten off, a small, lonely

figure in the encroaching dusk. Iphigenia didn't hesitate to gather the girl to her breast and wrap protective arms around her. Ginnie trembled and Iphigenia imagined she was fighting tears.

"It will be all right, Ginnie. Your father will get here to meet this man's demands," Iphigenia said, hoping Monte would indeed show up in time.

Barkley laughed. "Might as well make yourselves comfortable . . . while you can."

Iphigenia's skin crawled. She knew then that Jonah Barkley didn't plan to let them go, not even if Monte gave him what he wanted. She pulled Ginnie toward some rocks where they sat huddled together.

"Why did you come for me?" Ginnie asked.

"Because you were in trouble."

"But I've been so horrid to you."

"Yes, you have," Iphigenia agreed, analyzing their situation. Both men stood with backs turned, several yards in front of them, watching for Monte through the growing dusk. "But I understand how difficult it is for a child to lose a mother." Even as her own child might, she thought, eyelids stinging. Poor Hope. "I did things purposely to hurt my own father. First, because I blamed him for my mother's death, then merely because I wanted to remind him that I existed."

"I'm sorry for being so mean."

"I am certain you are, Ginnie. You know, I never meant to take your mother's place." Surreptitiously, Iphigenia pulled the mirror pendant from where she'd hidden it beneath her shirt. "No one could do that."

The mirror glowed with a greenish light—or else the last rays of the sinking sun were hitting it just right.

Ginnie's eyes widened, then she stared up into Iphigenia's face. "Cassie thinks you can take our ma's place. She wants to forget the past."

"Murdock," Barkley said, interrupting the conversation. "Damn light's going fast. You climb up there." He pointed to a ledge far above their heads. "You'll have a bird's eye view till it gets dark. I don't want any unpleasant surprises."

"Me, neither."

When the mirror continued to glow, Iphigenia quickly covered it with her hand as Murdock moved to the canyon wall. He used broken rock and indentations to climb up to the ledge. He was too busy to pay attention to them, and Barkley's back was still turned, though the older man seemed to be fidgeting, trying to chase away some uneasy feeling. She released the pendant.

"No, Ginnie," she said, taking up where they'd left off. "Cassie has not forgotten your mother." Then she stared down into the little mirror. An angry Xosi glared back. "But it is possible to love many people, whether or not you are related to them."

"Like I love Xosi," Ginnie said, her gaze straying again to the glowing image.

Iphigenia would swear that Xosi's visage changed, softened, that she appeared genuinely touched by the girl's admission.

"I only hope that Xosi is clever enough to protect you," she said, praying the significance of her words got to the ghost and that a spirit, indeed, could be of assistance.

If Xosi had anything to offer, she kept it to herself. Iphigenia heard no phantom words in her head, which was undoubtedly best since she had no idea whether or not Barkley might be able to hear Xosi, as well. His back was stiff, stance uneasy, and she wondered if he was experiencing anticipation at facing Monte down, or whether he sensed something unusual going on.

Flipping the mirror around against her chest so that the men would not see the glow, Iphigenia pulled the knife from its sheath and slipped it to Ginnie. The girl needed some way to protect herself. Then, through hand signals, she indicated Ginnie should take shelter behind a ridge of rocks.

Silently, Iphigenia rose and removed the revolver from her waistband and, aware of Ginnie following her instructions, crept up on Barkley. Her heart thundered in her chest, the mirror responding upon it. She felt a tingling and surge of heat, as if Xosi were working herself up to a frenzy. When several feet remained between them, Barkley whipped around. She raised the gun to chest level, and steadied it with two hands.

"Well, well, the little lady is not defanged, after all." He punctuated the statement with a laugh.

"I shouldn't think you would be amused with a weapon pointed at your heart."

"Know how to use that, do you?"

"Well enough to shoot off a rattler's head—and at more than double the distance."

His smile faded. "But that was only a snake. This time, you'd have to pull the trigger on a human being."

"I do not see that distinction," Iphigenia said, her blood racing through her at an unprecedented pace. "At least a rattler warns you before he strikes."

From his elevated perch, Murdock suddenly called, "There's Ryerson now!"

Iphigenia made the mistake of dividing her attention. She'd barely gotten a glimpse of a rider in the distance when Barkley struck. One hand shoved her gun arm away from him, while the other went for the weapon itself. In the scuffle, Iphigenia pulled the trigger and a bullet went wild.

"Iphigenia!" came Monte's faint shout from a distance across the creek.

She hung on to the gun with a ferocity she hadn't

thought herself capable of. While she couldn't get the barrel pointed at Barkley, neither would she let the villain have the weapon. Finally he let go, and while she was trying to regain her balance, let loose with a fist. His knuckles smashed into her jaw. Her head snapped with the impact, and she saw stars. And before Iphigenia could recover, Barkley had wrested the revolver from her hand.

As he turned his back on her, she screamed, "Monte, a gunman up in the rocks!"

"Shut up, you bitch!" Barkley roared, turning and grabbing hold of her shirt front.

To Iphigenia's amazement, Barkley let go a howl that set the fine hairs at the back of her neck straight up. He shoved her, shook his hand as if he were in agony, which he must be considering the heat she was feeling.

The pendant had taken on a life of its own.

As she stared down, the little mirror glowed brighter and brighter.

"That's it, Xosi," she whispered. "If you can do anything to help us out of this mess, this is the time!"

Monte saw Barkley manhandling Iphigenia with a growing sense of fury, but he didn't forget her warning. Rifle drawn, he approached the flooded creek that had taken on the proportions of a fast-moving river. He slowed his mount and stared up along the canyon wall until he caught a dark silhouette that was not part of the rock. Guiding his still-moving horse with his legs, he took aim and fired. The whine of the bullet echoed along the canyon.

The gunman fired back, but Monte executed some fancy moves to dodge the return bullets, then hung low over his horse's neck. Even in the encroaching darkness, he could see part of the old rope and board bridge was out. The creek itself was too fierce to cross at this spot because of the spring rains, but he couldn't let that stop him from saving his daughter and the woman he loved.

Realizing he hadn't seen Ginnie, he scanned the canyon. A faint greenish glow like the one he'd seen in the attic caught his attention.

Xosi!

What the hell was the ghost doing out here? Causing more trouble, no doubt. And that was Iphigenia with the mirror. She must have gotten it from Ginnie.

Monte concentrated on the bridge. He moved along the right, gathered his horse under him, and jumped the moldering boards in the middle. He heard more rotted wood crack and a strange moaning as the ropes swayed and strands popped. On the other side, more bullets greeted him.

Breaking away from the flooded canyon's mouth, Monte came up under the gunman's perch. Worried as he was about Iphigenia, going straight for Barkley would be a fool's errand, for it would put him out in the open, make his back a perfect target for the man in the rocks above.

And Monte was nobody's fool.

He dropped the reins and slipped silently out of the saddle.

"Murdock!" Barkley yelled. "Where the hell did the bastard go?"

"I dunno. He disappeared on me."

"Anything moves, shoot it!"

With his back to the rock's face, Monte carefully made his way up a steep incline, watching intently for activity in the gloom above. He moved like the Comanche he was at heart—silent and lethal—and held his breath waiting for the gunman to show his hand.

The canyon was silent but for the rush of the creek. Monte listened intently. Then he heard a faint scrape—the sound of boot against rock. Elevated and to his right, the shadow of a man's shoulder came into view. Monte froze. Aimed. A moment later, Murdock took another step.

And Monte squeezed the trigger.

The gunman dropped his rifle, but stood there, poised, as if waiting for something.

"Murdock? What the hell's going on?" Barkley called.

To which he received an immediate answer: the clatter of a gun dropping against rock as his hired murderer toppled from the ledge. Murdock's body landed face first in the shallow flood water on the canyon's floor.

Monte immediately slinked around the wall, keeping his back pressed to the rock. He could barely see through the dark. If not for the pendant's gleam, he would have had difficulty locating Iphigenia.

"You shoot at me, and you might hit your woman!" Barkley warned. "You might as well give up now."

"Don't listen to him!" Iphigenia screamed.

Her plea was followed by a sharp crack—the sound of Barkley hitting her. The bastard had no shame using force on a woman, but then he never had, Monte remembered, bristling. His stepfather had treated his mother in the same ill fashion. Wanting nothing more than to kill the cold-hearted murderer with his bare hands, Monte set down the cumbersome rifle, drew his revolver and moved away from the canyon wall, sloshing toward them through the ankle-deep water.

"You hurt her again, Barkley, and you'll never get the land."

"That mean you brought the deed with you?"

"I did. But I don't have it on me." Monte realized how foolish he'd been, thinking he could use it to bargain. Handing over the document would be the death of them all. He only prayed Ginnie was still alive. Though he'd left the deed in his saddle bag, he lied. "You could search the rocks around here for years without ever finding it."

Stepping onto dry earth, he drew close enough to see his stepfather pointing his revolver at Iphigenia. Her breast was heaving, and with it, Xosi's pendant. Monte had refused to face Xosi when she came calling in the middle of the night, but now his eyes were drawn to the tiny hand mirror that had somehow captured her spirit. The polished silver gleamed with a life of its own. If Barkley noticed, he ignored it.

"I could just kill you all and bury your bodies," Barkley threatened, "and most likely get custody of Stephen and Cassie since they're my step-grandchildren . . . not to mention the R&Y."

Monte gave Barkley his full attention. "You'd commit even more murders."

"He'll probably blame them on the curse, as well," Iphigenia said.

At the mention of the curse, the mirror flashed, suddenly flaring to life. The greenish glow grew and took wavering shape in the form of a livid woman.

Xosi.

Monte was stunned. Literally a shadow of her former self, she was still arresting. Could Barkley see her?

Obviously. The older man gaped and his gun hand shook.

Taking advantage of the murderer's diverted attention, Monte flew into action, butting him in the side with his revolver. Barkley went down to one knee. He was quick for his age, Monte would give him that, for he was up and firing in seconds. Again, seeming distracted by the sight of a fading Xosi, his shots went wild.

So did Monte. Heedless of his own safety, he slipped his revolver into its holster and tackled the armed man full force. They went flying to the ground and rolled into the mucky water. Barkley's gun flew out of his hand and landed somewhere nearby with a big splash.

"He has another gun, Monte!" Iphigenia cried. "That was one of yours he just lost."

Monte tried to punch Barkley's face with his fist, but the older man ducked. He elbowed Monte in the ribs, leaving him breathless, then shot to his feet. Monte threw out a leg and tripped him, and was on Barkley before he could retrieve the second gun. He kneed the man where it was bound to hurt most, and slipped the weapon out of its holster.

"Here, catch!" he called to Iphigenia.

"Got it. I'll find your other one," she said.

Recovered, Barkley tore into Monte with a few well-placed punches. Monte's head whipped back and his hat went sailing into the creek. He blocked the next blow and returned an even harder one, directly into Barkley's chin. The older man staggered. And as Monte stalked him for more of the same, he was aware of Iphigenia wading through the water, searching for the discarded gun.

Barkley caught him in the gut. Monte doubled over for a moment, but refused to let the pain stop him. Barely breathing, he increased his efforts until he had Barkley down and exactly where he wanted him: wallowing in the mucky water, unable to rise.

"Would you stop at nothing to get your hands on those water rights?" Monte asked, dragging the man up by his shirt front and shoving him back onto dry land.

The moon slid from behind some clouds, illuminating Barkley's crazed expression as he drew himself upright. "Once I thought I would," he said, panting with the effort, "but then when Amanda died so easily, I realized life didn't mean much to me. At least not other people's lives."

Stunned, Monte heard himself as if from a distance. "You killed my wife?"

"I was trying to scare her into wanting to leave Texas. Her horse spooked. Purely an accident, not that I cared—"

"Murderer!" came a screech bouncing off the canyon's walls. "You killed my mother!"

That's when Monte saw Ginnie fly toward Barkley's back, knife raised. Everything happened so fast. Barkley whipped around and grabbed the girl's knife arm. Before Monte knew what he was about, Barkley had spun her around and was holding the weapon to Ginnie's throat.

"One more step and your daughter's dead."

"No!" screamed Ginnie, struggling to free herself. But she was no match for a grown man. Kicking and screaming, she was dragged inexorably toward the dangerous bridge. "Pa, help me!"

"Barkley, it's not safe!" Monte yelled, fearing for his daughter's life. "Let her go and I won't come after you." Another lie.

His only answer was Ginnie's heartbreaking sobs.

Aiiee! came a wail from the darkness. *Take your hands off my* chica!

Monte whipped around and stared at Iphigenia, who stood frozen in ankle-deep water, a revolver in each hand. From the silvered mirror, a greenish glow whirled and danced, once more separating from her, this time a shapeless force that seemed to be gathering power.

Xosi could not let Jonah Barkley harm the girl she had grown to love. He would hurt Ginnie, maybe kill her. Then Ginnie might be imprisoned in the same kind of netherworld as Xosi herself.

But no, Ginnie hadn't lusted after riches or power, only love. And Xosi knew she alone was responsible for what had happened to her. Though she had never murdered anyone in cold blood, like Barkley, selfishness and greed had been her downfall.

The curse went back to that fateful night in the Aztec

ruins in New Mexico Territory, when she and her brother Tezco had sought a part of an ancient sacrificial wheel for the madman Montgomery. They had needed the artifact to seek a far greater treasure. And in removing the golden wheel piece from its sacred chamber, they had released the old gods . . . or demons.

From that night on, Xosi had seen both terrible visions in her mirror, as well as foreshadowings of events to come. Tezco had been equally haunted, and she had feared for her brother's very sanity if not his life. Still, her greed drove her. She had made one last attempt at snatching forbidden riches and in doing so had condemned herself. Little had she known that when Montgomery cut out her heart, she would be trapped in a curse of her own making.

But Ginnie was a true innocent. Surely if she died, she would go to a place of rest. Unless Xosi had brought the curse on the girl's head . . .

Dios, no!

She could not take the chance. She could not let Ginnie die.

"Unhand her, bastardo!"

A few feet along the bridge, Barkley glanced over his shoulder, real fear tightening his features. "Stay away from me, you witch!"

As well she should. Even nearing the water, Xosi shook inside. The water threatened to destroy her, to suck what tenuous life was left from her. She knew she could not cross the creek herself and survive.

But Barkley was dragging Ginnie, holding a blade at her throat. The girl was sobbing, holding her arms out to Xosi.

Xosi could not remember ever having done an unselfish thing for someone other than Tezco in her life.

But she would never have peace if she closed herself off from the plight of the chica she loved even as much

*as she had her own brother. Ginnie had for months
provided her only link to the real world. And the girl
loved her as she would a mother.*

*Feeding on the fear and the fury of the four people
surrounding her, even knowing she would put an end to
what little existence she had left, Xosi gathered her
strength and rushed forward, determined to be Jonah
Barkley's worst nightmare.*

Monte was rushing after the ghostly green haze that
was still growing in size and power, and Iphigenia
wasn't far behind. She sloshed through the water, her
gaze glued to the sight of the translucent whirlwind rising from the earth and shooting directly over the bridge
where Jonah Barkley dragged Ginnie ever closer to the
rotting middle. Part of her was aware that she was witnessing a most unusual sight, though she didn't have
time to think much about it.

Raising a hand against the glowing haze, Barkley yelled,
"Get away!" and stepped on a board that cracked and
pitched beneath his weight. "Get away from me, I say!"

With a screech, Ginnie somehow freed herself and
fell forward, away from her captor.

"Hang on, Ginnie!" Monte yelled as he stepped onto
the bridge. "I'm coming."

You have caused enough death for one lifetime!

Iphigenia stopped, transfixed as she heard the
words. The glowing haze took shape, and a larger than
life Xosi floated over the man who backed toward the
hole in the bridge.

"This can't be real—you're some kinda trick!"
Barkley yelled, voice shaking, even as Monte helped his
daughter up and gathered her in his arms. "I don't
believe in ghosts!"

Though you believe in evil, horrible man. You worship it!

Suddenly Xosi ignited into a bright red blaze, her burning image sweeping over Barkley, embracing him, completely surrounding him. He screamed and screamed, slapping at himself as if trying to put out the flames that were really some sort of illusion.

Xosi shrieked louder and louder, her voice causing the hairs at the back of Iphigenia's neck to stand straight up. The sound was that of an inferno . . . inescapable death.

"Aah!" Barkley screamed, beating harder at the flames licking him.

You can't survive my blaze!

"Water will damn well put you out!"

With that, Barkley purposely pitched forward into the creek. Xosi still hovered over the bridge. Even as he was swept downstream, the reddish glow softened to gold, then flickered to green as the current dragged him under.

Iphigenia thought it was ironic that the water Barkley had killed for would prove to be the death of him.

Xosi remained visible, though her glow had become dim. And Iphigenia saw her face change, saw it grow more peaceful and beautiful. The ghost began to drift and waver, her image fading. By crossing the water, Xosi had given up the last shreds of her own existence. She aimed a loving look at Ginnie, who was sobbing in her father's arms.

"Xosi, don't go!"

I must. Do not cry for me, chica, *but remember me kindly.*

The remaining light faded into the night. Realizing that Xosi had been misguided rather than evil, Iphigenia slipped the mirror necklace off and threw it out into the swirling black waters. "May you find peace."

Beside her, Monte added softly, "Go with God."

17

Iphigenia awakened with a start. Deep afternoon shadows filled her bedroom, and a slender figure hovered around her dresser.

"Ginnie?"

The girl started and whirled around. "I'm not trying to steal anything, honest."

Iphigenia believed her. "What *are* you doing?" She sat up and slipped her feet to the floor.

Ginnie lifted something from the dresser and hugged it to her chest. Then she took a step toward the bed and held it out. "I was returning this."

Iphigenia took the keepsake and stroked it lovingly. "My mother's music box."

"I'm sorry I took it."

She knew Ginnie's returning the treasure meant something—not only that the girl was free of her own mother's death at last, but also that Ginnie no longer was filled with resentment or hate for Iphigenia.

Perhaps they could make a fresh start. Rather, they could if she were staying. During the long ride back to the ranch, taking a circuitous route far downstream of the unsafe bridge, Iphigenia had had plenty of time to think about rescuing her own child.

She would have to be going only too soon.

Her throat constricted as she thought of leaving the people she loved. Ginnie's trying to make amends only made things worse. "Have you seen your sister?" Ihigenia asked. "She was very worried about you."

Ginnie nodded. "I made up with her and Stephen. Cassie asked me to move back into our room. I said yes."

Iphigenia smiled. "Good."

"I told Pa I was sorry, too, for causing trouble. And for blaming him for Ma's death. He said he understood."

"I'm sure he did. He loves you very much."

"He loves you, too." Ginnie stared down at the floor. "Do you love him?"

Yes. But she said, "I suppose I do."

"Then you'll be staying on?"

Surprised that Ginnie would broach the subject so calmly, Iphigenia asked, "How would you feel about that?"

"I think you should. For Pa and Cassie and Stephen."

"If I stayed, it would be for you, as well."

Ginnie lifted her head. "I guess that would be okay . . . now that Xosi's gone." Tears ran down her cheeks.

Iphigenia knew Ginnie felt as if she'd lost a mother twice. She cupped the girl's face as she said, "Xosi loved you very much, you know. She helped save your life."

"And lost hers because of it."

"No, Ginnie, Xosi really died in Mexico. I think you know that. You were only acquainted with her spirit."

"Then why did her spirit come here?"

"Unfinished business." Iphigenia knew it was not as simple as Xosi's refusing to be separated from Monte. "I think when a person's soul is caught between heaven and earth, it's often because they still have to prove themselves worthy of a higher life. Xosi did that when she gave up her connection to this earth for you. I'm sure her sacrifice freed her spirit to go to God."

Ginnie sniffed and nodded. "I'll miss her."

"But you'll always have her with you, here." Iphigenia touched Ginnie's chest where her heart beat.

Just then the sound of pounding hooves and a carriage approaching the house alerted Iphigenia. Surely not more trouble. Monte had said he was going to Pine Bluff early to telegraph the law about the situation.

"I had best get dressed."

"I'll go see what's going on," Ginnie offered.

Ginnie left her alone and Iphigenia chose a modest green day gown that didn't require too much fuss. As she slid into the garment, she heard raised male voices outside but couldn't make out whose. She ran a brush through her hair and gathered it in a simple twist. The voices were now coming from inside the house, if she were not mistaken. After slipping on her shoes, she rushed out of her room and down the corridor.

She stopped short outside the parlor where she was greeted by a shocking sight—Monte standing practically nose to nose with her father.

"It's time Iphigenia left this Wild West of yours and returned to civilization and her much safer life in New York. That's where she belongs," Horace Wentworth was saying.

"That's up to her."

"You can and will release my daughter from this absurd marriage. I don't care how much it costs me."

Monte's bronzed features darkened with fury. "I don't want your damned money."

"Then what *do* you want?"

"Father! Enough!" Furious, Iphigenia stomped into the parlor, where the entire household had gathered to watch the spectacle. Obviously their marriage was no longer a secret from anyone. "How dare you try to buy off Monte as if he was some needy beggar! He's more man than you've ever met in your life. And he owns more land than you've ever thought to possess. His stature in Texas is equal to your own in New York."

Though she wasn't certain that was true—Monte was cash poor, as he'd told her—she couldn't tolerate the idea of her father looking down on the man she loved.

"Iphigenia." Horace Wentworth had the grace to appear embarrassed. "I didn't know you were there."

"As if that would have made a difference."

Sighing, Iphigenia realized her father wasn't alone. His slickly dressed gunman-guide Graves was standing by the door, and directly behind her father, she spied the hem of a dress peaking out from the sofa. Though she couldn't see her, she realized a strange woman sat next to Cassie. Iphigenia was startled, for her father had been too wrapped up in his work over the years to seek female companionship. Aunt Gertrude had always served as his hostess.

But Horace Wentworth's newfound interest meant nothing to her. "What is it you want, Father? Why have you returned here? To torture me some more?"

"Is that what you think?" Her father nodded and swallowed hard, and Iphigenia would swear she was witnessing genuine emotion from someone who had to be the coldest, most distant person in the world.

"What else could it be?" she asked, aware of the tension in the room.

But not all bad tension. For Carmen was holding Ginnie affectionately as she sometimes did Cassie. And Stephen was trying to smother a smile.

"I brought someone to see you," her father said.

He stepped aside and Iphigenia's eyes widened. For there on the sofa next to a beaming Cassie sat a pretty young woman holding a baby in a lace-trimmed gown and matching bonnet.

Her baby.

"Hope?" Stunned, Iphigenia nevertheless rushed to the young woman, who, smiling, held out her child. "Hope, dear Lord, it is you!"

Gathering the baby to her breast, she pressed her close and silently began to cry.

"I took care of Abner Frickett for good," her father was saying. "Now I have a legal document that says he has no claim to Hope. And while I was at it, I slipped Naomi enough money to get her and her children far away from the odious man. Her choice, of course. Couldn't force her to it."

Iphigenia couldn't believe her father had actually come through for her. She couldn't believe her daughter was actually in her arms. She removed the bonnet and smoothed the silken blond hair from Hope's brow, then kissed the soft skin of her forehead. Hope gurgled and sucked on two fingers. Iphigenia inhaled and was dizzy with her sweet baby scent.

She stared at her father through tear-filled eyes. "You did this for me?"

"Of course I did it for you. And I hired Miss Lanigan here to take care of the child for as long as you wish."

Horace Wentworth cleared his throat and looked around the room as if he were uncomfortable discussing something so personal with all these witnesses.

"Why don't we go into the kitchen to see what Carmen is making for supper," Monte suggested.

Stephen protested. "But, Pa—"

"That includes you."

Cassie rose and pulled Miss Lanigan along with her. They followed Carmen and Ginnie and Stephen out of the parlor.

"I'll just wait outside, Mr. Wentworth," Graves said.

Monte was the last to leave the room. Before disappearing, he gave her a searing look that Iphigenia only wished she understood.

Filled with more happiness than she had known was possible, Iphigenia perched on the sofa, adjusting her daughter on her lap so that Hope lay against her arm. She trusted she was holding her correctly, for she had no experience with babies. But from the way Hope smiled at her and squealed, she figured she was doing fine.

"You're so beautiful," she murmured, awed anew that she had created this perfect little person.

"She is, isn't she?" her father said, taking the chair opposite. His fingers fidgeted with the wooden arms. "Reminds me of you when you were her age. Your mother even had a similar garment for you."

Startled, Iphigenia met his gaze, softer than she ever recalled seeing it. "You remember what I looked like twenty-seven years ago?"

"Of course I do." Again he seemed embarrassed. His white mustache twitched. "I remember everything. You were my little girl."

Tears struck the back of her eyelids again. He'd never before been so sentimental in her presence. "I never thought you cared."

He sighed, looked uncomfortable. "I guess I tried to shut myself off from caring when Dahlia died."

"But I was your child."

"And you were her miniature," he told her, his expression sad. "Every time I looked at you, I thought about what I had lost. Still, it wasn't fair of me to distance myself from you, I know. I regret that I was not more demonstrative, Iphigenia. Dahlia was the only person who ever brought out my softer side. Losing her nearly killed me. And once she was gone, I could not bear to wear my heart on my sleeve again . . . not even for you, my dear."

There was silence then, but for the baby's gurgling. Iphigenia wasn't certain which was worse—thinking her father was cold and distant, or knowing he had pretended to be for his own protection.

For some reason, she felt doubly cheated.

"So why did you search for me when I left New York?" she asked, thinking he should have been glad to get rid of his greatest reminder of the woman he'd lost.

"I was sick inside from worrying," he admitted. "Worrying that I had brought you to some terrible fate. I thought I could correct things."

Her spine stiffened at that. "Like trying to buy off my husband?"

"You don't belong here."

"I don't belong in New York with all its airs and strict society rules." Only the baby in her arms kept her from raising her voice. "I like the West. I have never before felt so alive."

"Then you're staying?"

Iphigenia hadn't considered what she would do now that she didn't have to be on the run with little Hope.

Would Monte want her to stay?

He'd married her so that she could collect her trust fund and therefore ransom her daughter. But her father had corrected the situation for her. And she had no idea of how Monte viewed their new circumstances. He'd been offended at the suggestion that he take Wentworth money, yet he hadn't said anything about being married for any other reason. Perhaps he would be relieved to be rid of her sharp tongue and stubborn streak.

Though uncertain of her and Hope's future, Iphigenia *was* certain of one thing. "I shall not return to New York with you, Father," she said, smiling when Hope grabbed onto her bodice as if in agreement.

Iphigenia had no desire to go back to her old life. She felt as if she'd already made a new one in West Texas with Monte and his children, and could only hope he felt the same. If he didn't love her, he at least desired her, and his children did need a mother, and of course Hope needed a father. She would find a way to make Monte see the logic of their staying together, she decided, and perhaps in time he would come to love her as much as she did him.

"But I forgive you for the past," she went on, "and I thank you with all my heart for the return of my daughter."

As Iphigenia met her father's gaze, she swore that Horace Wentworth's eyes were filled with unshed tears.

He cleared his throat. "As you reminded me, little Hope is my flesh and blood."

Thinking of her child, of the necessity of being able to support Hope if she did have to leave the R&Y despite her resolve, Iphigenia took advantage of his weak moment. "And I have faith that you will be reasonable and see fit to release my trust fund. Mother wanted me to have money of my own when I married."

Her father peered at her intently. "Do you really love this Monte Ryerson?"

Once again, he surprised her. He seemed almost . . . accepting of the possibility.

"More than I can ever tell you." Or Monte himself, Iphigenia thought, a lump sticking in her throat.

"Then the trust fund is yours," he said gruffly. "I'll make the arrangements upon my arrival in New York. Where shall I have my banker send the money?"

Relieved, Iphigenia took a big breath and hugged Hope closer. "The First Bank of Fort Davis will do."

"No need to do any such thing," Monte countered from the doorway.

Iphigenia looked up. She hadn't heard him return and wondered how long he had been standing there. Long enough to hear her admit her love for him? Well, if he thought she no longer had a mind of her own, he had another think coming.

"Yes, there is," she argued. "Father, do not listen to this man."

Monte was ignoring her and scowling at her father. "I told you I didn't want your money."

Her father gave Monte one of those cold expressions that used to distress her so. "We are discussing Iphigenia's trust fund."

"Keep it." Monte drew close to Iphigenia and Hope. "I can take care of my own wife and kids."

Iphigenia's heart soared. Monte sounded as if he wanted her to stay, that he wanted to take care of her— though he would have to tell her so much more directly. Still, necessity had forced Iphigenia to be practical over the past months, and she would not allow him to win this dispute.

"Monte, that money came through my mother's family." Glancing up, heart beating oddly at his very nearness, she connected with his angry gaze. "Passing it on in trust is tradition. Mother meant the money for my protection . . . and for that of my children."

For a moment she thought Monte wouldn't relent.

His rough-hewn features were set hard. She refused to look away until they softened and he nodded, if reluctantly.

"All right, then," he told her father. "But make sure you put the money in your daughter's name. I won't take a penny of it."

"Iphigenia Ryerson," she clarified.

"You have my word," her father said, trying to hide a smile but clearly failing.

Iphigenia stiffened. Was her father merely telling her a tale that he would send the money? Or was he smiling at her? Or at them? Odd as it seemed, she swore he now appeared to approve of the match despite his original opposition.

"Then everything's settled," Monte said, calling toward the kitchen, "You can all come back out now."

Iphigenia was thinking that things weren't settled at all, at least not between the two of them, when Cassie rushed back into the parlor, the others following.

"Pa told us you got married in Fort Davis!"

Iphigenia flashed a surprised glance at Monte. They hadn't discussed what they were going to do about their personal situation. "We did."

"Then you're our new Ma."

Cassie bent over to hug and kiss her, while Stephen and Carmen stood nearby, grinning and congratulating them. Only Ginnie stood alone, separate from the rest, her expression uncertain.

"Why don't we ease into things," Iphigenia suggested for the Ginnie's sake. "Start by calling me Iphigenia and let's see how things work out."

Ginnie smiled and moved closer to her family.

*   *   *

Later, slipping into her night clothes, Iphigenia was still thinking over the emotion-filled day. Her father and his entourage were spending the night on the R&Y. Since Ginnie had moved back in with Cassie, the attic bed had been given to Miss Lanigan. Stephen had volunteered his bed to her father and had taken Graves with him over to the bunkhouse.

And little Hope was already waiting in Iphigenia's big, otherwise empty, bed. Iphigenia couldn't help wondering what was going on in Monte's head.

Despite his announcement of their marriage to his family, Monte had not sought her out alone. The fact worried her, though she tried not let it. Once her father was gone, she would have plenty of time to deal with a recalcitrant husband. She couldn't help feeling disappointed, however, that Monte hadn't given her as much consideration as he had his own children.

Sitting on the edge of the bed, she ran a finger along the baby's leg and said to a sleepy Hope, "If Monte Ryerson thinks he can just ignore us, he's wrong."

"Who said I was gonna ignore you?"

Startled, she whirled toward the open door. "That's the second time today that you've appeared unannounced."

"You'd better get used to it." He stepped inside. "I don't have the manners of most New York society men."

She feigned shock. "You mean you'll just waltz into my bedroom any time you please without so much as a by your leave?"

"*Our* bedroom. The one down the hall. I don't believe in husbands and wives having 'civilized' sleeping arrangements." His grin was wolfish. "I'm half savage, you know."

Her heart thundered in her chest. She looked away

and fussed with Hope's little cotton gown. "I wasn't certain you wanted to remain married to me at all."

He drew closer. "I wouldn't have married you if I wasn't sure."

She faced him, searching for the truth in his eyes. "I thought you married me so I could get the trust fund and ransom Hope."

"That was one of the reasons."

"But you said you believed marriage was for two people who loved each other."

He appeared taken aback. "Did you lie to your father about loving me?"

"You were listening!" she accused.

Hooking her under one arm, he pulled her up off the bed. "Did you lie?"

Heat spread from where he held her to every inch of her flesh. "No," she said breathlessly. "But that makes only one of us loving the other."

His expression softened. "Like I said, I wouldn't have married you if I wasn't sure."

"Sure?" Heart thundering with hope, Iphigenia wanted to hit him. Why wouldn't he say the words she so desperately wanted to hear?

"That I love you, you stubborn woman."

Hearing them, she gaped and he took advantage of her open mouth. Before Iphigenia could say a word, Monte was kissing her. Sweetly. Feverishly. Lovingly.

And Iphigenia was returning the intimate embrace, her heart fuller than she ever thought possible. She branded each nuance of his lips and tongue and hands into her memory, though now she knew she'd have many more to anticipate.

When Monte broke the kiss suddenly, she breathlessly asked, "So, you are certain you want to stay married to a sharp-tongued, impossible woman?"

"I wouldn't want to be married to anyone else."

Feeling she needed to remind him of something they hadn't discussed since Fort Davis, Iphigenia pressed, "Not even a woman who could give you more children?"

His forehead furrowed. "Now what do we want with more than the four kids we got? Believe me, they're going to be a handful as it is." He looked at Hope, who was sleeping like an angel. "Especially her, if she takes after her Ma."

He was talking as if they were already a real family. "Well, maybe if her Pa were very loving and very attentive, she wouldn't be like her Ma, at all."

"She'll be the apple of my eye," he promised, "but I hope she has *some* of your qualities. If you weren't who you are, I wouldn't love you so much."

She snuggled into him. "So why don't you show me?"

"In *our* room."

Monte leaned over to lift Hope. He cradled her to his chest, experience giving him an ease with the baby that Iphigenia still didn't have. He smiled down at Hope, and tears sprang to Iphigenia's eyes. Monte was already treating her like one of his own. What more could she ask for?

A short while later, with Hope tucked into the cradle Monte had brought down from the attic, Iphigenia realized there were myriad things she could ask of Monte in the privacy of their room, all of which he would gladly give her.

Their finding each other had driven away all the shadows from their hearts.

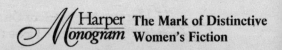

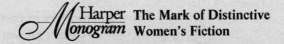